# ANYA OF ARK

KRISTIAN JOSEPH

To Phoebe,
Welcome to the Ark
and Merry Christmas
From Kristian Joseph

*For my niece, sister, mother and aunty. My partner Lauren,
who is forced to read all of my drafts. In addition, the
countless other Anyas who inspired this story.*

# THE CHOICE

Water splashed and waves crashed against the mass of a wooden raft as a solid horizon lit the day. Morning drums bellowed across the sea, bringing a grand rhythm to the floating village. A contraption built from salvage and desperation, it was the size of a small city, designed to move with the ocean's moods. A mass of scrap wood and plastic, held together by rusted nails and all else left floating from a world swallowed deep down below. Most of all, the raft was forged by hope: the last speck of man's undying will to survive in a world of water. Its name was the Ark.

On small kayaks off the northern deck, Hunters fished with spears in the early morning sun, and Makers fixed any weaknesses in the raft as the waters fought against them. Those who inhabited the Ark called themselves Arkers; they wore seal skins and fish leathers to stay warm at the core although they had grown used to the icy breeze that cursed them. Every Arker was tough, but it was hard for the adults, who still remembered the warmth of beds and endless luxury before the flood – the technology and great machines that had been taken for granted until the warming began.

It was easier for the young with no knowledge of dry land or memories of grass. It made them stronger, more prepared: immune to the cold, the constant splashing and wet hair. They were children, making the most of their surroundings no matter how cruel. Most of the young were only just waking to the sound of drums, but one had been up since daybreak. One girl sat on the Ark's edge, her wild dark brown curly hair blowing in the wind to reveal freckles and round cheeks as she dared to dream. Her name was Anya, and it was her sixteenth birthday. Anya wasn't particularly special, brave, strong, fast or tall. She was an ordinary girl to most, having never excelled in what others had wanted her to do, such as cooking, or crafting.

Instead she sat watching the Hunters on their little kayaks as the deep sea and bright day sparkled in her crisp blue eyes. She watched the Hunters move with grace, standing in narrow makeshift boats light as a feather. Their feet at one with the ocean, perfectly balanced and swift. Anya watched them strike the sea with makeshift harpoons, a sharp blade at one end and a rope at the other. Their spears cut the water with elegance as they picked out fish after fish. The Hunters moved swift and quiet, fixed on the task at hand without care for the cold, wind or water.

Amongst the many Hunters, Anya watched only one. Her brother, Jake, a man, more a boy of eighteen, with long blond hair and a skinny surfers body. He was only just starting to take a Hunter's shape as his arms and chest were filling out. Anya had watched him every day since he had chosen to be a Hunter two years ago on his sixteenth birthday. She was there at every moment, for every great catch, and every tattoo he earned for moving up the ranks.

For hours Anya would watch and wait for him to finish his morning duties. Today the Hunters worked harder, for their nets were hardly catching. On most days they relied more on the nets than the strength of spears, but over the past few days the nets had been empty. Anya didn't quite know why: the elders spoke of many reasons, and the Makers too. She saw by the colour of the ocean that it was growing lighter and shallower, changing from a vast blackness to a more blessed blue. She supposed that in this part of the never ending, unmapped abyss there were just less fish, but most of the Arkers were far more superstitious.

When Jake noticed her sitting there looking out, he stopped what he was doing, put his spear on his back and jumped from boat to boat, unsettling the other Hunters along the way. With no patience and no time to waste, it was much faster than paddling. Leaping the distance between each of them, he skidded on by in his bare feet before jumping to the next and last empty boat. His jump brought a splash and the boat soared towards the Ark as he surfed, before making one final leap into the air and landing right alongside his sister.

"Happy sixteenth birthday!" Jake scuffed up her hair with his coarse hand; gave a lazy smile and then a hug as his skinny frame loomed over her.

"Thank you" she replied, rather nervous, knowing this was the day she chose her path.

"Feeling old yet?"

"Not as old as you think you look with that moustache." Anya smiled and began to laugh as Jake shook his head and stroked his poor attempt at facial hair. It was blond, fuzzy and thin, but her words were only meant in jest.

"I have something for you," he said, reaching into his satchel and pulling out something wrapped in cloth. To Anya's surprise it was a necklace, glimmering in the morning sun. Her eyes glittered as he passed it to her. It was an emerite stone, like emerald, but it would glow bright at night, especially in moonlight. It was encased in gold, and heavier than she was expecting. It was her mother's, and she had seen it hang in her aunt Lyn's shack for years, swaying with the ocean as it glimmered. Looking at it had always given Anya strength, and took her mind off the storms.

"It's … it's beautiful," she said with a smile. "Did Aunt Lyn –"

"She said you could have it, sea-sister, it was Mother's after all."

Anya knew that her mother never took it off except for the night the storm almost took the Ark. It was hard to speak of their parents, but sure enough thunder and lightning reminded them of what they lost. Anya was still afraid of stormy days, of thunder and lightning, but today the sun was shining bright and beautiful, the sea was calm, and everyone took full advantage of the warm weather.

"Aunty and Uncle will be waiting for you, lets race." Jake gave her no head start and began to run. He scaled wooden shacks and swung from ropes as Anya tried her best to keep up. He went from plank to post, barging past Makers repairing the raft from the day before. The Ark was bustling with life as all the adults moved in the morning sun to the sound of heavy drums. Anya stopped on the edge of a platform in front of a jump she knew she would not make. She climbed down and started to run again until barging straight into another girl, Riley. Riley flew up in the air before landing hard. Her bucket of fish guts followed, spilling all over her long red hair as she shrieked with surprise. Riley sat up and squinted for poor eyesight and spied the fuzzy outline of none other than Anya Fairheart.

"Fishes! I'm so sorry!" Anya exclaimed. She tried to help her up, but Riley pushed her away.

"You clumsy fool, Anya! Why, I oughta … one of these days I swear I'll …!" Riley shrieked again getting to her feet, and Anya tried to wipe some of the fish guts off. But it was pointless: only a dunk in the ocean would relieve the smell now.

"I said I'm sorry, I swear by the sea –"

"Every day you wake me up early with your nightmares. I swear if your uncle wasn't who he is I would throw you off a crow's nest, or push you off this raft, or feed you to the sharks, or, or …"

Anya knew her nightmares woke the other girls. They often whispered and giggled behind her back; she didn't seem to fit in with their arts and crafts or their talk of boys. So, she took to getting up and out early.

Even then Anya was clumsy, even just changing her brown jagged leathers. There were no mirrors for getting ready, and anything she did seemed to be loud and without a care for her heavy flat clumsy feet.

"One of these days, one of these days I ... I ..." Riley continued, always in the habit of making empty threats. Anya zoned out at the mention of noises in the night, and it was safe to say she missed ten more such threats. Riley's threats were endless; she was short-tempered and always tired, and now, before she could finish, a fish flew through the air above them. It splattered right between Riley's eyes, almost knocking her down once more. Jake was sitting just above them on the roof of a shack, unable to contain his laughter. He almost fell down, rather proud of his aim. Riley screamed and shouted again. To Anya's dismay, Riley's mother joined them from the hut just underneath Jake's legs as Jake rolled back to remain unseen. She plodded to the scene like the over-protective mother she was and began to scream and shout in unison with her daughter.

"My baby! My poor baby! What have you done to my baby!" Riley's mother had fiery red hair too, and somehow managed to stay round on a diet of only fish. "One of these days! One of these days! I'll be having words with your uncle, you little shrimp!"

Anya looked worried and Jake howled so loud that Riley's mother turned to face her driftwood shack. She eyed the roof but failed to notice the slimy fish that had hit Riley between the eyes, right below her foot. She slipped, up into the air she went and back down through the wooden planks, bum first. Wedged in place just short of the waves below, Riley's mother couldn't move.

Anya froze until Jake jumped down, grabbed her by the hand and forced her to run. Anya didn't look back as they raced over slippery planks, across the rickety raft toward their aunt and uncle's quarters. They moved through crowds of Cooks carrying many fish to prepare for dinner and Makers busy planning to maintain the raft. In open space they picked up speed and ran, but Anya tripped on a loose plank and went crashing into a barrel which tumbled and rolled at speed.

"Oh no," Jake sighed as the barrel began rolling right back at them before seeming to right itself.

"Who dares awaken the great Lord Turtle Head!" shouted a voice from within, and at that moment a man's head wearing a turtle shell like a helmet popped out of the barrel, his legs extended out from the bottom and arms from the sides. The man stood in a heroic pose. He had a huge brown beard and leather straps was all that kept the barrel around his body. "I said who dares wake Lord Turtle Head!" the man shouted again. "Everyone knows I need sleep during the day in order to keep the Ark safe at night. Plus I need my beauty sleep." He said the latter part while stroking his beard languorously.

"Sorry Turtle Head –"

"It's *Lord* Turtle Head, and thou who wakes the turtle, pays the price!"

"What do you want?" asked Anya as she and Jake began to step away, knowing that getting involved in one of Lord Turtle Head's schemes was always a disaster.

"Ooh, aah, one, one dollar."

"We've never seen a *dollar*. No one has seen a dollar for thirty years."

"Hmm …" Lord Turtle head stroked his big bushy beard in contemplation, "that's exactly what someone with a dollar would say. I don't trust you Anya Fairheart, there's something fishy about you, something fishy indeed. My turtles say very strange things about you."

"Whatever you say, Lord Turtle Head."

"Now I'll give you two days to bring me my dollar, if not, I'll tell my turtles to get you. Oh, and that reminds me," Lord Turtle Head stepped closer, and he looked around to check whether anyone was listening. "You both need turtle helms, the sky is falling, I have spares in here, now where did I put them." Lord Turtle Head rapped his knuckles on his turtle shell helmet before disappearing back into his barrel. Then suddenly many items were launched from within; rusted tools, fishing lines, a dozen large fresh fish and rocks. "No one, no one ever listens …"

Jake and Anya ran the moment Lord Turtle Head went back into his home and they didn't stop. "What's that guys deal?" asked Anya and Jake couldn't help but laugh.

"He thinks he can talk to turtles and that the sky is falling, he means no harm I suppose. Uncle said he was a very smart scientist before the flood, but he lost his marbles."

"How did he fit all those things in his barrel?"

"No one knows, I wouldn't want to go in there," Jake replied as he shuddered.

Lord Turtle Head left their minds when they saw her aunty and uncle's shack. Aunt Lyn finishing a wooden sculpture with shaking hands whilst rocking on her self-made rocking-chair. Lyn's long silver hair hung to her waist and her soft warming smile was a delight. She was a tall and slender woman with no children of her own but so much love to give.

"Aunty Lyn!" Anya shouted, running right to her. Lyn struggled to her feet; her joints were sore, and she was shaking, having gone years without any medication or a diagnosis. Despite her ailment, she was still one of the finest Makers on the Ark, with all the time in the world and the patience to match.

"Hello, my sweet," she replied, hugging back so tight and not wanting to ever let go. Lyn was over-protective of them, knowing she was fortunate to have this much family left in a troubled sea that took almost everything. Anya felt a little bit embarrassed and rather nervous, as her birthday was the most important day of her life. "Happy birthday, my darling, I see Jake gave you your present." Aunt Lyn lifted the emerite necklace with her shaking hand to witness the light. It was strange for her to think back to all those years ago and know that this would be the only light left at night aside from the stars.

Lyn smiled and held back a tear. "You've both grown so fast. Here, I made you this." She presented the carved sculpture: it was some sort of land creature Anya would never know.

"Thank you, Lyn! What is it?" It was a fair question, Anya loved to imagine such creatures, having been given one a year since her parents' passing; this one was round, had four legs, two strange long teeth and a long nose.

"This is an elephant."

"An ele-whaaat?" asked Anya, being way too young to know land at all. Her brother Jake was the same and although the adults painted fond pictures with stories, such stories were lost on them without ever having known a tree, a building, a car, or a beach.

"An elephant!" Lyn said, remembering that such creatures were long gone. "These are its tusks, and this is its trunk." She laughed at Anya's puzzled gaze, but the laughter quickly turned to tears, tears she found easier to hide on other days.

"Why are you crying?"

"I just wish your mother could see you, you look more like her every day," said Lyn. She leaned in and stroked Anya's cheek before guiding her hand down to the necklace tucked into Anya's leathers.

"They are watching us from the water, as always," Anya replied.

"As always. Keep it safe, and remember: today is a special day, so enjoy it. I know you've been thinking long and hard about what you want to be; I've seen your work; you will be an excellent Maker."

Anya didn't know what to say; she was good with her hands but being a Maker was never something she had wanted. It was so easy for Jake; he was a man; he was born to be a Hunter. It was a reality too unfair to swallow, and though women whispered of a world where they could once be whatever they wanted, somehow that world had washed away.

"Where's uncle?" asked Jake with excitement. He looked more like his uncle than his father, and he didn't have his father's smarts, that much was sure.

"Isaac is on the stage watching the water, he will be expecting you."

They turned and ran along the rickety planks, racing each other, with Jake in the lead once more. Anya almost slipped on a loose piece of wood and Jake stopped as he saw Uncle Isaac in the distance. Isaac was a large man, full of character, truthful and wise. The Ark had aged him as it had many; now he had a big bushy grey beard and hair to match. He was strong but worried about his succession within the tribe. He had to stay on top of everything, as he truly was the best man left to lead his people, though he had never wanted any of it.

Before the great flood, Isaac was a mechanic, and his brother Richard, Anya's father, an engineer. They built the raft together as the world began to flood. Back then it was nothing more than thirty feet long, and as the water rose around them Isaac was nothing but cynical. As the world fell apart around them and their families, Richard kept it together whilst most killed each other for small boats. On a car-park roof, from old wood and empty barrels he built something better. Isaac and everyone else owed Richard their lives, for without him they would all be dead. Even in the face of knee-high water he believed in the Ark, dismissing all the small boats; he was an innovator where Isaac had been a cynic at first.

Isaac's mind soon changed when they set sail on the raft, yet he still had no faith that it would hold together in the storms; Richard however, did. He knew it would grow as it had: an organic kingdom. With good scavenges, the raft would float forever, as it grew piece by piece and person by person. Isaac missed him now more than ever. When Richard was taken in the storm, he had never wanted to lead, but the people looked to him. So now Isaac stood on the Great Stage they had built together, looking composed, but still so lost without his brother.

The Stage was a raised platform, on one side facing the endless ocean and on the other side the largest open space on the Ark, where the masses could be addressed, and meetings were held.

Jake had stopped running as, in the distance, he saw who his uncle was talking to. It was Tyson, the largest Master Hunter on the Ark. He towered over Isaac, with black dreadlocks as long as Anya was tall, while his hands were as big as planks. Anya knew her uncle had never liked him; they had never formed a bond as most had. Isaac and Richard had argued about letting him on the Ark in the early days, but Richard had fought to let him on. Since then, there was a lack of trust between them – and everything was about trust on the Ark. Tyson never smiled, he was sharp and to the point, valuing strength above all else. Jake disliked him too, and his son, Miles. Miles was always so self-centred, and he had a soft spot for Anya. Jake, being the over-protective brother, didn't like him one bit.

Because of Tyson, they stopped in their tracks and put their backs to the Ark's side close to the water's edge, hidden from view. Jake signalled to Anya to stay quiet with a finger to his lips. "Let's see if we can hear what they are saying," he whispered, and before Anya could say no, Jake swung silently under the raft and along the scaffold. It was dark here, except for the light cracking between the planks. Anya saw a whole mile of the Ark moving up and down with the ocean; the wood creaked as if it were alive. The ocean below was rough and unforgiving, so Anya was careful as she swung from pillar to post, scrambling to follow Jake before coming to a halt underneath Isaac and Tyson. She peeped through the plank's gaps with the boy.

"We're low on food," said Tyson in his deep bellowing voice.

"I know," replied Isaac as he looked out to sea, trying to hide his worries.

"The nets don't catch."

"I know."

"We're near the shallows …"

"I know." Isaac's few words made Tyson step forward; he was easily agitated and impatient at the best of times. Isaac folded his arms, knowing not to step back or show the slightest sign of weakness. At times like this he missed his brother and his way with words. Tyson was no friend; worse, he was a rival in a world where strength was everything. It took strength when the ice melted, when the water rose, when it kept rising and the highest cities flooded. When men killed for boats, rafts, anything that would keep them going. It took strength during starvation and sickness. When nine billion people had become a mere two hundred, strength had been everything.

"If you say *I know* one more time –"

"Then say something I don't already know."

Isaac stepped forward; he was tough but growing old and not in any mood for the younger hot-headed Hunters with dreams of power.

"We need to speak of the shallows, we need to speak of the shadows. My Hunters have seen things in the water – we need to know, Isaac."

"Eyes play tricks and the shallows are forbidden." Isaac shook his head; he would never accept the rumours of monsters. It had only been thirty years since they were on the surface, where they would drive to work and worry about bills; where they could hide within the warmth of walls … but all that seemed a lifetime ago. Tyson, however, took it very seriously; he would never agree with Isaac, and he was ready for war.

Below them, Anya didn't understand, but, as a Hunter, Jake had heard what lay beneath, the reports of glowing eyes in the night. Still, it wasn't uncommon to see things out in the sea. The elders often saw boats, or planes, sometimes even shooting stars and mermaids. The eyes often played tricks when they looked out upon nothing for so long.

"What if we dive, what if we can touch the bottom? There could be medicine, tools."

"No, Tyson, I will not risk our brothers," said Isaac

placing a hand on his shoulder. He was right not to risk anyone to dive into the unknown. The Ark had survived without the old ways for decades; there was no need to remind the people of what had been lost.

"Our men will risk everything for medicine, think of Lyn's struggle." Though brutish, Tyson was persuasive, too. Isaac knew they had all lost so much, even parts of themselves, but still he was weary of Tyson's certainty. He didn't know for sure, but he guessed that they would go anyway, that they might return with supplies – and if they did, Isaac would look weak. But if he encouraged them and they didn't return, it would be just as bad ... although at least they would have tried.

"Very well. Take – and take only the most skilled: Gregory, Pierce and Cayden."

Tyson nodded. He was about to take his leave when the support below Anya fell down and she splashed into the water. Tyson booted a plank with his bare foot, splitting it in two; it fell into the water, hitting Anya on the way. Jake darted out of the way and they saw only Anya looking up at them, helplessly trying to keep her balance. Tyson huffed, stormed off the Grand Stage and stomped into the distance back to his shack.

"Anya, what are you doing down there? Get up here now." Isaac was angry, so Anya climbed up in panic. Jake stayed behind, trying to avoid getting into trouble. "Jake, you too!"

They both made their way back along to the Ark's edge and over the side. Anya feared that Isaac was going to yell at them, but as soon as she drew close his stern look turned to a smile. He opened his arms and picked her up, swinging her round and round.

"Happy birthday, my sweet!" he said, before bear hugging her tight.

"You aren't mad at me?"

"Only while Tyson was within hearing distance."

"Thank you, Uncle," Anya replied, feeling his warm embrace as he continued to hold her as if she weighed nothing. When he saw Jake, he put her down and began play-fighting, shadowboxing, ducking and diving, and then rubbing his long blond head of hair. Anya had always felt that, as a boy, Jake was his favourite, but she didn't say anything.

"Jake, I need to speak to Anya alone; today is her day. Go practice your spear work."

"Yes, Uncle," Jake replied in a slightly disappointed tone. He jogged off back towards the Hunters at the Northern dock. Isaac looked down at Anya with a smile, before looking out towards the sea.

"Come, enjoy the sunrise with me, today is special." Isaac placed an arm around her, guiding her toward the platform's edge. "I only wish your mother and father were here to see this, they would be so proud."

Anya looked out into the sunrise as it split the horizon, flaming yellows and reds bouncing off the blue ocean as far as the eye could see. She missed her mother and father, but she could barely remember them; her uncle, however, remained as heartbroken as the day the storm came. Isaac knelt to her eye level.

"Today is a special day, the most important day. Tonight's ceremony will be hard for me: you won't be a little girl anymore, how can I ever be ready for that?" Isaac was right, he would never be ready; he was the closest thing they had to a father and accepting that she was growing up as he was growing old was harder than he had ever imagined. "I'm sure you will be the best of Makers, just like your Aunt Lyn." He was proud and excited but tried to hide it, forever reminding himself that it wasn't for men to show emotions, he had to be strong for his people. "You will be the best; you will make great things like your father and I …"

Isaac's words failed to produce the intended effect. Anya stared down at the floor, afraid and upset. She didn't want to look up at him now, everything he had said showed that he didn't really know what she wanted, so Anya sighed and shook her head, feeling so alone.

"What's the matter?"

"I …" she said, unable to find the words and knowing both the disappointment and the argument that was coming. "… I-I don't want to be a Maker. I want to be a Hunter."

Isaac took to his feet, rested his hands on his hips and swallowed the sea's cold breeze, which cut away the words he wanted to say. He frowned, tried to keep calm and look out to the ocean for guidance. He could foresee the embarrassment at the ceremony tonight: the laughter of the other Hunters, the shunning from the elders. In all their eyes he would look weak, but in his heart, he knew that it was the society bestowed upon them that was broken, and not her.

"Anya," he said with a sigh, placing his mighty hand upon her shoulder, "you can't be a Hunter."

"Why?" It was all she had ever wanted, all she felt destined for, but it would break Isaac's heart if she tried to explain why.

"You know why."

"And you know nothing."

"It's too dangerous; the elders won't allow it. The tests, the training, you won't be able to –"

"At least let me try." She held back the tears as her heart sank and so did Isaac's. He wished there could be another way, that he didn't have to pretend to be so strong, that he did not have to protect her, to save her from the pain of failure and the embarrassment.

"No, I forbid it," he said folding his arms.

"It's all I want to do, Uncle."

Isaac looked more tired every day and Anya supposed that he only saw the girl in her, and not the adult. There was so much he wanted to say but couldn't. Anya didn't understand, she never would. All she wanted was to be herself; she didn't want to be told what to do or how to live.

"Hunting is a man's job; the tribe won't allow it."

"My mother was a Hunter –"

"Your mother hunted, as we all did before the laws of the tribe," said Isaac with a sigh.

Her name was Fiona, and Anya had heard stories about her from the other women. How strong she was, how she did everything she could for the tribe, even in the storm.

Isaac, bless his heart, turned to Anya with an honest smile of pride, but he could not condone her choice. He could not say it, but he admired her will. Anya was stubborn; if her mind was set on something then there would be no other way. She got that from her father. But this …

"I can do this; I can be the first one."

"No," said Isaac, dead set in his tone. His mind was made up and Anya choked up on the inside. She wouldn't accept it, she couldn't.

"I know I can do it."

"Tyson will make sure the trials drown you. I won't be unable to protect you. I won't speak of this again. You will be a Maker; now go and help your aunt prepare for the feast."

Anya was lost for words. Trembling, she tried to hide her tears and be strong, but she felt weak and small. She turned and ran. Isaac called after her, but she kept moving, pushing past elders, Makers and anyone who got in her way. Anya didn't look back as she ran for the east crow's nest, desperate to hold back the tears.

When she arrived, Anya took a moment to catch her breath. Her lungs were cold. The east crow's nest wasn't the largest, but it was the first, and held a special place in her heart. Her father built it on his own from rusted metal and wood. It wasn't high like the north and south crows' nests, it wasn't grand, but it had been there in the beginning, when the Ark could be measured in metres instead of miles. It was the first lookout post, where her father had scouted out supplies, driftwood and those they could save.

The old east crow's nest was a place where Jake and Anya would play as children, where they would hide on cold, lonely nights without their parents. When Anya was down it was the only place where she felt safe. Clenching the rope tight in the cold wind, the sky began to darken as she climbed. When Anya reached the top, she huddled there and buried her head between her knees to wish it all away. She loved her uncle; she loved her brother – but she wished the tribe was not the way it was. Her mother and father would never have wanted it this way and it shouldn't have to be like this. Anya took her necklace from around her neck and wrapped it tight around her hand; she stared into the emerite gem, wishing to be anywhere but here. No matter how much she wished, how much she closed her eyes, nothing changed.

Anya stayed up there for hours, thinking, waiting, wishing. Isaac tried not to attract too much attention to her disappearance, but he told his most trusted men that she was missing, and they looked everywhere for her. The boy who climbed and found her was Jake's age; his name was Miles and he was the son of Tyson. Tall and slick, with dark brown eyes, long thick brown hair and a charming smile, he always acted tough and cocky, which, as much as Anya hated it, she loved it, too. He swaggered over the side after an easy climb and looked her up and down. Cheering people up wasn't his strong point.

"Anya, you need to come down," he said, pushing back his hair.

Perching on the edge of the high crow's nest, cool and calm, he always seemed to look bored with every-thing, and that intrigued Anya. She blushed. When she made her wish, she definitely didn't want him to see her like this. This was the exact opposite of what she wanted; she had had a crush on Miles for years and yet he had never really said a word until now.

"I don't want to talk about it," she said, hiding her true feelings in his presence.

"Well, I do. I heard you wanted to be a Hunter."

Anya could tell by his expression that the idea of her being a Hunter was alien to him, irregular and foolish. "Me? No, no, not true."

"Well, good. Hunting's for brave men," he said with that smile. "It just wouldn't – it just wouldn't be you; you know."

Anya tried to compose herself as Miles took a seat alongside her. He put his arm around her and leant close. She felt uncomfortable, rushed by a complete disregard for her feelings.

Then the loud fake cough of a saviour sounded. When Jake heard what had happened, he knew where she would be. So, without saying a word he had climbed to the top, unaware of who he would find when he got there. When he saw Miles, his eyes locked on with a silent fury as Miles stumbled to his feet. Anya blushed; she didn't know what to say.

"Miles, get down. Now," said Jake, with no patience about him. Miles sneered and moved towards him. They came face to face for a moment and there was a strange, silent animosity in Miles's eyes.

"I'll see you soon, Anya," Miles said before climbing down and out of sight.

"He is slimy, do you know how many –"

"That makes two of you then, doesn't it, Jake!"

"Well –"

"Miles can change."

"You have a lot to learn if you think he can change," said Jake, dangling his arms over the edge and staring out across the Ark. It seemed to stretch forever from here; he saw the north and south crows' nests towering into the clouds, the shacks, social spaces, docks and sails all around.

"So why are you up here, sis? What did Uncle say?"

"He said I can't be a Hunter; he says I can't learn to fish or swim or sail like the rest of you. It's all I want to do."

Jake looked into his sister's eyes and could see how much this meant to her; he could see she was growing. She wanted to make her own choices and he imagined how he would feel in her position. Still, the tribe's ways were set in stone and he had to protect her as best he could, even from things he would choose to change.

"We've spoken about this before; I wish it could be different. You know that hunting is no job for women."

Anya felt low, even lower now that Jake had said this. He was all she really had, and his honesty hurt more than anything else. She felt the sway of the raft once more, the motion of the crow's nest in the wind as the rain started to come down around them. Anya gripped the emerite necklace tight, hoping once more to be anywhere but here.

"I know who I want to be," she murmured with tears in her eyes.

Jake looked back at her with a smile. "Nobody knows, no one. I know what you're thinking: life isn't fair. the truth is there are some things we can't choose, and I know you will be the best Maker in the world. You will be able to spend all day with aunt Lyn, just like you used to."

As Anya listened to him, she tried to hide her sadness with a fake smile and a nod. It was no use crying or moaning up here, it was no use trying to change the Ark. Jake stood up and offered her a hand; after much hesitation, and to her shame, Anya took it. They climbed down together in silence, but Anya still wanted to be anywhere but here. At the bottom she clasped her necklace, closed her eyes and wondered what tonight would bring.

## 2

## THE CEREMONY

I n the evening, stars bounced from the never-ending blackness of the ocean to illuminate the Ark. The waves could be cruel or kind, and tonight the water was tame. Within Lyn's crooked shack, Anya could hear the drums beating outside and her heartbeat in unison. The acapella songs of the Arkers blended too, to form a unique orchestra. She sat on a crooked, aged chair facing Aunt Lyn as she applied all sorts of strange oils and powders to her face. Anya felt anxious, but she didn't resist. Make-up was applied around her eyes; it was the first time Anya had ever worn any, having never wanted to. It was made from the oil and fat of seals and she hated killing animals for anything but food. Despite her silent protest, Anya had a radiant beauty: her freckles complemented dark skin and her hair curled freely down over her shoulders. It was a shame that she couldn't see it for herself, for there were no mirrors on the Ark. Lyn couldn't help but smile back at her, for her niece held a hidden beauty that shined even when Anya tried to hide it.

"You look amazing, Anya," said Lyn.

"Thanks," Anya replied, half-heartedly. She didn't want to talk, when she was sad or over-thinking, she went quiet, and Lyn would rather make small talk than address a problem she couldn't solve. Anya hadn't seen or spoken to her Uncle Isaac since earlier on, but Aunt Lyn had heard what had happened and knew she couldn't make it go away. Still, with her iron spirit, she would do everything she could, and every time Anya dropped her chin in sorrow, Aunt Lyn was there to lift it right back up again.

"Today is a special day. You will remember this for the rest of your life," she continued, remaining positive although afraid to address what went unsaid out of respect for her husband. Aunt Lyn wouldn't say it, but she knew what was really wrong: it was a social problem underlying the whole Ark; the position of women in the tribe was an issue that no one dared address.

"The sooner it's over with, the better," replied Anya. Aunt Lyn ignored her negativity and draped a large cloak of leathered rainbow fish over her shoulders. It was heavy and glimmered even in the shack's darkness. Anya found it to be heavier than she had been expecting, but many before her had borne its brunt band now it was her turn to take the burden. She wondered what Jake would think of her looking like this. He would surely laugh – but that was just an extension of her own insecurity. Anya didn't like dressing up and she didn't play well with other girls. She thought of Miles and whether he would still like her, though it was the idea of him that she enjoyed more. She remembered that he and Jake would both be sitting with the other Hunters, ready to feast first. Anya wished she could sit there instead of with the Makers; she wanted to use a spear and learn to glide on kayaks as they did. The muffled sound of drums in the distance met her beating nervous heart and caused the shack to shake.

"Don't forget your necklace," Lyn said.

Anya had almost completely forgotten. She took it from the mantelpiece and placed it around her neck. Lyn stood at the shack door and looked at Anya once more: her necklace, her long curly black hair, and her glimmering rainbow-fish cloak. She nodded and pushed open the door for Anya to begin her walk. Moonlight and stars filled the sky as the sounds of drums and song flew in. Two lines of Makers and Crafters joined hands, forming a tunnel for Anya to walk through. Lyn turned back and crouched to Anya's level once more, held both her hands, and gave a warming smile.

"This is it, are you ready?"

"I suppose," Anya sighed, before making her leave. The Ark rumbled with a cheer in the moonlight. Anya saw the faces, the joined hands, and began to walk between all the smiles and good wishes. The drums grew louder, and the sound of singing took over. Anya had seen such ceremonies many times, but everything was different from the other side. Nothing could prepare her for the many faces and steps ahead, but every ounce of anxiety left her as she traversed the tunnel to the encouragement of her peers. She turned back to look for

Lyn, but she had disappeared, lost as each member of the tunnel she passed separated to walk behind her.

Anya watched her step because of the uneven wood-work below; careful not to fall in front of the crowd. She passed every face on the Ark; all had been a part of her life, no matter how small. There were tears, smiles and words of encouragement that made her feel more at ease. Some were perched high in the crows' nests, and small children gathered in front of their parents. Every adult member of the tribe had tattoos, and each had a special one on their left arm. It signified their position and rank. It was easy to tell the juniors, with the thin outlines of their trade tools, and the older masters whose tattoos were thicker and filled in. Makers had hammers, Carers had needles and thread, Chefs had spitting fire, and the Hunters their spears.

It was hard to fathom just how many people there were here, all singing and celebrating for her. She felt overwhelmed, knowing they were watching her every move. Today would be the most important day of her life, and so, for courage, she gripped her mother's emerite necklace tight in her hand. Focusing on its warmth, she walked through the masses, and when the crowd parted, she saw the banquet area for the feast.

Anya reached the Grand Stage's steps, where the elders and her uncle awaited her. The cloak was getting heavier and she knew the whole tribe was watching. One step at a time she went until she reached the top, where only this morning she had spoken with her uncle. It was different now because of the dining table, the seashell decorations, the forever fire lamps and alongside her uncle were the elders, the oldest and wisest on the Ark. She turned to see the crowd – all these people gathered here for her, for something she didn't want to do. They were cheering, chanting, dancing, already enjoying the night's festivities with cups of seaweed wine to keep them warm and dizzy. The stars were bright, the ocean was calm, and everything seemed so perfect, except for how she felt deep down. She gave Uncle Isaac a look, and to her surprise he smiled as if trying to apologise in his own way for this morning.

Anya turned back to the crowd. The adrenaline took over and she could not feel the evening chill or the gentle ocean sway. When the drums and choir came to an end, there were cheers and applause. Anya sat down at the head of a grand, weathered table surrounded by elders. Uncle Isaac faced her from the other side, and alongside her was Elder Frederick, the most respected elder of all, who headed all ceremonies. He wore a skinned walrus as a cloak, which weighed him down tremendously. He was bald, wrinkled, but still had strong sea legs, as they all did. She watched Elder Frederick bring the crowd to silence with a hand signal. Elder Frederick looked around with squinting eyes, surveying the crowd; when he began to speak, others could not help but listen, for he commanded their respect.

"May the sea guide us, may the ocean speak for us. May the winds and the waves bless us. Now feast!" Everyone stomped on the floor and banged their fists on the table, the crowd roared and rumbled and began to sing songs of the sea once more. The loss of the land had brought new songs, and with all the time in the world to practise, the melody was beautiful, rhythmic. When the food was ready, they all began to quieten. The Hunters were served first, laughing and joking, hungry from the long day's work. Watching from up here revealed how boyish they were, rude, impatient, demanding and somewhat ungrateful; but they worked every day from sunrise to sunset to feed the Ark; it was a job only the strong could do.

Next the children were served. They sat together on the floor for the lack of new benches to satisfy their growing numbers. The Carers and Makers took their seats too, far less rambunctious than the Hunters, and Anya noticed that next to her proud Aunt Lyn was the seat she was set to take after dinner. Last of all, the head table was served with a whole steamed swordfish. Anya sat, patient and nervous, enticed by the smell, among the elders. Her uncle cut the beast with a large hunting knife and with skill carved a piece for everyone. They passed along Anya's piece, and she looked down upon the succulent slice of fish, but she wasn't hungry. Her uncle stared with pride as Anya nibbled, but she couldn't find the room in her stomach, and felt sick. Sick for the words of this morning, sick for the choice ahead.

"Today is a special day for you, Anya," said Elder Frederick before taking a bite. Anya remained polite and gave him a grin, struggling to force a smile; she wanted to shout at him about the tribe's inherent problems, its inequality, but instead she grinned.

"Thank you, Elder."

Anya sat quietly among the sound of other conversations, finding it hard to concentrate. She was unable to eat, unable to appreciate the moment and be happy. When all eyes were off her, she took her piece of fish and threw it backwards, off the Ark and into the sea. When all the food was gone there were more songs and dancing with spinning spears. Juggling flips and tricks took her mind off things for a little while as she watched the tribe members jump from ropes above the Grand Stage. She watched and waited, taking in the Ark in all its beauty; it was singing, and it sang for her. When the moon was at its brightest the festivities came to an end. Anya wanted nothing more than to take off the cloak, which was starting to itch. She wanted it to be over, but she didn't dare say so. Despite her wants and wishes, the world continued to move without her. Young Hunters moved the table, and she stood alone with Elder Frederick. As the others departed, she felt so detached from it all. The Ark waited in silence and only the crashing of waves could be heard. Anya couldn't move, she saw a thousand eyes, but she grasped the necklace in her hand. She caught a glimpse of Jake and knew everything would be okay. The crowd was quiet, the sea was calm, and everyone was staring in anticipation.

"We are here on the sixteenth birthday of Anya Fairheart, a child of the Ark. I's a special day for us all. We wouldn't be here if it were not for your mother and father. They gave us all a chance to form a new world and made the ultimate sacrifice. We are in their debt, and we are in yours." Many bowed their heads at Elder Frederick's words, paying homage to the minds that made the Ark. All their lives were spared because of them, and that brought tears to many.

"Today was your day, and tonight is your night. Tonight, you are a woman, a member of the tribe." Anya could see the teary faces of many young women who had shared the same rite of passage, as Elder Frederick continued. "So, people of the Ark, do you accept Anya?"

"We do!" the Ark roared back in unison, before going quiet again.

"Will you swim with her?"

"We will!"

"Will you feast with her?"

"We will!"

"You are welcomed by us, blessed by us, loved by us. So, tell us, what is it that you wish to be?"

These were the words that she dreaded. Words that echoed around her mind and across the ocean. Frozen in place, at one with ice, she looked down at the speechless crowd who awaited a quick answer and then waited in anticipation. Anya clutched her necklace tight and thought of her mother and father. She looked for Aunt Lyn and saw her looking back with a proud smile and tears in her eyes; she gave a nod of encouragement to settle her stage fright. She had to say something ...

"I wish, I wish to be a Hunter."

The crowd gasped; those still eating spat out their food. Children asked questions, some whispered, and others tried to shush the crowd. The Hunters bellowed with laughter as Jake sank down amongst them. The

Makers were in shock, the Carers too; neither the old or the young knew what to say, and an eruption of shouting started to bury her. Anya wanted to cry but she held back the tears. She should not have said it. But it was done, and she could never take it back. She saw the anger in Isaac's eyes, the disappointment of the elders. Anya dropped the rainbow fish cloak to the floor. She could not take the laughter and the staring any longer.

"Women cannot be Hunters!" shouted a voice from the Hunters' table. Others cheered in agreement. Tyson and the Master Hunters grinned but remained silent out of respect for Isaac. Then, amidst the chaos, Jake shoved the one who had shouted, and a scuffle broke out amongst them.

"This is a mockery," said one of the female elders from behind, and that hurt the most.

"Enough!" Isaac's booming voice cut through the torrent of ridicule. Those fighting were held back, and the Ark was silent once more. Everyone waited for him to speak and Anya jumped from the stage to run through the crowd.

"Let her go!" Isaac shouted, and the crowd parted. Anya saw disappointment in the eyes of those she passed. They shook their heads and folded their arms and some of them refused to move out of the way. She had let them all down and ruined everything. Isaac looked on from the Grand Stage; he wanted to call to his niece, tell her to stop, tell her everything would be alright – but that would cause revolt. Her decision threatened their traditions and his place as leader. He feared for her, but more so for an Ark with a ruthless leader.

Cayden, one of the master Hunters alongside Tyson, stood up to face Isaac across the crowd. "This is blasphemy!" he shouted, whilst flipping a table for six with ease as the crowd dispersed to escape his rage. Isaac watched him tower above them, pushing through the crowd to make his way back to his quarters. It was Tyson's role to keep the Hunters disciplined, but he stood by and did nothing. Isaac could only let him go as the other Hunters followed, and Tyson gave Isaac an unwelcomed stare, before he too turned to leave.

There were no further celebrations, no more cheers or songs to be shared, for the night had been cut short. Under the surface, arguments brewed in marital shacks as women who had dreamed of being Hunters, or at least equals, considered their position in the tribe. They told tales of the olden days, now drowned, when men and women were almost equal. But the men who felt women should not hunt remained stubborn. Isaac, who had fought so hard to keep things together in times of struggle and depleted resources, was suffering the biggest strain of all. It began to rain, and a stormy sea followed their dispersal. Everyone headed inside their shacks to take shelter, to their hammocks wrapped in sea leathers. Though the walls of their shacks were full of cracks that the wind whistled through, most stayed warm.

Ignoring the weather, Anya ran fast and far away from all of them; she would have left the Ark if she could, but instead she climbed the same crow's nest as this morning. There she hunkered down and cried. She wished more than anything that her mother had been there to hold her, and that her father had been there to lead them – but they were gone. No one would stand with her now, no one would take her side. It was her against the world. Even the weather was against her; it grew worse, and the crow's nest swayed side to side. Anya feared a storm. She felt the thud of someone climbing, and a wet hand reached the top before the frizzy blond hair of her brother appeared. He climbed up to sit upon the edge, resting a hand either side to steady himself.

"Hey, sis," he said gently, knowing she was upset. Now he knew how much it all meant to her, and how foolish it had been to try. Anya didn't reply. "The weather's pretty bad up here." Jake knew Anya would be afraid if the storm continued to gather. The nest swayed and creaked in the wind.

"I know."

"Being a Hunter isn't all it's cracked up to be ..."

"That's easy for you to say, you *are* a Hunter. You had the choice to *be* a Hunter."

"It's ... it's a difficult job, a man's job."

"You're a boy," she said, losing all patience. Anya was angry but she didn't mean to take her frustration out on Jake. He sat down next to her and gave her a hug. They had climbed up here many times before, when the other children had teased them, or when they were unable to sleep, or on the anniversary of their parents' passing, when it was all too much for them.

"I remember the last time I saw Dad; do you remember what he said?"

Anya hated it when he said this. She remembered what he'd said, but Jake always used it to try and cheer her up.

"You said he told you to always look after me."

"He did. Being a Hunter is hard, and even if you could be, would you really want to do it? I mean, it's warmer amidst the windbreaks, making stuff."

"I really do," said Anya with pure determination in her heart.

"Even if they let you do the trials, they will taunt you. They will break you down and they sure as hell won't teach you. Tyson will make it impossible. The trials are made to test the strongest of Hunters. Do you think you can perform the blindfolded spear dance? Climb the mighty crow's nest? What about the high dive, and the long swim?"

Jake's words resonated with her, but they were bitter to swallow. Anya felt that she was strong enough to withstand their taunts, but she knew that no one would teach her. A tear rolled down her cheek as she made a fist; it wasn't fair. The Ark was a prison. She looked out to the ocean and saw the Hunters' kayaks tied up at the Ark's edge. She saw the elders hobbling, the raft being repaired, and all the crowded shacks below. No matter how stubborn she was, and how little she wanted to believe him, Jake was right. But then he said something she didn't expect.

"*I* will teach you." It took Anya a moment to

process what he'd said, so he said it again: "*I* will teach you."

"When?" Anya's eyes lit up and she wiped away her tears without a moment to lose.

"We start tomorrow."

"Thank you, Jake, I won't let you down, I promise," she said, suddenly ecstatic, and ready to learn the Hunters' way. They talked for a little while longer and Anya found the courage to face the descent down the mast. Despite the shame, the embarrassment, the doubts and whispers, tonight was hers, her birthday. It was time to grow up, time to join the tribe, and time to change the tide.

## 3

## BLINDFOLD

Everything was black. Anya clung to a large wet log that moved freely with the ocean. Crouched over, with a spear tied to her back, she was afraid of separating her hands from the log to stand up, for standing meant falling and falling meant the icy reality of failure. Her lungs tightened, her cold limbs were shaking, and the large old log below her continued to spin no matter how hard she tried to keep it level.

"Come on, come on, get up, if you can't do the spear dance, how do you expect to do the others?" asked Jake, he was standing a few feet away on his kayak with his arms folded, a ragged fish leather poncho sheltering him from the harsh winds.

"I can't," replied Anya as she trembled. She couldn't see a thing in the blindfold, and she feared another cold dunk in the morning sea after five spills already. Facing another fall was the worst thing in the world right now, and the feeling kept her frozen and unable to fathom standing.

"You need to be strong. Do you want them to laugh at you? Do you want them to taunt you?"

"No."

"Then stop giving them a reason to."

Anya gritted her teeth, and anger drove her upwards until she was on her feet. Then she went to grip her spear, but her movement and stance were tight and timid instead of being relaxed. She managed it for a few seconds, before the log spun around and she plummeted into the sea yet again. With a scream, she shivered and cramped up, before clasping the log for dear life.

Anya felt like a failure, to herself, to Jake, and most of all to her uncle. Jake pulled her up onto his Kayak and she wrapped herself in a thick rag for warmth. Her breathing was fast and sharp.

"It's hopeless, I'll never stay on my feet in this wind."

"It'll just take time."

"I don't have time." Anya was right: that was something she didn't have, for the trial was always the week after a sixteenth birthday. If the trial was not passed in that time, there was no way she would be a Hunter. In normal circumstances, master Hunters would be with her all day to show her everything she needed to know, they would also be the ones who would judge her at the trial, but she had no opportunity to build such relationships.

"You're good with a spear at least, if you can just balance, I have no fear that you can perform the movements. How do you feel about the high dive?" said Jake, trying to change the subject.

"Terrible."

"What about the rope run?"

"Even worse."

"Well, we have to try," said Jake as he rowed back to shore.

Anya sat shaking; it was warmer now than before, but she was still very cold. *Why did I ever say the words? Why did I ever say I wanted to be a Hunter? she thought.* Clasping the emerite necklace, it was warm, and she wondered what her mother would do. Her mother would tell them all where to go. She would overcome such animosity, become a Master Hunter and show them how wrong they were.

As they journeyed closer to the Ark Anya held her head high until the sight of a group of Hunters at the north dock made her lower it a little. They were getting ready to go out for the day. Usually the Hunters would be getting on with things, untangling nets and sharpening spears, but today they were still as statues. They watched Jake row closer in silence, and as they pulled into the side none of them said a word, silent in their disapproval.

Jake tied up the boat and they made their way to the south of the raft. The Ark was busy but exceptionally quiet. Everyone seemed to be getting on with things but everyone they passed was silent and distant. No one said hello or wished them well, no one smiled, everyone seemed down, as if Anya's decision had changed everything. When they reached the south crow's nest, Anya stared up at the swaying mast stretching high into the sky. It was hard to see the top, and harder still on one's neck. It towered above everything except its northern twin. A mix of wood and nailed metal poles, both nests had taken years to construct. This one was immensely tall, a mile higher than the one she often retreated to, and she even had to cajole herself into climbing down from that nest.

Jake led the way; he began to climb without hesitation, scaling it quickly. "Come on, we haven't got all day," he said.

"I'm right behind you," said Anya, but she wasn't. She stood at the bottom staring at the swaying tower that seemed to disappear into the clouds. After a large gulp she placed one hand on the lowest hold to boost herself up. Anya tried to move but her legs were like jelly, stuck in place for fear of failure, of being stuck halfway and having to call for help, of a crowd gathering to laugh and heckle her.

She stepped away and reached down to ring the bell of shame. One ring, and she waited, afraid to open her eyes for the embarrassment. Above her, the metal cage, but a dot, descended from the top of the crow's nest. Rusted and old, swaying in the wind and knocking against the mast, it clinked as metal did. It juddered, dropping a few feet and then slowing, free-falling a little more, and swinging around. It came down slowly and Anya winced as it bashed against the mast. The cage came to a halt on the Ark's deck. She stared down at the symbol of her defeat before stepping inside and locking the door behind her. It was only when she was on the other side of the cage did, she see Tyson close by with his arms folded, and when she saw him, he shook his head. Soon he and all the others were like ants and she was high above, flinching in the wind and at each knock against the mast. Even so, in that moment, she didn't ever want to come down.

Anya felt the wind blowing, cutting through the cage against the sound of creaking metal. Seagulls flew by; it was a surprise to see one so close up, as they often stayed up high. It was hard not to look down, and when she did, she felt sick; this was too far above deck. Anya closed her eyes until she felt the cage come to a halt. She undid the buckle for the cage door to swing open, and then she saw the gap between the cage and the crow's nest. It was a vast, unforgiving drop, and she feebly crawled across, hating herself. Anya stayed low, terrified of looking over the edge. Just being near the edge brought a sense of dread, so she kept her eyes forwards, to where Jake stood, a few steps behind an old man wearing an old navy hat and anorak that had been patched and re-stitched time and time again, weathered by the ocean. Anya found the strength to stand, nice and slow whilst feeling the sway of the nest.

As Jake and Anya stepped out of the cage, they were welcomed by the gruff voice of the nest's sole inhabitant.

"Well well well, Jake and Anya Fairheart," said Wilson in in his gruff voice. "Took you long enough"

"How did you know it was –"

"I saw you eye the climb a mile off. I see everything I do, that's why I'm up here. Let me guess, you want to go for a little swim lady?"

"I want to dive" Anya declared.

Wilson didn't respond, he merely stared out at the ocean with a glum look. Jake turned to Anya and whispered, "he doesn't hear too good." Wilson heard just fine, but he often drifted. Many said he had been hurt in some great war, some tall tale involving the navy, but the only thing anyone knew for sure about Wilson was that he liked to be alone.

Jake placed an arm on Wilson's shoulder. He turned around and Anya saw his icy blue eyes. Though Anya hadn't seen him for a long time, she recognised him. Many years ago, when her parents were still alive, but now he was old and red-faced, his skin a weathered leather of the sea. Wilson's hair and beard were white as snow. He did not smile when he saw Anya, and he soon turned his attention back to the ocean, his cruel mistress.

"What are you looking for?" asked Jake.

Wilson sighed and continued to stare at the ocean as if he could see something they could not.

"There's something dark beneath the sea. I see their eyes at night, their numbers."

Anya could tell right away that Wilson wasn't all there. It was no surprise, given where he spent his days at the top of this crow's nest. There was a small sheltering cabin, and a pulley system for any supplies he might need, but not much else. It was isolation. He would stay up here only for a few days before his wife passed. She had died of the flu – that was all it took back in the early days of the Ark, when only the strong survived. He seemed to blame himself for the storm, that was the last time he had come down, and with blame, he convinced himself that they may have had a chance at steering the Ark away from it. After that week's turned to months, and months soon turned to years. Wilson had made a promise to himself, to never stop watching but no one really knew what he was looking for. Most said it was the worst seas and weather, for icebergs, he would never say it was for the foolish hope of land.

"Anya has come to do the high dive," said Jake, eager to change the subject.

"Have you?" said Wilson as he span around and hobbled with a wide stance towards her and backed her up against the rails to size her up.

Anya winced from his bad breath, despite trying to act brave, "I have," she replied. Wilson looked her up and down and shook his head. It was easy to see the fear. Her legs had gone stiff and she was moving against the nest's windward sway instead of with it.

"No, you haven't. Divers don't use the cage to come up. Look at yourself, afraid of the edge. I already know how you're getting down; only fooling yourself and that's fools work. Are you a fool Anya Fairheart?"

"No."

"Requesting the trial was foolish."

"How did you know?" asked Anya.

"Slow learner too, as I said, I see everything," replied Wilson with a fierce impatience. "Your foolish move has upset more than you know, girl, and I see it hurts you too."

"Nothing will hurt me," Anya snapped before turning to the edge in an attempt to impress him; but she froze, fixated on the distance to the depths far below.

"We're one tribe and what hurts one of us hurts us all." Wilson put a hand into his pocket and retrieved a rock that he kept for such occasions; he placed one hand behind Anya's head to force her to look down.

"What are you doing? Let go of me!" she said, trying to resist.

"Watch," Wilson commanded with pleasure. He extended his other hand over the edge while maintaining eye contact with her, and then he let the rock go. Anya's eyes followed it all the way down; it seemed to drop forever.

"Wait for it. Wait for it …" said Wilson. He clicked his fingers at the exact time the rock hit the water, with a look of satisfaction. "Do you know how hard it hits your belly? You put your faith in your feet to make it or you end up like Roger."

Roger fell. Roger died. Anya knew he was only trying to scare her, but it was working, the drop was too far. She would never do it; it was a waste of time trembling up here. The wind was cold and the drop unforgiving.

"Or what about the rope? From the south nest to the north? You may end up like poor John." Wilson guided her with his hand and Anya saw the long rope. It stretched all the way from the south nest to the north, the two furthest points on the Ark. Another pulley system to get goods across quickly, every Hunter had travelled the distance. All except John: John lost the use of his legs and took to being a Maker.

"I-I can't do it," said Anya. Everything had seemed so easy when she was on the ground, but now it all seemed so foolish. She had seen the way people had looked at her, the way she was shunned, and she hated it. Even Jake bowed his head: he had put his faith in her, and it seemed to be for nothing.

"Take this piece of advice, my sweet. Stay on the Ark where it's safe. Dark times are coming, you have a good heart, but lack strength." Wilson hobbled towards the side of his shack next to the cage, making a few minor adjustments to the pulley system connected to the cage.

"I suggest you get in; I can't see you making the journey down. One small slip, and *splat*. I don't mean to scare, but one day you will appreciate my honesty." Anya looked at him, then the cage, and then the steep drop. She tucked her tail between her legs and shuffled sadly inside, and Jake did the same. "Oh, and Jake, tell your uncle I've ran out of rocks. It' a lonely life up here and I need more to throw at Lord Turtle Head." Wilson chuckled to himself before saluting them both, then he kicked the lever. He sent the cage cascading down at speed. As Anya held on to the bars in desperation, her stomach churned with disappointment.

"Do you think you can make the swim?" asked Jake, knowing the tide would be strong.

"I can try," said Anya, desperately trying to keep her mind off the drop. The cage came to a slow halt at the bottom and Anya opened her eyes once more. She saw a number of Crafters and Makers watching in silence, taking a break for a moment from fixing a breach in the

Ark. Jake glared at them and sure enough they put themselves back to work as the pair left the cage. Already at the south side, they headed for the nearest dock and the kayaks in silence. Here, they were well away from the Hunters. They dropped off and went out past the south side of the Ark, and then the kayak drifted about two miles behind the Ark's anchor until they were in rough seas.

"Are you sure you want to do this?" asked Jake, doubtful now, given the day's failures. Anya took off her necklace and wrapped it tight around her hand brace before giving a nod. She dived off the kayak, into the ocean, and began to swim, with no fear of the cold. Stroke after stroke she ignored the icy feeling even as it consumed her. Anya was a strong swimmer despite the cold; she kept breathing, kept a rhythm, and pushed herself on. She moved with the waves, coming up to breathe again and again, but soon each breath was harder than the last. She seemed to swim forever but despite how hard she pushed herself the Ark came no closer.

"Come on Anya, try harder!" Jake shouted from the kayak in front of her. He kept looking back to check on her and saw that she was making no headway.

*I can do this, I can do this*, she kept telling herself, but her arms and feet were cold. Trying to ignore the spasm, the pins and needles nevertheless took hold and there was a pain in her chest. Soon she hyperventilated, struggling to stay conscious until a mighty wave took her. Before she knew it, she was out and in darkness. Jake dived in to rescue her, pulled her back onto the kayak and rowed her back to the Ark. Anya came around with a cough and a splutter. She lay still, too cold and too tired to move upon the kayak. Jake was rowing and though he said nothing, Anya knew he was worried. She tried to breathe and regain her strength; Jake took the kayak to where the Hunters had been earlier that day. Their entire day's work had been done, and they would be eating now, so it was safe to return without being heckled by Hunters. Anya collected herself before making her way off the boat and onto the Ark.

Defeated, tired, and without a shred of hope, she reached the first shack, where Jake stopped in his tracks. Two twenty-year-old twins called Julian and Julien, both Hunters, stood in their path. It was impossible to get their names right or tell them apart for they each had bright red hair, brown eyes and fair skin. They were both bigger than Jake and had up until this point left Anya and Jake well alone, but now they blocked their path.

"If it isn't the two little Huntresses," said Julien as Julian began to laugh – one would always laugh when the other made a poor joke. Jake tried to move around them, and Anya did the same, but they wouldn't budge. Jake tried to step around them again with his head down and sensing his weakness they pushed him to the floor.

"Get off him!" Anya shouted as she sprang to protect her brother, scratching Julien. It left a long red mark down his face and he made a fist as if ready to strike her, even though she was half his size.

"Leave them alone!" came the deep voice of a thick set shadow. To their surprise, a Junior Cook called Tomas revealed himself. He stood there with a heavy stick. Tomas had thick brown hair, green eyes and had more facial hair than the other three boys. He was a stocky young lad, too thick set to move like a Hunter and none too sharp. He looked like a caveman with a club, big enough to cause even the twins a problem though he was only Anya's age, and the twins, being cowards, backed off and ran away, laughing as they did.

Anya saw Tomas and recognised him, though they didn't know him well. He was quiet, spent most of his time helping his family; in fact, she had never heard him say a word before. He offered his big hand down to Jake, but Jake ignored it and got himself to his feet.

"I could have taken them," said Jake.

"No, you couldn't," replied Tomas, straight and to the point. Anya couldn't help but laugh for his quick reply. She was grateful, for Tomas had done something few would have done.

"Burn," said Anya.

"And you, you swim slow." Tomas wasn't joking. It was his way; he wasn't one for flattery or casual conversation.

"Were you watching us?" she asked, and Tomas met her question with a sharp nod. He was about to speak again and offer another wise lesson, but someone else was coming. Tomas raised his stick in case the twins returned, but to his surprise it was Miles. He pushed his long, windswept hair back as he arrived, and smiled. It seemed so convenient to Jake – how he had missed the commotion. No doubt he had been watching, or at least within hearing distance. He barged past Tomas, giving him the look a snob gives a barbarian, before addressing the siblings.

"It's a good job they left before I got here. I was going to deal with them," said Miles as Jake took to sighing. Anya half believed him for his smile, and Tomas chuckled.

"What are you doing with this brute?" asked Miles, and Tomas grunted, raising his stick half ready to strike Miles on the head.

"He saved us," said Anya, and her smile made Tomas lower his weapon.

"Only because I didn't get here in time."

"Everyone knows Miles is useless, only passed his trials because of daddy," said Tomas.

"Enough brute, no one likes the lies of a legless Maker's son." Tomas lunged forward again, and Anya stepped in front of him. Myles, in order to defend himself quickly stepped behind Jake, "don't hold me back, I'll take him," he said with his fists held high.

"Enough!" Anya shouted and the commotion came to a quick end.

"I didn't come here to beat up this overgrown buffoon, now listen, my father came back from the shallows, he said that there are buildings, even ground."

"Ground?" asked Jake in disbelief. They had never stood upon anything except the raft and the idea of solid ground was quite the mystery.

"Yes, ground! We could go there; we could be the first to see it and bring something back. Something so amazing that I, I mean we, will be heroes. They may even forgive you, Anya."

*Forgive me?* Anya thought.

"No," said Tomas.

"No? What do you mean, 'no'? Brute."

"There are things in the shallows."

"Fairy tales, children's stories. Are you a child, brute? A baby?"

"Everyone knows that Miles, son of Tyson, is baby" said Tomas, raising the stick high once more. Anya put herself between them to lower the tension, she wanted to hear what Miles proposed.

"There will be riches, untold riches, and we can be the first to get to them. We can do something great," said Miles.

"I don't know …" said Jake. Anya knew he was thinking of Uncle, who would forbid it. Her mind however was filled with thoughts of glory: if she could bring the tribe something amazing, maybe they would forgive her and take her seriously. Maybe the Master Hunters would train her for the remaining six days before her trial.

"Let's go," she said.

"Goodbye," said Tomas, knowing that even listening to them was foolish.

"You have to come with us, brute. Hunters work in fours, isn't that right, Jake? They might even make you a Hunter," said Miles. His voice pained Tomas: being a Hunter had always been his dream, but though he was considered not sharp of mind, he was no fool and so he shook his head.

"Come with us," said Anya. Tomas wanted to say no, he wanted to say something that would indicate his opposition but all it took was Anya Fairheart to ask him to go. Miles and Jake readied the kayaks. Miles ushered Anya into his, and Jake reluctantly accepted the burden that was Tomas. They set off shortly after to explore the shallows. Anya was excited at the prospect of solid ground; she could not believe it. *Maybe I can find something to give to Uncle Isaac and Aunt Lyn for letting them down?* She wrapped her necklace tight around her hand and matched the pace of Mile's ore strokes as their kayak cut swiftly through the sea.

They journeyed with haste; the Ark was anchored for the afternoon so they could find their way back. Jake kept looking over at Miles and Anya. They were both laughing, and that annoyed him, as did Tomas's silence. He had no good conversation, his only contribution weighing down one end of the kayak. Looking at them both made Jake unsettled; he knew Miles could not be trusted. He knew that Miles, being Miles, would not have told them everything, but still he rowed.

Jake was half right: Miles had told them only what he knew, having relayed what his father, Tyson, had said in passing. There was much that Miles didn't know. The Hunters had gone to the shallows today and were gone for hours; but of the four that went, only three returned alive, in a state of shock, covered in blood and urgently wishing to speak with Isaac.

## 4

## SHALLOWS

The water was calm, the afternoon overcast, and the sun disappeared behind a vale of grey as the four sailed from the Ark. Their oars cut through water rhythmically and Anya set the pace. She turned to see Miles following her lead and behind him the Ark was barely visible. This was as far as she had been, as far any of them had been. A sense of adventure and a fear of the unknown took each of them as they sliced the sea's foam in unison. The smell of rotting wood had gone, and the scent of salted air took over to drive them forward. Tomas was sat behind Jake and his weight brought the bottom end down and the front end slightly out of the water; Jake had tried to make conversation with him but speaking to Tomas was like talking to the ocean. He was quiet and calm. He frowned an awful lot, but deep down, behind his rugged exterior was a gentle heart. There was something about him; his strength said more than words ever could, and his rowing beyond made up for the heavy ended vessel. In truth, his power outmatched any Hunter that Jake had seen, but he wouldn't say it.

The further they went; the more Anya had a strange feeling. It was like a chill, not due to the cold but the eerie nature of this vast open space. There were no waves here, the water was oddly calm, and strange green algae floated on the surface. Anya picked it up with her oar and held it close. It was the first time she had seen such a thing.

"What are you doing?" asked Miles.

"What does it look like I'm doing? I want to know what it is."

"It's slimy, it might be poisonous, put it down," he said, and so she did. Plants very rarely floated to the surface; some elders thought that plants and trees had evolved to stay underwater. Elder Frederick once told Anya that trees created oxygen, but now there were no trees above, only floating rotten trunks. He went on to say that algae produced most of the world's oxygen, and that was why everyone drowned rather than suffocated. He also said it was ironic to see mankind so determined to destroy trees and pollute the ocean, given that it would swallow the land.

Then Anya thought of something he said about the water. How at sea, for many years, the water was black, but the past few months it was dark blue. Here, in the Shallows, it was getting lighter and Anya's excitement shook the boat. Miles didn't feel the same way. The further they went, the more agitated he became; he no longer moved with the boat, and trembled, having lost his sea legs.

"Be careful!" he snapped, to Anya's surprise. She turned to see that he was pale.

"Are you afraid?"

"No."

But he was. He tried to hide his snarl and smiled, turning to the other boat a mere two metres away. Tomas mouthed the word 'baby' and grinned, so Miles scowled back at him. As they took their eyes off the water, Jake's boat jolted, thudded and scraped against something solid. Miles was quick to hold his oar against the motion of the water to avoid the same mistake; his boat came to a stop slowly, only just grazing its underside. Where they had scraped the underside, Anya saw the colour of the water change. They were on the edge of a huge dark square of water. The square was a black hole stretching far ahead of them; it swallowed the bright sea that surrounded its edges.

"What is this place?" asked Miles.

"I don't know" replied Anya.

"We should go back …"

"It was your idea."

"Oh no," said Tomas as something hard knocked his kayak. He looked down to see that the kayak had a crack running right through it.

"We're sinking," said Jake. "But don't worry, we can take turns swimming back with the other kayak, the Ark isn't too far. Is yours okay, sea-sister?"

"It's fine," Anya replied, with no care for the kayaks; all she cared for was the dark square. She lowered a foot over the side and into the cold water, and there, about a foot deep, it stopped dead. Miles looked on in terror at what she was doing as she dipped her second leg in and went to stand. She didn't know how to stand on something so still, and, off balance, waved her arms in attempts to compensate for the lack of constant movement. The ground was solid and strange, it wasn't wood or metal, it was still, and that made her nervous.

"What are you doing?" asked Miles, and whilst he stayed in his kayak, afraid, he watched Tomas and Jake do the same as Anya. Anya moved forward and dropped a further six inches. She edged out with caution and soon realised the whole dark square would be like this. She turned around and smiled at the others before they jumped down to join her. Wary at first, disoriented by the stillness, the three of them moved forward, crouching low, hands out to aid their balance. Then, as they grew more sure of their footing, they began to splash and paddle on the dark mysterious square. Soon they laughed and cheered in celebration of their discovery.

Anya waded through the water and saw green circles ahead floating; she didn't know their names, but they were lily pads, and as she went to stand on one, she fell right through.

"Come on, Miles!" shouted Jake, and despite his fear Miles finally stepped out of his kayak. Timid at first, he joined in, and the four of them were now gods on top of the world. Anya heard a strange croaking sound and bent down. On one of the lily pads she saw a frog, and then many more. She lowered her hand and it hopped on, and she watched in wonder as its neck expanded. She knew what it was, for aunt Lyn had carved a toy one for her birthday. Anya turned to the others with the frog upon her hand. Jake and Tomas were amazed but Miles jumped back and squealed.

"Get it away! That thing will kill me!"

"Baby," said Tomas, "frogs do no harm."

"Frogs?"

"Yes, frogs," said Tomas, as Anya gently put the frog back on its lily pad. She wanted to explore, and, looking out, saw reeds and plants. In the distance were strange, large bushes, so she waded through the water to get a better look at them. The four of them moved in a line with Anya at the front and Miles lagging behind. They walked further and further from the kayaks, one of which was slowly sinking and now half submerged, but none of them seemed to care, except Miles.

"What is this?" asked Tomas as he crouched down and ran his hands in the water. He placed his head under, and everything was dark. Making a fist, he pulled up algae and moss and then let it fall from his hand back into the water. Together they moved forward in the hope of wonder and discovery. Anya led the way, and she became entranced by a large green thing with pink spots. She knew it was a bush and saw to her amazement that the spots were flowers with yellow centres. She had never seen anything so beautiful, so she plucked the biggest and most beautiful one. Unsure of what to do with it, she placed it in her hair and tucked it under her headband. Tomas and Jake continued to forage, but Miles froze and then shrieked.

"Something touched my leg! Something touched my leg!" He panicked, quivered and yelped. Jake began wading towards him in the hope of calming him down as Miles flailed.

"It'll just be a fish, calm down," Jake said before he slipped from the edge of the world and disappeared straight down to be swallowed as if he were never there. With a splash, a crash, and half a scream he was gone.

Anya and Tomas desperately waded towards where he had been.

"Jake!" Anya shouted whilst scrambling through the marsh.

"This was a mistake! We're all going to die, we're all going to –" pleaded Miles, but on his last word Jake sprang from the water, clinging to the side of the hole. He coughed and spluttered, desperate to speak before Tomas pulled him back out.

"It's another world! It's another world!" he exclaimed in disbelief, whilst trying to breathe.

Amidst the excitement they had lost sight of Miles, who had waded through the shallows back towards the only remaining kayak.

"Miles!" Anya called, but he didn't turn around. Taken by a fear of the unknown, Miles had nothing else on his mind but getting back to the Ark as quickly as possible.

"I told you: baby," said Tomas.

"How will we get back?" Anya shrugged, and Jake put his arm on her shoulder.

"Miles won't go without us, let him cry on the boat. You need to see this!" he said. Anya looked at Tomas and then back to Jake.

"What's under there?" she asked.

"Another world!" he shouted, unable to contain himself, "let's go!" And before Anya could say a word Jake dived back in. Anya turned to Tomas and he met her gaze with a silent shrug, so she wrapped her mother's necklace around her fish leather forearm brace and followed suit.

Anya dived headfirst, and when she broke the surface everything changed. All around were old white walls, desks, chairs, computers, keyboards and bundles of wires, all overgrown with algae. There were whiteboards, carpets and wallpaper, colours on the walls the likes of which she had never seen before. Everything was overgrown, tinted green, and Anya swam between a jungle of metal, brick and plastic. It broke their very understanding of reality, of all that was. All they knew was rotted wood and cold; but this was concrete, this was something more.

They explored, each taking their own path. Anya made her way through the long cloudy green room, marvelling at the past. It was all so strange and wondrous to see what humanity had lost. Everything was so perfectly crafted – such perfect straight lines and edges. Within the room, nothing was made of wood, and the metal that was there was rusted but still so well preserved. She looked forward to see Jake staring at the room's edge. There he floated, entranced by something. He turned, pointed at his eyes with his fingers, and then back to the room's edge.

When Anya joined him, she understood what it was. Through the windows ahead was a town, a city of buildings, overgrown but beautiful. *This must be the highest point in the world*, she thought to herself. There were many smaller buildings and rusted metal mounds: cars, smothered with green. Mother nature had taken everything back. Anya watched Jake press his hand against some invisible force field and then he realised that it was glass. Windows had been explained to them, but they had never seen one for themselves and Jake had never felt glass before. He pressed his hand against it as if connecting with a world swallowed whole. Then he remembered to breathe, so he gave a thumbs up and pointed to an air pocket he had spotted on the way in. There was only so long even a trained Hunter could hold his breath, and he took calm breaths as Anya and Tomas joined him. The pocket was big enough for the three of them, and their breathing echoed in the small space as they tried to be calm and not upset the bubble.

"What is this place?" asked Tomas.

"I-I think this is what the adults called work," Jake replied.

"It is magical, it's —"

"Control your breathing, Anya," said Jake. "Did you see through the glass?" Anya nodded and before she could reply Jake took a breath to go under again. Anya took another moment to settle herself and swam to the glass window. She put her hand against it before looking down to the depths beneath. Anya didn't understand where she was. None of them did, they had never seen land, a town, or an office block before in all their lives. In a world devoid of such things, it was hard for elders to make youngsters understand; but now they knew. Here they were, on the top floor of a huge office, at the edge of a town washed away by the sea. Floating above a foreign and forgotten land – the place of their ancestors.

Whilst Anya and Jake continued to explore, Tomas went to the window and pushed his hand against it. It popped out of place and floated out in front of them, dropping down slowly, creaking and echoing in the waters as it did. Tomas froze in fear of its slow descent, as Anya swam off, cringing at how clumsy Tomas could be. She went back the way they came, to follow Jake as he made for the surface, but Tomas remained frozen at the window. He saw something down there. Glowing dots, far below. Almost losing his breath, he pulled himself away, thrusting back toward the exit. Unable to shout. Unable to scream.

Anya was still floating, at one with the water, when she saw something spectacular. The wall ahead was a full-length mirror. It was her reflection, and she had never seen herself before, except in the water. She looked past the floating rags she wore to see her bronze skin, freckles, blue eyes, and the flower in her long brown hair. She saw her beauty, how she was coming of age, and smiled. In such a moment, it was easy to forget that she needed air until, in the corner of her eye, she saw something which made her want to scream. Staring right at her was a dark green figure with glinting yellow eyes. Tomas came to her side and pulled her arm in panic, kicking frantically for the exit. They swam for their lives, scared that at any moment the monster would drag them down.

Tomas was so close to the surface he could see Jake's hand reaching down, so he took hold. Jake pulled

Tomas out, but to their horror the weak, waterlogged roof began to collapse around them. They scrambled to get out of the way as it caved in. Anya was still under as the water went dark and clouded with dust. She turned to find another way, but then she saw the monster. The green-skinned yellow-eyed creature had webbed toes and fish-like scales. It was almost reptilian, almost human – and then the roof came down and a beam pinned her to the floor.

Anya kicked and struggled, flailing to get free, but blind for the dust. With panic she began to choke and drown, before passing out. The last thing she saw were two yellow eyes staring into her soul with sorrow, but Anya couldn't hold on, and she had to let go. She became a sleeping princess trapped underwater; another lost soul swallowed by the sea. She was gone, cold, lifeless, no more.

The yellow-eyed creature looked at her body, it turned away and back again as if contemplating something. It came closer to inspect her; lifted the roof beam as if it were a feather and threw it to one side. It took its webbed claw to Anya's heart and from its eyes came a bright blue glow. The brightness shined from its claw and onto Anya's chest before it was gone again, and then the creature swam away. Anya lay lifeless and cold in the water, but then her eyes burst open as a pain seared through her chest. She looked around, aghast, her only instinct to push for the surface, and so she did. Tomas saw her and dragged her from the water with all his might. Anya coughed and spluttered up saltwater as the colour came back to her cheeks.

"There are hundreds of them!" he shouted, shaking and afraid before he pulled Anya up and onto his shoulder. Tomas started to run with haste, his heavy feet slowed by waters resistance.

"Hundreds of what?" asked Jake, then he heard a splash and turned to see a claw burst from the water. "Run!" he screamed as he quickly joined Tomas.

"I was already running!"

Anya opened her eyes, she felt dizzy, but when she could focus, to her horror she saw the creatures explode from the water, screeching and screaming. Up and down, in and out of the water they came, relentless, terrifying, and in numbers.

"Oh god, this is how we die. This is how we die," said Jake, pushing through the water with all his might. They looked around and realised Miles was gone. There were no kayaks ahead, they had nowhere to run and the monsters were close behind. Tomas was tiring fast as the screeching deafened them all.

"Put me down, you will move faster" Anya instructed.

"You will die" Tomas replied.

"Well, so will you if you don't put me down!" Without hesitation she jumped down from Tomas's shoulder, landed on her feet whilst almost stumbling and continued to run. Anya could feel the pouncing of the creatures in and out of the water close behind. Tomas was faster without carrying her, but none of them were fast enough as a tremendous screeching sound signalled the end. Running became pointless, as they struggled to move fast in shallow water. Jake led the way with Tomas close behind and Anya struggled at the back, her head was spinning, her heart burning. She could barely breathe and knew that any moment they would take her down. Soon the razor-sharp claws would settle in, and Anya wondered whether they would tear her limb from limb or whether she would be eaten.

When all hope was lost, Anya heard the roar of a familiar voice shouting, "spears!" Amidst the chaos, none of them had seen one of the small wooden ships, the *Iron Lady,* approach from parallel to the square. It was the Hunters' ship, and aboard it were the fiercest Hunters on the Ark. Uncle Isaac, Tyson, Pierce, Cayden and four more, all armed with sharp wooden spears. The boat turned and ropes were thrown down over its side. Jake and Tomas climbed aboard as quickly as they could scramble. Anya grasped the lifeline but struggled to pull herself up, her chest burning from where the monster had touched her. A webbed claw made for her shoulder and Isaac threw a spear that coursed through the monster's hand. It screeched the most hideous sound in pain. Others lunged forward at pace, but Tyson yanked the rope into the air, pulling her on board with one mighty heave. Anya got up, she was unable to take her eyes off the creatures, and unable to believe what she was seeing. There were so many screeching and clawing at the boat like rabid animals. The Hunters thrust their spears at the beasts, keeping a tight perimeter, while the others used oars to push the *Iron Lady* off from the side.

Anya looked up at Uncle Isaac and saw a different man. Not kind, nor quiet, but angry and menacing.

Deep down all the Hunters were afraid of the creatures, but they hid it well in the face of war. As the boat sailed, the Hunters turned around to face their enemy and the creatures screeched loud, an awful sound which echoed across the sea. Their sharp teeth glistened, as eyes of orange and yellow seemed to glow. Then they retreated, back underwater into the darkness, never to be seen again.

There was silence after the scream as everyone tried to process what they had witnessed. Anya held back tears; she was pale and cold, cold to the core. She remembered being trapped as the roof came down, those glowing yellow eyes, and then … nothing. A quiet, blank infinity. But then, to her disbelief, she came back, and she clutched her chest in fear of it. She looked around to see Cayden, a large Master Hunter with a blonde mohawk staring down at her. His blonde mohawk and braided beard making him appear quite the warrior. Pierce, another Master Hunter alongside held his spear high with a wide stance in victory. His hair, a forest green, fluttered in the wind.

"Filthy fucking things," he said.

"Aye," said Cayden.

Anya turned to her uncle. She didn't know what to say, so she said the only words she could fathom.

"Thank you, Uncle. I –"

"Don't speak!" bellowed Isaac. "Did they touch you? Did they touch any of you?" Isaac asked, shaking her by the shoulders, enraged. His eyes were red. Jake and Tomas didn't dare say a word; they shook their heads as the other Hunters looked away.

"No, no," said Anya quietly, all choked up. But they had, and she touched her chest for the piercing pain the monster had brought. Anya felt afraid, too afraid to tell them.

"What is it, Anya?" asked Isaac, for he knew something was wrong.

Anya crossed her arms, and to her dismay she realised, "I ... I ... I lost my mother's necklace," she confessed to her shame, caressing her wrists where the necklace had been. There was nothing worse, nothing worse than losing it, and for a moment she forgot about the monster. There was no peace without the necklace, she had the flower tight in her headband, but that was nothing compared to something so irreplaceable.

"Miles," said Tyson in his deep gruff voice, summoning his son. Miles came shuffling over, shaken, defeated, unable to look up at any of them. The other three youngsters stared at the floor, afraid to look directly at Isaac or Tyson.

"Miles said you kidnapped him and made for the shallows, is this true?"

Jake and Tomas stayed silent, but Anya couldn't. She was still so full of adrenaline. "No! We went together, as a team of Hunters. We lost one boat and Miles sailed away." said Anya, surprised by Miles's betrayal. Tyson folded his arms and gave his son a scolding look, before laughing. His glare first and then his laughter made the other children flinch and begin to understand why Miles was the way he was.

"This girl stayed while you ran away?" chuckled Tyson with a loud, sinister laugh.

"But Father, I –" Mid-sentence, a mighty backhand struck his cheek to silence Miles as he whimpered in fear.

"What happened today, you never speak of it," said Isaac, putting himself between them.

'But Uncle –" said Jake.

"But nothing. To the tribe, to each other, to no one. Understood?"

"Yes," mumbled Jake.

"I said *understood*?" said Isaac, raising his voice, and the four of them chimed back:

"Understood." But Anya's mind was on events past, wanting nothing more than for it all to go away; but it would not. She saw those creatures now as clearly as ever, and she knew she could never unsee them.

"Now sit and stay quiet until we return," Isaac continued, and the youngsters didn't dare disobey. They sat cross-legged in the middle of the ship, back to back, unsure of what to say or do. Miles was still shaking, terrified by what he had seen. Jake was quiet and Tomas just seemed his usual distant self. Anya couldn't shake the monsters from her mind, nor the stinging pain in her chest. After a while Cayden approached the four of them; Anya wasn't sure whether he took pleasure in scaring children, or whether humour was his way of coping with the worst of situations.

"Do you want to know what happened to old Greg?" he asked with a big smile. But the children said nothing, too afraid of Isaac's wrath. Anya, however, nodded; she needed to know.

"One of those monsters put a hand through his

chest and tore out his heart like it was nothing." Cayden chuckled as he mimicked a beating heart with his fist, and Anya tried to ignore her own palpitations. "I'd count yourselves very lucky." Cayden chuckled for the horrified expression on their faces, before backing away once more and playing with his knife. Anya felt the pain in her own heart as he said it, she watched the Hunters pace backwards and forwards, manning the ship. The journey was long, and Anya knew they would probably never have made it back on their own. She overheard Tyson and Isaac talking as they kept a lookout for the Ark.

"What are we going to do about them?" asked Tyson.

"Nothing, we go far from here."

"There will be supplies down there; we need everything we can get from the shallows. And they killed one of our best – we should kill them all."

"No," said Isaac, "there are too many of them."

Tyson looked rather spiteful; it was hard to ever know what he was thinking behind those constant angered eyes. He hated not getting his own way, hated being the strongest but not the one in charge. Everyone knew he wasn't the brightest, but that didn't matter anymore, for the Hunters only cared for strength.

The trip back to the Ark seemed to take forever. Anya's breaths were long and dry, her heart was burning, and at every moment she felt as if those creatures were about to jump over the side of the vessel and come for her.

She could not wait to see the Ark again and was

relieved as Pierce called its name from behind a tele-
scope. When they finally arrived and pulled up to the
Ark's edge, everyone turned out to watch. Bad news
travelled twice as fast as good on the Ark, and everyone
heard how the little girl who wanted to be a Hunter had
foolishly made for the shallows, how she led them into
danger after one of the Hunters didn't return earlier that
day, and how a brave group of Hunters rescued them
from her mistakes. Anya felt pale and feverish. The long
day had taken everything from her, and when she
walked the *Iron Lady*'s plank at the south dock, she saw
all those judging eyes, but only cared about Aunt Lyn,
who ran forward in tears to embrace her.

"Oh, Anya, what were you thinking? Why would
you want to do such a thing, what are you trying to
prove?" she entreated.

"I did not know," Anya replied, sobbing, unsure of
what to say, before reaching into her hair for the flower.
It had dried on the journey and looked beautiful, bright
pink and yellow, and still in one piece. She passed it to
Aunt Lyn, and she smiled upon seeing such a beautiful
reminder of the past. Lyn put it back into Anya's hair
and held her close once more.

"It looks better on you, child, it looks better on
you."

## 5

## FEVER

After the shallows, with those green-scaled, yellow-eyed monsters and their haunting screams, everything changed. Anya couldn't eat supper; she wasn't hungry. She seemed without energy, without motivation. Jake, Miles and Tomas had disappeared for fear of being seen with each other again. The Hunters' wrath made them all separate; it was for the best, as there was nothing any of them had wanted to say to each other anyway. Not after what they had seen, what they had been through.

Their journey into the grand unknown began with curiosity but had ended in disaster. Anya spent her time sitting alone on the edge of the Ark watching the sun set. She sat cross-legged, looking out to the horizon in the direction of the shallows, thinking of those beastly creatures and how she would never forget their screams. She thought of the one she had seen up close, its reptilian skin, the way it looked through her. She brought up a hand and clutched her chest where it had seared her skin. A stinging pain took hold, and no matter how much she wished it away, it didn't go. She thought of her uncle, and then the trial, she would never be a Hunter now – but behind closed doors things were happening beyond Anya's control. Many whispered in secret about the inequality between them and the Hunters. Wives confronted their husbands, banding together to support the girl who wished to be a Hunter. This was all unknown to Anya, who had given the flower to Aunt Lyn.

Lyn shared the flower with friends, Makers and Crafters who had told stories to their children of flowers, although none of them had ever seen one. Anya had brought home the unimaginable, a beautiful pink and yellow flower brighter than anything they had ever seen. It gave them hope, and they spoke of the girl who wished to be a Hunter, who had brought them the impossible. Anya became a silent hero. Wives stood up to their husbands, and even Aunt Lyn raised the prospect of Anya being a Huntress with Isaac, who brushed it off for fear of the other men. Kamara, Tyson's current partner, was even brave enough to mutter it in his presence, but when he told her to speak up, she didn't dare.

Anya sat watching the sunset, thinking over everything, unaware of the problems growing upon the Ark. Amidst her thoughts, she forgot how tired she was. When she went to stand, a migraine came, and she felt the heat of her forehead. She struggled to make it back to her shack. When she arrived, it was late, and everyone was asleep; in silence she crawled to her space to sleep. The ocean's gentle rocking calmed her; she did not dream but tossed and turned all night. In the morning, Jake came to wake her early with the intention of practising for the trial. He looked at her as if she was marked for death.

"Are you okay?" he asked, but he knew she wasn't. Anya was pale, her rags soaked with sweat. Her arms were heavy, weak, and Jake put a hand on her forehead. There was a burning heat on her brow, and he went to get help.

"I'm fine," Anya muttered, but Jake had already left. She pushed her hands down as if to fight being horizontal. She got to her feet and stumbled over the other girls who blocked her path. Riley awoke again, as did the others, but they didn't scowl or whisper – instead they shuffled out of the way, out of respect for what she was doing. Anya pushed forward, struggling to keep her balance. When she got outside, the brightness of the day was blinding, the raft's rhythm unnatural. Stumbling towards Jake, he seemed but a blur amid all the woodwork of the raft. She only knew it was him for the outline of his long blond hair. Every step became a struggle and she couldn't hold herself up any longer. Anya fell hard onto the raft's planks and hit her head. She was barely breathing.

"Help! Help!" Jake shouted as a crowd gathered but no one wanted to touch her. It was up to him to pick her up and carry her to the only place he could.

When one fell ill on the Ark, there were few options to stop the spread of sickness. If it was the flu or another, similar disease, the ill were granted isolation and prayed for. Anya was carried to the sick shack, a small rickety building, somewhat neglected, a lonely place. There was a bed and seal leathers to sleep in, enough supplies for a week, and nothing but a hole in the planks to go to the toilet. Jake laid Anya down and left her to fight the fever; and a wicked fever it was. It struck hard and fast, causing Anya to shake and her heart to pound. Red hot, no splash of icy saltwater seemed to diminish the headache and she was unable to catch her breath. Unable to eat, speak or stand, she felt hopeless. Only rest could help, but staying still brought an unbearable chill, which led to spasms. Her cough was chesty, the fever high. Anya tried her best to fight it, but everything went black and then she began to dream.

With such sickness came hallucinations, and Anya dreamt that she was flying high above the Ark, a seagull soaring in circles to the clouds and back down. The gull was old, fuzzy, and moulting. The Ark was its home: it had led a happy life, raised its young, loved and lost its mate but now its flight had become a struggle. It flew up high before diving down, and then came the sickness of falling, the dive toward the sea, until it broke the ocean's surface. It sank deeper and deeper into the depths until it found its peace.

Everything was black, everything was cold, until its ability to feel ceased altogether. A different feeling took hold: a sight with sound. The dark depths were a thing of beauty, filled with life, filled with peace, a never-ending wonder. A great whale soared within the ocean, flowing and flying through a motionless calm. The sea was its endless blank canvas, an infinite playground where the grace of slow movement was everything – a peaceful, tranquil harmony. Hungry, the whale opened its mouth and swallowed the ocean, letting in plankton and saltwater as it did. Beautiful long noises met the sound of others nearby, whispering, telling stories. Then the strangest noise travelled through the water, humming and singing. Unfamiliar voices seemed to echo back and forth throughout the ocean. It was a harmony never heard before, so different to the rhythms and songs of the Ark. The tones began to separate, disperse, and became different voices, whispers of the unknown, the dead perhaps calling Anya's name with a sweet hypnotic tone. They argued, cursed, sang, praised and made peace with one another. Then she heard a familiar voice: her mother.

"I love you, Anya, but you can't stay here, not yet. You have to wake up," she whispered, fading away and becoming lost in the sounds of a thousand others. Anya was at one with the ocean; there was no need for anything except to swim, but against her will the whale rose to take a breath. It made for the surface, there was nothing she could do to stop it, no matter how hard she tried. When the whale burst out to breathe again, Anya's eyes opened. Shaking but alive, she coughed, spluttered and turned onto her side. She took up the bucket of fresh water and downed most of it. She felt better, stronger, and she poured the remaining water over her head, before looking desperately for the flower. She noticed it had fallen from the bedside, having grown dull and faded, and as Anya went to take it in her hand it fell to pieces. She remembered she had lost her necklace, too, and that hurt even more.

Anya heard crying: it was Aunt Lyn sobbing on the other side of the door. Through the keyhole Anya could see her., so she knelt down to take the key and opened the door. On the other side Aunt Lyn rubbed her eyes in disbelief. Seeing Anya alive and well took away all the pain. Aunt Lyn had sat outside the shack on the hardwooden floor despite the cold night winds and heavy rain. She had prayed, hoped and worried, refusing to leave for as long as Anya was inside.

"Anya, my sweet, you're alive!" Aunt Lyn shouted, before embracing her in disbelief. "Are you okay?"

"I feel fine, but you shouldn't hold me like this," said Anya, not wanting her aunt to contract the same sickness. But Aunt Lyn smiled and began to chuckle.

"I don't care, I only care that you're better. It's a miracle. You were as good as dead. Now don't you think you'll be going anywhere; you need more rest."

Lyn took a long curious look at her. Anya was a little pale but other than that she appeared to have made a full recovery. Lyn looked worse for being worried sick and having lost so much sleep.

"I've rested for long enough … How long was I out for?"

"You've been out for six nights."

"Six nights?" Anya gawped in disbelief, but it was true, she had spent days tossing and turning, sweating, coughing and spluttering, all the while dreaming of other-worldly creatures. She had felt the end, had felt peace. Anya knew from the way Lyn looked that she had waited outside the door the whole time. They would have had to drag her away.

"Six long nights."

"Six nights! I, I can barely remember any of it. You waited for me this entire time?"

"I will wait for you forever, Anya, wherever you go." Lyn grabbed her cheek and smiled once more. "Here, I made you something," she continued, before bending down to the side of her rocking chair to reach her bag. She withdrew a wooden sculpture with her shaking hand. Aunt Lyn presented her with a carving of a whale, and it stopped Anya in her tracks for a moment, as she remembered her dream.

"Is everything okay?" asked Aunt Lyn.

"I'm fine, it's just, what we saw at the shallows."

"Your uncle wouldn't tell me what happened out there, but Jake did. Those monsters, maybe they are people, maybe they were angry because we went into their territory. What happened when the roof caved in?"

Anya remembered all of it; the monster's eyes in the mirror, swimming for her life and becoming trapped under the beam. She recalled darkness, a bright light and then feeling alive again before climbing out to run away.

"Whatever happened to you, we can talk about it."

Anya backed away as she failed to hear Aunt Lyn's words and replayed every moment in her head, but she wasn't afraid, she was oddly calm and realised that six nights meant seven days, and today would be the final day for the trial.

"Thank you, Aunty, for everything, thank you," Anya said, backing away once more to leave Aunt Lyn worried.

"Where you are going? I want you to rest."

"There isn't enough time, I must speak to Uncle."

"Well, maybe it isn't such a good idea, maybe you should stay," Aunt Lyn said, and Anya ran forward to hug her once more. Then she moved from the shade into the piercing light of day. She ran fast, as Lyn looked on with pride, happy that she had pulled through, but sad that her beloved niece had left her there with the whale sculpture still in hand. Lyn fell back into her rocking chair, where, for the first time in a week, she fell asleep.

Anya went past shack after shack, through crowds and cooking circles. It was a beautiful day, and everything felt so new. Those who saw her went silent, holding their breath for fear of a fever spread from the shallows. Everyone turned to stop and stare, for the girl who wanted to be a Hunter, who had gone to the shallows, and even defied death, was alive. Anya didn't care for whispers, but she had not seen what had happened in the past six days and no one would stop to tell her.

A funeral had taken place for Gregory, the Hunter who had lost his life on the first voyage to the shallows. His wife Fiona swore and spat, cursing the elders, cursing Isaac for his lies. They had tried to cover up what had happened but rumours of yellow eyes in the night could not be washed away. Four had gone and three returned, none of them the same. Pierce was silent, where Cayden told tales of monsters, and Tyson grew more paranoid by the day. Trouble brewed in the homes of Hunters, for talk of women's rights came from questioning wives with Anya's wish for change. The hunting men met in hopes of deciding how best to silence their women. The fishing catch was down, and many said Anya's wish to become a Hunter had cursed the Ark.

Uncle Isaac was growing tired and weary; he thought Tyson and the others were plotting something. All he had ever tried to do was protect them, but this blue world was very different to the blue and green of old. Arguments in council meetings became rife. Isaac wanted to ignore the shallows, but Tyson rallied behind talk of monsters. Isaac insisted on letting the women of the tribe raise their concerns, but Tyson threatened to meet their defiance with swift action. Hunger, and Gregory's death, fell upon Isaac's shoulders and at every turn. No matter how hard he tried, he seemed to have the wrong answers. All this, whilst Anya lay upon her deathbed. Isaac had never felt more alone. His big brother Richard, so smart and diplomatic, was gone in the storm and he would never have him back. With Lyn by Anya's side, and Jake trying to get over the horrors of the shallows, he didn't have anyone to talk to. The Hunters allied in numbers, and the long rule of Isaac grew weaker by the day. He knew that they would all stand with Tyson – it was only a matter of time. Isaac wondered what Richard would do, what he would say.

Anya was oblivious to all this. Jake, Miles and

Tomas hadn't spoken either, having been sworn to secrecy. Lyn had stayed outside the sick shack day and night. She would have frozen if it hadn't been for the elders giving her a blanket and food. Isaac had sat alone without her council, and he was hardly sleeping. Despite this, Anya, with her fierce furrowed brow, marched through the people of the Ark and up to the Grand Stage, as the crowd looked on in silence.

"Anya," said Elder Frederick in surprise; he was the first to notice her, and the others followed suit. Isaac turned around in disbelief.

"Anya, I thought you were –"

"Dead? No, I feel better, much better."

"You were very lucky; I have seen such sickness take many. Why aren't you resting?"

"I wish to do the trial, Uncle" she said, giving no time to pleasantries. Isaac hung his head and frowned. He rested his hands on his hips, before taking a deep breath to calm himself.

"Anya, this is not the time, there are much bigger things we need to –"

"I'm ready."

"It's too late," said Isaac, fearing another dispute. He shook his head and sighed, not wishing to discuss this any further. Silence took the Ark as the elders looked away, not daring to say anything. Tyson, however, stood towering over her, looking down with that fierce expression of his.

"I think you need to rest, little girl," he said.

"I'm sick of resting, I'm sick of waiting. I'm fine."

"Anya," said Isaac.

"Listen to your uncle: The Hunters don't need some little girl who runs off to the shallows and has to be rescued."

"Miles is a Hunter and he ran away! At least I didn't leave us there to die!" Anya's response was short and sharp, her fierce nature easy to beckon. But though she aimed to ridicule Tyson, he smiled as if amused. Nothing was quite making sense to her and she was oblivious to the game of politics being played.

"I see your senses have not recovered. Three children went missing on one kayak, and Miles followed you and called for help. You would be dead if it wasn't for my son," he said with a smile.

She knew it was nonsense and that Miles had run away with his tail between his legs. They would be dead if the *Iron Lady* had not appeared. So, in a way, in Miles's cowardice had saved their lives, and she forgave him despite his actions. That still didn't change what had happened; the truth was the truth and the people had a right to know. Anya was not the type of person to hide things or tell lies to protect others.

"That … that …" said Anya, so frustrated that she was tongue-tied.

"Anya, apologise. You have done more damage than you know," said Isaac, but Anya didn't want to apologise to such a wicked man. She was too stubborn, just like her father.

"If the girl wants to do the trials, let her fly, Isaac, or let her fall."

When Isaac heard those words from Tyson, he knew that he had got what he needed: someone else to say it.

No matter the hidden intentions of his foe, Isaac wanted Anya to do it and prove everyone wrong. And if she did, it would restore his name.

Isaac took a long look at his niece and saw the fire in her eyes, the determination.

"Very well," he said.

## 6

## TRIALS AND TRADITIONS

Anya stood upon the kayak as Jake rowed her to the old log. There were a number of kayaks already there, all belonging to Hunter's who had turned out more for a joke than to provide support. They were already drinking seaweed wine, dizzying about the day and becoming rather rowdy. It never would have been accepted at any other trial, but Anya's was an exception. In the past, when a candidate had attempted any of the trials, a member of the council, or a Master Hunter would announce the games, their importance and all else, but no volunteered today.

"Good luck" said Jake but he didn't hug her. With her chin held high Anya climbed up onto the log, her foot almost fell, and the crowd reacted in jest as she corrected herself. At the top she crouched with the spear on her back and the blindfold in hand ready to go. She looked for an elder but instead she found Tyson, Pierce, Cayden and many others. Uncle Isaac wasn't on any of the kayaks, but he was watching from the Ark's edge.

"Wait!" a voice shouted. Everyone turned, to their utter disappointment they saw a barrel bobbing up and down, floating toward them. It was none other than Lord Turtle Head, paddling with his arms and home-made flippers. The younger Hunter's began to laugh, only to be told to quieten down by a warning look from Pierce.

"What's he doing here?" Cayden muttered as many moaned and groaned at his appearance.

"Wait! Wait! She owes me a dollar!" Lord Turtle Head cried.

"No one's seen a dollar in thirty years," Tyson bellowed as he shook his head impatiently, only wanting them to get on with it.

"My good man, I want my dollar and this trial cannot continue until I have it, no sir."

"I don't have a dollar" said Anya from her log, rather glad for his appearance.

"Well what else do you have?"

"Not much to be honest."

"My turtles told me you had some information, tell me what you know!"

"Here he goes, about his *bloody turtles* again," muttered Cayden as he pulled on the long braids in his blonde beard.

"*Shh*," said Pierce, "if he hears you, he won't stop his turtle talk."

"What's that about my turtles? You shouldn't be out here you know; here I have some turtle helms for you all …"

"Enough!" Shouted Cayden, "the Trial must begin."

"Very well. Instead of a dollar, I will settle for announcing the trial."

Anya looked at Lord Turtle Head and then at all of the Hunters, she knew that they would despise his intervention and so she had little choice. "Very well," she said.

Lord Turtle Head looked up with excitement, he cleared his throat and jumped up to stand on the rim of his barrel. He revealed his brown fish leather briefs, his swollen belly and skinny frame with his hands held high in the air.

"Ladies and gentlemen, children of all ages. We gather here today for the ultimate test, the Hunter trials, the showdown. Watch as she faces the spear dance of balance on a loose log, witness the epic crow's nest climb to the clouds, the highest of high dives and the merciless mile swim. Will she conquer all, taste glory, and leave the wimpy Hunter's quaking? Or will she die an incredibly painful death." Lord Turtle Head paused for a moment on that thought. "Ahead is our mighty challenger, she's no stranger to danger, the queen of mean, the damsel of destruction. She floats like a butterfly fish and stings like the sea –"

"Oh, just get on with it!" shouted Cayden.

"May I introduce the challenger, Anya of Ark!" Lord Turtle Head put a hand to his ear to hear the crowd roar back, but there was no noise, only the sea.

"Erm, thank you Lord Turtle Head, I think," said Anya.

*This is it*, Anya thought, with her feet either side of the log that had defeated her before. The small crowd heckled her, and everything was black, for the wrap wound tightly around her eyes. Though her fever had passed, the pain in her heart still stung. Anya tried to calm her breath, to relax, to breathe. Many of those around cast doubt, but something within had changed. Having danced with death she had come out the other side to feel fearless. There was a peculiar feeling, an innate determination bringing her a sense of calm and balance. Now it seemed that it had only ever been nerves that had held her back.

"She's going to fall!" shouted a Hunter from the back. Anya cleared her mind to forget about them. *It's just me; no one else matter*s as she crouched down low, unsure of whether to stand. Despite all the odds, Anya got to her feet, spear in hand. Staying still for a moment to control the log's movement, she was quick to adjust. Her toes felt the cold splash of the waves, her hair swept back in the sea breeze, and she was up and ready to fight. Standing tall and strong, Anya advanced across the log, holding her spear ready, and then she struck out, extending it with delicate ferocity. Strike – strike and move. Strike – strike and move. She spun the spear around her and lifted one leg from the log. The world stopped as Anya balanced, and there was silence but for the waves, as all the heckling Hunters went quiet. Anya moved her feet with every slight movement of the log.

With a sigh of relief, she threw the blindfold down in triumph, before jumping from the log onto the kayak closest to her where Jake was waiting. No one dared to celebrate or smile, given the sour nature of the Arks Hunters, but to everyone's surprise the little girl had done it. She had faced the first hurdle head-on, and though he didn't show it, Isaac was proud. No one had expected her to do it, not now. Not after the illness. Even Anya could not believe it. There was no applause and no celebration. The Hunters' minds were in shock, but right now Anya was blind to anything but her own success.

The kayaks separated into a flying V formation and rowed back to the Ark in unison. Jake paddled as Anya looked at those in the kayaks around her: they were quiet, solemn, and shared none of the celebration she felt inside. Jake himself didn't dare cheer; though he was proud, he seemed wary of his hunter brethren. Lord Turtle Head however was chanting her name on the way back whilst doing a form of back stroke.

"What did you think?" she asked Jake, in need of his approval.

"You did well," he said, surprised about how easy she had made it look.

"Did Uncle see?"

"He did," sighed Jake, "but he is not himself, no one is."

Anya overlooked his worries; she felt proud and was already thinking of the next task at hand. She seemed oddly calm and relaxed. The situation only dawned on her when they reached the north dock and she stepped foot on the Ark. Many of the tribe were watching, although pretending not to watch. Anya saw Tomas amongst them, and he smiled; it was the warmest thing she had seen all day but there was no time to stop, to talk or rest. Anya was taken right away to the north crow's nest. There she would climb, attempt the rope walk to the south, where Wilson would be waiting, and then perform the high dive.

Anya looked up to the crooked north crow's nest high above. Part of her felt a fool for trying to do something like this, something she had not prepared for; but it was not impossible. It was not as daunting as before, either; where fear had been, there was something else, and instead of an obstacle she saw a path. The only thing that made her worry was the stinging in her chest, which came with every breath. As she stared up at the nest, a large hand met her shoulder; it was her uncle.

"Are you sure you wish to continue, Anya? No one will judge you if you give up now. It's quite a climb."

"I'm ready," she replied, fiercely determined, and she took her uncles hand to hold it for moment before she brought it down from her shoulder. They faced each other, and many things went unsaid. Though Uncle Isaac tried to be strong, Anya could see the real emotion behind his eyes, his love, his pride and in her eyes, he saw the same.

Isaac knew that she was growing up; he had to let go, let her do things he wished to protect her from, even if it meant challenging the Ark's traditions.

"Send my regards to Wilson when you get to the other side," he said.

Anya turned and began to climb, "I'll tell him to smile once in a while."

"You can always use the cage to come back down," said Tyson, as the Hunters sniggered, with Miles cowering behind them. Anya knew had to prove them all wrong. So, she pushed on. She went up and up the creaking wooden structure and didn't dare to look below. She could not see the end above her, and black clouds had gathered in an ice-ridden wind. Her hands and feet were soon freezing on the mere chips and indents in wood and metal, that many called holds. The rain came down, making it harder to hold on for her cold and shaking hands. Anya forgot how tall the mast was, how it went from side to side, bending over, and moving with the wind. Shooting pains in her chest returned as a chill took hold. Her footing slipped but she clung on tight, swaying high above as everyone below looked on. Anya fought against the slippery wood, desperate to get a hold. She wanted to give in, but her fingertips held on with unnatural strength as a pain pierced her chest. Anya panicked; her breathing quickened and all she wanted to do was get down and go home – and then she saw a seagull and remembered her dream. Breathing again, she took a moment to think of those below, the doubt among the tribe, from Uncle, from all of those who dared to stand in her way. And she climbed, fierce and determined to overcome it.

It was a perilous and unforgiving ascent, but Anya drew strength from her goal, despite the elements. Her hands were numb and sore, her feet blistering, but she kept moving. Relentless determination pushed her on; the only way forward was to take one hold at a time. To her disbelief, she finally reached the end of the climb and made it over the side of the north nest in triumph. With great relief she lay for a moment, her muscles shaking, looking up at the black and red sky.

"I did it, I did it," she muttered between short sharp breaths. There was even a small cheer from below, which helped her regain her strength and get back to her feet. She looked over the edge and saw the world with different eyes. She remembered the other crow's nest she had been too afraid to look at, too afraid to climb, when there had been only fear … but now there was beauty.

When she turned, a seagull was on the opposite edge, staring at her. The seagull flapped its wings and flew up, swooping past Anya. The bird disappeared into the distance, leaving the nest and making its way toward the other which looked like a twig in the distance from where she stood. Anya's eyes locked to the old weathered and unsafe rope. On foot, the distance was a leisurely walk across the Ark, but via rope it was something else. Anya had climbed ropes before, but only twenty or so feet off the ground. The fear of failure had always kept her far from such things. She saw that to her right was another cage, and looking at it made her think how easy it would be to give in, to sail down and forget all of this, bury her head in rags and save herself from falling; but today was not that day. She turned once more to the rope, to the unknown, to something she thought she would never do. Instead of running, Anya was ready to fight; she climbed back up onto the nest's side and almost fell just from looking down. The nest bent and creaked with the wind as her belly turned upside down. She turned, put her back to the world, placed two hands tightly on the rope, and with all her faith she jumped upward, wrapping her legs around it.

"I'm on." Anya turned her head to see the Ark far

below, "wait, I'm on!" Anya forced her eyes shut and winced. She stayed still for a moment, as this was her last chance to turn back. "Turn back now and you're safe. Turn back now and they will forget about all of this," she said, at war with herself for a moment. But a part of her refused to say no. Despite the illness she had suffered, there was a hunger inside.

Anya shuffled slowly along, feeling the sway of the rope in the icy breeze. Ten or fifteen feet or so … if she was going to turn back, now was the time. Black clouds smothered the sky above and it began to rain. It was impossible to wipe the water from her eyes as she continued.

Time passed with great struggle and determination, at first the backs of her knees and the palms of her hands were a little painful, but soon they were burning on the rope. The pain was sharp, and soon she wanted to let go. Anya tried to look at the sky to keep from thinking negatively, but heavy rain came and made her cough when she tried to breathe. Until that moment, she had thought drowning in the sky would have been impossible. Turning to see the nest she had come from; it was hard to believe how close to it she was.

"No, I thought I had made it a lot further. I'm not going to make it," she told herself. Her hands were beyond sore. Sopping wet, with no way to get dry, her grip faltered. The wind made it worse, a relentless icy chill. She wanted to rest but there was no way; every second her hands hurt more and more. Anya shivered and stopped not to catch her breath, but in the hopes of giving her arms a rest but she could not. One slip and she would fall to her death, though if she was tired, she could call out and Wilson would have her pulled along – if she didn't slip from fatigue first. Anya would never call out; she would never surrender; but she had plateaued. The possibility of a fall became all the more appealing – more so than a cry for help. Anya thought of giving up and then to her disbelief the sky began to clear, the wind began to settle, and she could hear the crowds roar below. They hadn't given her any encouragement when she was on the log, but now they started to believe. Then an angel called out, a saving grace from below.

"You can do this, Anya!" she heard Jake shout. And his words were echoed by others. Anya pushed on. She moved slowly and calmly, trying not to over-exert herself. It was tough, gruesome, and she left a line of blood along the rope. When her legs were shaking and her hands could take no more, she bumped her head on the mast of the south nest. She had done it. Anya could not believe it, she had done the impossible, the unthinkable. She got herself over the side and fell down from exhaustion, when she could she wiped the blood on her fish leathers.

"I see you made the rope," said Wilson, leaning on the other edge of the nest with his arms folded and his hat pulled down just over his eyes. He looked Anya up and down with a cold judgemental frown, giving no praise.

"I did," she replied, out of breath, her hands stinging for the cruel red marks left upon them.

"You made it look so easy, too. I never thought you had what it takes to do the trial, especially not now."

"What do you mean?"

"You have been ill for six nights, at death's door. Jake came and spoke with me, he said you might not live."

"I'm here, aren't I?"

"You are, against all odds ... You pushed for the trial with no care for the tribe's current problems."

"What problems?"

"Your uncle struggles to keep command."

"Now listen here you old wrinkled waste of space, don't you dare take away this moment with such rubbish."

Wilson shook his head. He took another glance at her and moved back, as though something terrible drove a wicked fear into his heart.

"Don't take another step," he warned, raising his hand to stop her, desperate to get away, although there was nowhere to go.

"What? What is it?"

"When I saw you on the log, I thought you would lose your balance, and upon the climb I thought you would fall. Now I know what is carrying you forward, and I want no part in it." Wilson's warning came with a raised hand and finished with his finger pointing at Anya's chest.

Anya looked down at where her rags left the top of her chest exposed. To her horror and shame, there was a reptilian patch of green skin, rock hard and growing on her heart. It was right where the creature had touched her. Disgusted and afraid, she looked back at Wilson with grave concern and pulled her rags up to cover the spot.

"What do I do?" asked Anya, desperate for an answer; but Wilson didn't have anything for her.

"Your eyes already have a hint of yellow, girl."

"There must be *something* …" Anya was desperate, but Wilson shook his head. Old and wise, he had obsessed over those yellow eyes, those creatures up here on his own. He didn't know until now that this was possible, and he himself needed time to work through it. In short, there was no answer, and no cure.

"What is happening to me? What is going to happen to me?" Anya continued to plead for some sort of answer, but Wilson was smitten with silence.

"No one knows what's going to happen to you; you already have their strength. Climb down, end the trial, say your goodbyes, and in the night, swim. Swim free and far. If they think you drowned, you will be more fondly remembered."

Anya's eyes filled with tears as she desperately tried to hold back her feelings. She thought of Jake, Isaac, Lyn and Tomas. She could not do it; she could not let go of the glory of being the first Huntress; she was so close. It was in her grasp, through a burning desire to win. Amidst the sickness and being so close to death, Anya had been blind to the changes her brain was making. This instinct to win, to succeed, had not always been with her, but it was growing stronger than ever with the infection now – some unknown instinct.

"I can't."

"Then you will turn us all," said Wilson. "Don't be stupid, stay up here, leave tonight, I'll tell them you were too afraid to make the dive."

Anya thought over his words, and she looked down at her soaking rags as the clouds gathered once more. She made a fist and closed her eyes in silence. There was a moment when everything was calm, when nothing mattered, and then she ran forward for the edge. She lunged up the steps of Wilson's lookout and dived. Free-falling, she soared with grace. It was a leap of faith. Her eyes remained closed, the cold wind against her as the freedom of the fall took hold. Everything was at peace, at least for a moment.

With a crash, Anya broke the surface of the water feet first. Her toes hit the wall of ocean and her body followed in style. The saltwater washed away her tears and she no longer felt the water's cold. She didn't want to surface from the depths, but like the whale, she had to, and when she did, the crowd roared. Her curly dark hair washed around in the ocean as she saw all those proud faces watching, cheering her on. Rows of female companions, Makers and Crafters, Cooks and Carers; little girls filled with hope that they too might hunt. Many sat on the roofs of shacks, on the railings and floors, as Anya swam to the edge of the raft. Jake extended a hand to pull her out and Anya took hold, lacking the energy to pull herself out. A rush of adrenaline took over as Anya stood on the edge of the Ark, on the edge of the world, basking in glory. Lyn and Isaac were close by and even Isaac was smiling, proud after all. Though he would never tell her; he always knew she could do it. Isaac raised her arm up, which met with the crowd's applause. Tears of pride came from the women of the tribe, and people danced, chanting and singing, for today was a new day. It was her moment, and Anya knew the last challenge, the swim, would be easy. But as quickly as her celebration came, something took it away.

Despite the cheering crowd around her, the Hunters didn't smile. They stood still with spears in hand. Tyson stood with his mighty arms folded, muttering under his breath, and then his stare turned from derision to one of opportunity. Something had caught his eye, something that made even him blind with rage, remembering his trip to the shallows when Gregory was murdered. When Isaac had raised Anya's hand it had revealed the green on her chest, the scales of the beast, and Tyson had seen all he needed to.

"Isaac, take your hand off her!" he bellowed as the crowd went silent. Isaac caught his glare, but he didn't understand why Tyson would ruin this moment.

"What is the meaning of this?" he replied, before following Tyson's eyes down to Anya, where the green mark could no longer be hidden. He stepped in front of her to protect her as Tyson pushed forward from the crowd, followed closely by his Hunters.

"This tainted little girl, she is one of them, she is one of those monsters that butchered Gregory!" No one could appease Tyson's rage. He raised his arm, pointing right at Anya, and everyone saw it for themselves. Those who had praised her moved away, and as quickly as Anya had risen, she fell. Tyson looked at her as if she had torn Gregory's heart out herself, as did the other Hunters. People whispered under their breath and everything flooded back to her: the fear, the embarrassment. Everyone was staring, judging, and she felt like a freak once more.

"Don't do this," Isaac said, knowing that they would take her away.

"She has to go," Tyson replied, more cold than vicious. The memory of one of those monsters tearing out Gregory's heart as he fell lifeless into the ocean replayed in his mind over and over. The trauma it had caused had gone unspoken, but he had nightmares every night, unable to forget those scales and the deafening screeches.

"She is just sick, she must go to the shack," said Lyn from the crowd, in denial. For the first time in a long time Isaac didn't know what to say or do, although he would do anything to protect his niece, his family. Anya couldn't say a word; her throat was dry as salt.

"She will be one of them soon, she will doom us all!" said Tyson.

"No." Isaac's voice cut the air.

Tyson snarled, "I have grown tired of that word as I have grown tired of your old weak ways. Don't let your family blind you –"

"I said *no*."

That was all it took; for Tyson's short temper, it was the final straw. He didn't want to take it anymore, such weakness for a niece who so shamefully broke the tribe's traditions. The cursed girl had led Miles to the shallows and risked all their lives. It was clear to Tyson that Isaac had lost his way, that his weak leadership must come to an end, and all of the veteran Hunters were in agreement.

"Then I declare my right to lead the tribe," said Tyson, and Isaac's heart sank. Lyn tried to put an arm on Isaac's shoulder, but he brushed it off as Jake pulled her back. The crowd fell silent, no one dared to speak, and then the heavy beating of the drums began: boom, boom. Boom, boom. The crowd pushed back and formed a circle around them … Boom, boom. Boom, boom.

"If this is how it has to be …" said Isaac, and without hesitation he took off his top rags, revealing a stocky frame and fisherman's arms. Isaac was smaller, but he stood tall, his chin high, unable to take his eyes off the wrath of Tyson. Old but strong, this wasn't his first fight. He and his brother Richard trained for years together before the flood and everyone knew he was strong.

Tyson stepped forward, more gorilla than man, as the Hunters formed a ring holding back the rest. Isaac had known this day would come; from across the circle they stared at each other and Tyson looked ready.

"Let the ocean bear witness, let the sea god decide!" shouted Elder Frederick, knowing that he could take no sides, give no favours. "May one of you arise our leader. Now, show respect in victory or defeat."

Each of the men gave a fierce nod before edging forward with fists held high. Isaac had a boxing stance, where Tyson looked more an animal, a brawler; and so, it began. He came in swinging heavy fists, and Isaac took them all, protecting himself with his guard before stepping in. In range, he hammered a few blows against the beast's abdomen, but it did little. He was pushed back before receiving a mighty hook that connected like a brick. Isaac hit the floor but jumped right back up again unwilling to show any sign of weakness. He spat a little blood and pretended it didn't hurt, but it did. Members of the crowd shouted for either side, but the weight of the crowd was still with Isaac. Encouraged by knocking him down early, Tyson kept going forward, but Isaac charged with all his might, throwing a flurry of punches up close and personal. Each one hit Tyson hard and heavy as Isaac began to dismantle the beast, giving it his all until a heavy fist came back and cracked his nose. Tyson grabbed him by the shoulders and head butted him and again.

"Stop this, somebody please stop this Lyn shouted from behind. It was a distraction Isaac didn't need. Anya looked on, helpless; there was nothing she could do to end this, and had she known it would happen, she would never have surfaced from the high dive. There was a sinking feeling in her stomach as she watched them beat each other senseless like animals.

Amidst the screams, Isaac thought of Lyn. He clenched his fist and threw a hook with all his might, cracking Tyson in the eye and sending him to the floor. He was out. It was done. Despite all the odds, Isaac had come out on top. He turned to his family with a smile. They were safe, he had done it – but as soon as he took his eye off the game, Tyson was up. He ran for Isaac, threw him up in the air and speared him down to the ground, almost cracking the Ark in two. Diving on top of him, he threw fist after fist, until Isaac only saw darkness.

"You fool! You stupid fool!" said Tyson. "Those monsters are coming for us and you wouldn't do a damned thing! You wouldn't do a damned thing!"

The crowd watched in horror as Anya ran forwards to pry him off, but she was met with a backhand which sent her small frame flying. It took two Hunters to pull Tyson away. Isaac was barely breathing, and Anya ran to his side again amidst the chaos to tend to her uncle.

"Uncle, I'm so sorry, this is all my fault. I'm so sorry," she said, trembling, with tears in her eyes. Around her the Grand Stage was overcrowded, and those celebrating with Anya only a moment ago were now terrified by the threat of infection and the fight for a new leader.

"All hail, Tyson the Strong! He will save us from monsters, mockeries of trials, and will not let Gregory's death be in vain!" shouted Cayden.

"Hail!" the crowd echoed.

"Silence!" Elder Frederick shouted. "What's done is done!"

The Ark stopped short at his call for order, and the Hunters formed a wall all around with their spears, forcing the Makers and other lesser factions to move back, as Tyson stood triumphant. Anya knelt by the side of her bruised and battered uncle until the strong arm of one of the twins came down to drag her away. She kicked, scratched and screamed, as everyone looked on hopeless and afraid. Jake stepped forward, desperate to help, but Miles took him by the arm to hold him back.

"You monster!" said Anya as Tyson turned to look at her with pity and disgust.

"No, the monster is *you* ... Now seize her before she poisons us all."

Anya looked around for a way out, for somewhere to go, but there was nowhere to run to on the Ark. A fishing net was thrown and in an instant she was tangled before they dragged her along as the silent eyes of her people looked on.

"Get off her!" Jake shouted, pushing past Miles; but there was nothing he could do, it was too late.

"Take Isaac, Lyn and the boy to the cells," said Tyson as he wiped away the blood of his enemy from his sea leathers. The Hunters obeyed his command: Anya was slung over a shoulder carried away. Clawing at the net was no use. She cursed and cried as she watched all those faces staring, afraid and in silence, except for her pleading Aunt Lyn.

They took Anya to the *Iron Lady*, where she swung helplessly over the side in her net. When Anya looked up, she caught a glimpse of a familiar face watching way up high in the distance. Wilson raised his hand to salute her and say goodbye. Anya stared back through her rope cell and thought of everything he had said. She cursed herself for being so stupid, so thoughtless, and all she wished was that she had taken his advice, and swam away, far away.

## 7

## DROWN

A nya kicked and cursed in the net, struggling to get free, but it was no use. Time passed in hopeless resistance, and so eventually she calmed herself on the side of the *Iron Lady* as darkness came. She saw the ocean and a feeling of lonely helplessness washed over as she thought of her uncle. The evening wind was cold and sharp, but Anya could barely feel a thing except the pain in her chest. Her breath was cold and icy, and when the Hunters prepare to set sail, the only thing on her mind was her family.

Around her those once loyal to Isaac couldn't bear to look at her. Their movements about the deck were swift but gave no sign of victory. Anya had screamed and called them cowards, but her voice was hoarse; not one had risen to her insults, and so after a while she had conceded defeat. They had betrayed her uncle, they had betrayed her family, but she only blamed herself.

It could've been hours, but it felt like days before Tyson stepped onto the ship. Anya sat swinging in the net, watching him and thinking of escape. She was unsure of where they were going but knew they would not be going far. It was easy to think about repeating the swim, escaping the net somehow and clinging to the *Iron Lady* – she could hide at the top with Wilson, or live her life in the north nest. The rock-hard green skin upon her chest stung as a crackling cough and wheezing took hold. She had let them all down, and soon after that realisation came the acceptance of death. She was lucky to survive as long as she had, and if this was it then at least she could rest, spend eternity warm and dry with her parents.

The net swung in the cold ocean breeze as the boat travelled away from the Ark, Anya looked back to see her home one last time, it was but a dot in an endless sea. Hopes of escaping the net and swimming back became all the more impossible as Anya looked on. When Tyson finally approached, it was hard to put her hatred into words. He stood, bloody and bruised, leaning over the side of the *Iron Lady*, his heavy solemn stare one of pity. He was a liar, a monster, a no-good traitor and thief.

"Dry your eyes, girl, is this how you wish to be remembered?" asked Tyson without care or consideration, he washed his hands in a bucket of seawater to take Isaac's blood away.

"I will be remembered for far longer than you, the great betrayer, the thief. My uncle treated you like a brother, he saved your life, and this is how you repay him?"

Tyson hung his head for a moment in memory of

the past. He remembered it like yesterday, being stranded upon the rooftop while rain thundered down and the water rushed up, taking everything around him. Having lost his wife, child and everyone else, he was alone in the apocalypse, killing and stealing just to stay alive. On his knees he cursed God, begging as the waters rose … And then the Ark came by, much smaller than the structure today. He remembered Isaac and Richard's disagreement over whether to let him on, Isaac didn't like the look of Tyson, and it was Richard who made the decision to save him. Tyson remembered that day as he stared into the eyes of the little girl. "I did what I had to for my people; but you, you endanger all of us, monster. I'm only doing what must be done, what your uncle isn't strong enough to do."

Anya poked her face through the gap in netting, and she spat. It hit Tyson right on the cheek. He wiped it off with a look of hatred. "You wretched thing, but it doesn't matter, it will be over soon." With his words, his look turned to one of sweet satisfaction which made Anya tremble.

"This journey out to sea doesn't scare me, my uncle will save me," Anya was hopeful, but her foolish words only made Tyson laugh. "What's so funny?" She panicked, unaware of what was going to happen; she didn't like the way Tyson looked at her. There was a sweet sense of satisfaction in his gaze.

"You Anya Fairheart will never see the Ark again, you will never see your family again, they can't help you, no one can. You can scream, you can cry, you can beg, but by the time the sun rises tomorrow, you will be dead."

"What are you going to do to me?" Anya asked, too proud to panic and cry. "You can't kill me? I'll live in the crow's nest, with Wilson, I'll never come down, I promise ... I'll do whatever it takes."

"You aren't a girl, you're a monster. I will tell them it was peaceful Anya; I will tell them it was humane, but you, monster, you only have to do one thing – drown." Tyson kicked the lever as Anya screamed. She reached out a hand, but the net descended into the deep. The ropes were heavy, the water cold. It dragged her down, smothering her in the abyss. She tried to break free and with her last breath her cold trembling fingers managed to pull the net open. Anya untangled herself and made for the surface. She coughed and spluttered, gasping for breath, only to see that the *Iron Lady* was already too far, flying at full sail.

"Cowards! Cowards!" She shouted, but all hope was lost. Cold and alone, Anya thought of swimming after the vessel; but they would see her, they would stop her, and that was even if she made the swim. No man alive could make that swim. Her options dwindled and she took to floating, steadying her breath, defying the inevitability of going under. It was cold and quiet amidst the ocean waves and all Anya could hear were her thoughts. It was easy to stay afloat at first, but no matter how accustomed she was to her situation, over time the cold took hold. It reminded her how human she was, how human they all were, without the Ark. Still, she would defy Tyson's wishes to the death. Hate kept her going, but soon hatred washed away and with it, her energy. Time went by so slowly, and her body was already so tired after the trials.

It was so quiet, and so oddly peaceful as she watched the horizon. The only thing that kept her going was the thought of Jake, Uncle Isaac or Tomas coming to the rescue across the horizon, but they didn't come. Anya was alone with her thoughts, and it was cold. She wished she had her necklace: that would have kept her warm, but it was lost to the deep as she was. Anya took to prayer, but it was hard to know who to pray to. The Arkers had abandoned their old god with the flood, as none of their prayers were ever answered. Now they prayed to the sea, but still she heard the adults whisper and weep to their old god at times.

"D-dear God, I don't know if y-you're out there somewhere, it's b-bloody cold. I d-don't know if you ever had a p-plan for us, and I d-don't know what I did to enrage you like this, but f-forgive me for any wrong I have ever done and s-save my f-family."

Her voice became distant, trembling as the cold came off her breath. It was hard to keep her eyes from dropping, and her head from slipping under, but when she did, she pushed herself back up and looked out to the horizon once more for rescue. Anya thought of Jake, Isaac and Lyn, and then her mother and father. Anyone could come and save her, anyone, but no one came.

"I suppose this is it then," said Anya with acceptance. When the night was black it was beyond cold. She didn't know how long it had been, but it had been hours. All she had to do was to stay close to the surface, to keep breathing, but she was losing all reason. It didn't seem important anymore, any of it. She thought of the whale, how it would come up for air and go back under for hours. Going under didn't seem so unpleasant anymore. She felt the ocean calm and pictured the magnificent beast swimming deep beneath.

Anya found peace and let go of hate. She didn't blame Tyson; she didn't blame herself. There was nothing left to feel guilty for: it was just her now, her and the ocean. She could no longer feel a thing as her head bobbed under. Right before the end, she did the only thing she could, and closed her eyes. Like millions of others who had fought the ocean's cruelty, she gave into the darkness. Down she went into the never-ending darkness of the ocean, a journey into the next life.

There was nothing but peace, a simple, silent peace, and the cold went away, as did everything else as she melted into darkness. Anya felt at one with everything. No more hate, no more doubt – and as she sank, she looked up to see the surface that everyone tried so hard to cling to. From underneath, the surface seemed to be the wrong side. At the end, she had no choice to breathe in, then came the cold into her lungs and a massive weight took hold. That was the last feeling, the last experience, of cold. There was peace, there was darkness, and then came the end ...

## 8

## BELOW

Yellow eyes opened, awoken by a thousand haunting whispers. Clutching her throat, she forced a hand to her chest and found herself breathing without air. Eyes now cursed saw ultraviolet blurs beyond human understanding. When the blurring went away, a bright overpowering underwater world took hold, a world of greens and blues, yellows and oranges. Floating in a neon infinity, she struggled to remember anything. When she could focus her vision, she was shocked to see hundreds of bodies floating all around in an underwater graveyard.

Anya froze in fear when she saw that the bodies were monsters. Those green-scaled creatures of horror that haunted the shallows with their loud screeches, with sharp claws and teeth, were all around. Anya could hear whispers, they seemed to be their whispers, but their mouths weren't moving. She could hear their thoughts; their dreams and it was terrifying. She didn't know what to do, how to speak, how to breathe – but she was breathing.

"Is this, is this the afterlife?" she asked, though her lips didn't move. She spoke with her mind!

"No," echoed a soft female voice across the ocean, Anya didn't know where it came from. She looked around but none of the bodies had moved.

"God?" But she was far from heaven and far from hell, a purgatory for those left after the flood, those who fought against the wishes of the water.

"I'm not God," said the voice.

This unnatural and unholy place shocked her to the core, so she swam. Swam at lightning speed away from the voice, between the thick forest of bodies, and now overgrown buildings swallowed by the flood, covered by coral and surrounded by fish of a thousand different colours. Anya weaved down an alleyway and found herself in the middle of a crossroads. Here the world was filled with old rusted cars, and lined with pavements, lampposts and shop fronts. Large signs still stood outside buildings, but now fish and coral inhabited the remains of a lost civilisation having given it new life. It was an underworld of the unknown, a blinding rainbow, but Anya hated every second of it.

"Jake, Aunty, Uncle! This can't be the end, this can't." Anya continued to panic, forcing herself to swim, feeling alien to this place. It was hard to remember diving from the crow's nest into the sea as she tried to get away, for everything came in flashes of panic. Anya went to feel around her neck to touch her mother's golden necklace, but it was gone.

She moved through the coral reef, schools of fish all around, stingrays on the ocean floor. Everything was clear now, clear to see, to hear, clearer than ever before, but she didn't want it. It was a manic fantasy, a hallucination. To her horror she remembered Tyson kicking the rope and sending her into the darkness. The pain, the fear, her water-filled lungs dragging her down and out. She remembered death, how warm it was, how calm and peaceful.

Then Anya saw the tennis court, and then she saw the office … it was all real. Feeling sick, she pushed on, barely able to feel her own body. Ahead, one hundred storeys high, was the missing office window she, Jake and Tomas had looked down onto this place with such innocence. It had been a place of wonder a few days before, and now it was a place of desperation, a final refuge.

"This is a dream, or I'm dead," she said. In desperation, she made her way to the building, still hopeful of getting home. Looking back, she saw the bodies in the distance begin to move, so she moved even faster, faster than she had ever swum before. Anya made for the bottom floor to escape the monsters. She moved at speed through the front doors, passing glass stained with moss, and darted through the large open lobby, its stained red floors covered in reeds and coral. Large gold pillars supported the structure, and a staircase split the middle of the room. Anya shot toward the staircase; going up and up, she manoeuvred in the dark as scared fish retreated into dark corners and crevasses.

Memories of those she loved began to haunt her –

she had to return to them. Up and up she went, making for the top floor. She could taste the air, the freedom, and feel her family's loving touch. Behind her were bodies and screeching monsters. Anya darted through and stopped at the same desks as before. She made for the collapsed ceiling, so close to the surface, so close to going home ... but then she saw the mirror. It was the same mirror she had stopped at and stared into a week prior. The same mirror from which a floating angel with a flower in her hair had stared back at her. But to her shame, staring back at her now was someone, or something, else.

It was a yellow-eyed, green-scaled reptilian monster with sharp teeth, claws, and no hair. It was ugly; it was unthinkable. Anya put her claws on the mirror and scratched at it, desperate to change what was staring back, but there was nothing she could do. She tried to feel her nose but is wasn't there, instead she had nares. She couldn't stand the sight of herself and understood for the first time the beauty of her thick brown hair and her freckles. They were gone, replaced by the sins of a screeching monster, banished to the depths and far from her family. Anya broke down but she couldn't fall; she tried to cry but she couldn't shed a tear. Grieving, she mourned her family and her lost emerite necklace; that would have at least reminded her of home, but it was gone.

Then came the voices, the songs, laughter and prayers. Those down below were awake and they were moving. She prayed they could not hear her, she prayed they would not find her. The voices overwhelmed Anya, they took over and reduced her to nothing. She could feel them coming closer, it was impossible to explain how or why but they were coming. In the corner of the mirror Anya saw another monster. This one had eyes like hers but even more yellow; it had narrower nostrils, pointed ears and a scar on its shoulder. It looked into her eyes with great concern and Anya wanted to do nothing more than flee – but she froze. The overwhelming whispers of the others down below took over; she could not control them, they deafened her. Anya backed away as the strange beast came forward, raising its hands as if to show that it meant no harm.

"It's a strange thing, to be unable to cry," said the creature in the soft female voice Anya had heard before, although it did not move its lips. The voice was coming from somewhere else and Anya realised it was pure thought: telepathic. The creature stared through her and the shock of its haunting look made Anya forget about the others, for this one's hypnotic gaze took hold of her entirely. Then the other voices came back. "Listen to me, only listen to me …" The creature came closer, making Anya forget about anyone else, for the eyes were hypnotic. It took Anya a moment to snap out of its gaze, and then a shiver went up her spine for she had seen this one before – it was the one that had turned her.

"You! You evil monster. You cursed me. Made me lose everything, why? What did I ever do to you? Stay away, stay the hell away!" Anya's thoughts whirled; the only thing she could do was show her rage, her fear and loss. "You forced me to be this way! Why didn't you just let me die?" She trembled and backed further and further away, unable to contain her hatred; and then the other voices took over again.

"Listen to me, listen only to me, girl. I saved you," said the creature, coming closer. Anya had to focus on its voice no matter how much she did not want to.

"Saved me? You turned me; you tore my family apart. I have nothing because of you!"

"You were dead. Drowned. I brought you back to life. This place is safe, this is our heaven, your Ark was the struggle."

"You know nothing of my Ark, monster. Lies, all lies. You killed Gregory, he was a good man, a kind man."

"Yours attacked our home first, and we defended ourselves."

Anya did not know what to say, for she had lost everything. It wasn't fair; this monster had no right to do what it had done. She had been banished, afraid, alone, and was now being lectured by some horrible thing. "This is torture worse than death. I didn't ask for this, I didn't choose this! I'd rather die."

"Then return to your surface and die. None of us chose this life," the creature replied, turning as if to leave, and Anya lunged forward in fear of being alone.

"Send me back, please, just send me back."

"If only it was that simple. I drowned, we all drowned, but only the chosen come back." The creature came closer as Anya backed further away into a corner.

It reached out to touch her arm, but Anya batted it away with a hiss and sharp claws.

"Why have you made me suffer like this?"

"This isn't suffering. The cold, the illness, the lack of food, the wind, the water – these are suffering. People dying young, struggling every day, the Hunters and elders ruling. Your so-called *Ark* is suffering, clinging to a world long passed."

There was nothing Anya could say to change its mind, for it truly believed it had saved her. Anya looked around her: the world was water and the Ark was gone. Tyson had won, he had banished her. "It was ... it was my home."

"I came from a poor home too," said the creature. Anya gritted her sharp teeth and shook he head. Unable to listen, unable to believe, she scratched the glass behind her with her claws, desperate to find something to hold on to, some way to escape.

"The surface made you weak, and I have made you strong."

"You are not God!"

The creature looked back at the frightened little girl up against the stained mirror and saw in Anya a vision of herself. There was such fear and terror in her eyes, and the mention of God had been a harrowing accusation. "This is the way nature intended us to be," it said, before turning away as if about to leave. It had this strange way of looking through Anya, sensing something beyond the realms of human understanding that only made her worry even more.

"Wait," said Anya, desperate for any form of help,

any comfort or reassurance. No matter how much she hated the creature, she was afraid to be alone.

"Yes?"

"Please, please, change me back." Her request was met with a long cold stare as the creature debated her response and then shook its head. Though Anya felt that the creature had lost its humanity, there was a strange sadness in its eyes.

"If only I could, little one. I would turn us all and build a mountain to the sky for us to live again. If only I could."

The cold hard truth made Anya break; she wanted to fall on the floor and cradle herself.

"Then get away from me," she said, but the stranger didn't move. "Get away!" Anya screamed, and so the creature moved to the window.

"I am sorry, child, I truly am. If you need me, just think the name *Hali*."

Anya felt a ferocious primal rage building inside her, and so she screamed. The fury came from behind her eyes and she made her claws into fists, unable to control herself any longer.

Hali looked at Anya once more, as if there was more she wanted to say. "I will be here when you want to talk," the creature said, before swimming out of sight.

Alone again, Anya felt like a stranger in her own skin. A feeling of disgust took over, as she stared into the mirror. Anya had never felt self-conscious or wanted to look different. The Ark was a place for natural beauty, free of mirrors. This was a cruel shame, and she obsessed over every green scale. Burning yellow eyes with hints of red stared back, large fangs and claws to match. Shaking, she lunged forward and smashed the mirror, sending shards of glass all around. She bowed her head and again wanted to cry. Jake, Lyn and Isaac would not love her like this, nor anyone else in the tribe. Anya thought of Tyson and how right he was to get rid of her. She wanted nothing more than to be herself again, have her soft skin, feel the cold, the breeze and the sunshine. After taking a long hard look at herself, Anya knew there was only one thing she could do. She was unable to live this way, unable to fathom any way that this could work. She would rather test Hali's talk of the surface and reach for a flower one last time.

Anya turned away from the broken mirror and propelled herself through the doorway, where the rubble had settled below the hole in the roof. She stared up into the pool of bright sunlight, thinking of her family. What was above seemed to be a heaven, with brightness piercing through in all its glory. Anya took a few breaths, swallowed her pride and propelled herself toward the surface. Her claws pulled her up as she stood where they had once stood before, laughing and joking on top of the world. This time, however, the air was burning, the breeze dry and the sun singed her skin, causing unbearable pain. Anya wanted to dive back under, and she screamed just like the monsters had when the *Iron Lady* came. She trembled, before falling to her knees. Crawling now, the heat was too much and she fell back just below the surface. Then she tried again but the pain was even worse this time. All she wanted was the end, but she was not strong enough to stay up there, for above the surface was a burning hell on earth. Anya fell back into the water, burnt and broken, harbouring the bitter acceptance that there was no going back. Sunken and solemn, she slithered through the office where she would be trapped forever.

## 9

## ANOTHER WORLD

The sore red burns from sun's rays told Anya that she would never make for the surface again. She retreated into the darkness, wishing to rip off her scales in the hope of freeing herself from this unholy body, this curse, but she could not bring herself to do it. As painful as it was, the saltwater healed the sunburn, but she was still a stranger in her own skin. Alone and in pain, far from anyone who loved her, Anya lost the will to live. She wanted to end everything but was unable to force herself up to the surface, for any drive, any motivation had withered away with the pain. Anya retreated to the office and no longer wished to swim, so she held her legs close to her chest and bobbed along the floor with her eyes closed. Floating was uncomfortable: to extend or to crouch was unbearable.

Thoughts of the Ark came and went, making Anya sick as she tried to think of home. She remembered her family, the other girls, and even Riley. She missed the wind, the rain, even the cold and the struggle. Arguments and confrontations seemed so small now. Anya thought of Wilson and his tower, the trial, and how close she had come, although that was not really her. The budding strength of a horrible creature had given her a burning desire to win; that was what had got her so far and would have got her to the end. Tyson was right to get rid of her. Isaac would have kept her, but then more would have turned. She would have made them all monsters.

Anya felt her feet – now webbed claws – and her hands – once soft, now hard as rock. Her nose was no more, and her eyes were much wider than before. Anya could see more, hear more, but everything she loved was gone. This place was beyond lonely, beyond lost. Desperate to return home, she knew there was no way to turn back time. She stayed in the office block alone, trying to ignore the voices, trying to remain still, for hours. No matter how hard she tried, though, the ocean kept her moving. It was impossible to stay still, to ignore the ocean; it was all around her, inescapable, and trying to talk to her in new ways, ways she ignored. Out of instinct she shut out all the voices that clouded her mind and tried to handle a brief moment of quiet and solitude.

Hours passed by in a bitter and twisted depression. A pain took her stomach. It was a growing hunger, stronger than she had ever felt before. Anya ignored it like she ignored everything else her body was trying to tell her. She replayed her failures over and over: the look on Tyson's face, the moment he booted her into the ocean. A noble Arker's death, an eternity in the clouds had been stolen from her, and now she was down here. Hell had been described as a place of fire and brimstone but now she knew the truth.

Only so much time could be spent fixating on her mistakes, her shame. As time went on Anya formed an obsessive loop of such feelings in her mourning and denial, replaying events of her childhood in her head, every joyous moment with Jake, Isaac and Lyn. She remembered her parents and the storm that took them.

"What would they say if they saw me like this?" she asked herself. Her mind was full of thoughts about everyone she knew cursing her, those gasps and awful looks they gave her before the net came down. Then she thought of her mother, she would tell her to be strong, and her father would tell her to rise to any challenge. Everyone always said her father solved problems with an open mind. She wondered what it was like in the days of the flood, the days no adult would speak of. Those lawless days when the water rose, and people fought for boats instead of money. He selflessly overcame any problem to save those around him. *If I have an ounce of such strength, maybe I can survive*, thought Anya.

Having grown restless, she wanted to move. She opened her eyes and found herself unable to stand the blank walls any longer and so she decided to explore the building. She swam along the corridor and down the stairs to the floor below, to find nothing but endless offices. Everything was the same: depressing bland dark chairs and desks, and white walls that the grown-ups of the Ark joked about. The only beauty here was what nature had taken back. Anya wondered why the Ark's elders had spoken of these places with such fond memories; there was nothing to love about this building.

It was at that moment when Anya's yellow eyes looked a little more closely and saw something more. Upon the desk in front of her was a rectangular frame, a picture – she knew what a picture was for that one picture of her parents that Aunt Lyn kept. Anya picked up the frame and rubbed away the algae, to find a family of four. A mother, father and two young girls. The perfect blonde family smiling together and holding each other. She looked at the children's nice clothes, well-kept hair and toys.

*How easy it was for them, how easy*, Anya thought, knowing that she had been robbed of a real childhood, having to work from an early age in the burning cold whilst others died all around her. Anya knew true struggle and upon the Ark she would never have had a family, never have allowed herself to be a mother for fear of leaving behind a motherless child. She let go of the photograph from between her claws. Then she noticed that photographs were on every desk; a sad speck of individuality upon humanity's chains, now washed away.

Her thoughts were interrupted by the smell of something sweet, a strong scent that made her cramped stomach rumble. She wanted nothing more than to assuage her cravings, but then came the reminder of self-hatred, and she promised herself she would not eat. Instead she would starve, for that would be easier than the unbearable burning of the surface. Anya moved down through each floor looking at the pictures upon each desk. She noticed other small personal objects, too: personalised mugs and other remnants of the past. She lost herself in imagining the workers' stories as she made her way down to the lobby that she had rushed through upon waking that very morning. At the front desk she saw something she had missed. An entire wall was taken up by photographs, many of them covered in sea life, many of them disintegrated, but those that were plastic and built to last still remained, and there were hundreds. Above them the word "missing" was written, worn by time and tide.

Below each photograph were contact numbers and dates going back to twenty years prior. Anya knew right away that they were those lost in the flood, and she scoured the board to see the faces of all those lost. She froze and felt a tremendous heart-wrenching guilt, for one of the two blonde girls from upstairs was staring at her from the wall. Anya knew there was no way the girl would have made it in the flood; she had most likely drowned and yet her family would have kept searching until the water swallowed them too. She felt guilty, for she was still alive, and the girl was no more.

"May you rest," Anya said before floating away, depressed and downtrodden. It was hard to think of anything but the demise of the Old world.

The smell of something sweet and delicious took her attention again, and her hunger became too much, a burning sensation in her belly. She turned to swim around the pillars and past the lift, where she found a fire exit and opened the heavy door with great ease. Anya entered a dark stairwell where the words "week two" were written in large red writing. To her amazement someone had marked a thick red line along the wall.

"What is that?" she asked, so unable to get used to her voice reflecting through the water. Anya swam further, passing rusted tin cans of food and plastic wrappings. There were more messages on the walls: "30 days … it isn't stopping." Another red line made her realise it was for the water level. Further she travelled and with each flight was another message, another measurement: "eight weeks … boats gone." Higher and higher Anya went: "Three months, no food." She wondered about the writer, and then she reached the last message, which read: "sorry, world, trapped forever."

Anya wondered who had written such messages, and then to her horror she saw a skeleton, still clothed, sunk on the concrete stairs, huddled up against a fire exit. In panic Anya burst through the heavy metal fire doors with unnatural strength to escape the nightmare, so fast she dented the doors in half and tore apart a rusted metal chain which kept them shut. She flew down the corridor and beyond, desperate to get away. She hid around the corner and closed her eyes. There was no need to catch her breath, but she was afraid and alone. This eerie building, once a place of refuge, was now a place of fear.

"I want to go home, I want to go home, I want to go home!"

Anya tried to get a hold of herself and remember the ways of the Ark. It was cold and tough; this was nothing compared to what she had faced up there. Still, what she wouldn't do to have Uncle Isaac, Jake and Aunt Lyn by her side – but she could not. She was alone in this terrible underwater world, and so she took to swimming away once more. Making for the top floor with great speed, she glanced at where the roof had fallen in, where she had become stuck and had drowned before being given another chance by that monster. She replayed the events in her mind hundreds of times, unable to move forward. It was a bitter loop without escape … until she heard a voice.

Anya swam all the way along to the office windows to see the new world outside. A terrifying sense of dread took hold when she saw those wicked sea monsters that had cursed her. She hid from view by perching on a desk and peered over its edge, terrified of being seen. She watched as they congregated, communicated, held and spoke to each other in such a human way.

"I see through you, you wretched things. I hope you all die, you abominations. I hate you." Anya writhed in hatred, until she was all out of energy to hate. So, she took to watching her enemy, a group of them with broad chests and shoulders, males speaking amongst themselves. She wanted to know what they were saying but they were too far away. She felt the same feeling she had towards the Hunters on the Ark: that deep injustice. Then the group swam away from each other at lightning speed and Anya saw the biggest of them holding a gold trident. He stared in the direction of her building, before in a whirl of sand, he was gone.

Her brain was aching, her body weak. Anya was starving now, hungrier than ever before. The transformation had taken everything from her, and she had denied her body anything it craved. The will to move fast and free outside and to feast was growing, and she could not stop herself any longer. Animal instinct was taking over and there was nothing she could do to stop it. The hunger inside called, stronger and more carnivorous than anything she had felt before. Anya could still smell something sweet and delicious. It was almost hypnotising and too much to resist, so she opened her light-yellow eyes and burst forward from the wall. Strong and fast, flying along the corridor and down the stairs she went, floor after floor, following the most delicious scent. Whatever it was, it was moving. Anya turned a corner, and, to her surprise, there it was: a big, juicy-looking yellow and neon-blue vagabond butterflyfish.

All day its sweet scent had teased her, and there it was. The fish bobbed and flickered in its own world. Its movement was mesmerizing; it was all she wanted, all she craved. Trying to shake off her desire was impossible: Anya could not take her eyes off it for the cramping hunger in her stomach. She boosted off a wall and lunged at lightning speed, catching the fish with a razorsharp claw as it wriggled desperately, trying to get free. Meeting her prey eye to eye, Anya bit the head clean off and crunched it in her fangs, as blood spread through the water. It tasted amazing, liberating, better than anything Anya had ever eaten. In the end, all that was left were bones, and she let them float away in the water. She remembered how hard the Hunters found catching fish by hand on the surface.

Through the window, she saw a number of the creatures passing, so she jumped back, hiding herself from the enemy. When the coast was clear she journeyed back to the top floor to cling on to fond memories of a past life. At the top of the stairwell Anya stopped, for another flower floated by but this one was more withered. It must have made its way from the bush on the roof top, the dark square and into the water, to sink and drown as she had. Anya clasped it tight, and she remembered seeing herself in the mirror with a flower in her hair and how beautiful she was. She remembered giving it to Aunt Lyn before the fever took hold. She missed Aunt Lyn so much – the feel of her warmth against her. Holding one another meant so much in the coldest of worlds. Anya missed her hair, her eyes, her hands and everything else, but no matter how hard she tried, she could not cry.

After the flower, Anya thought of her mother's emerite necklace. It had to be here, it had to be around somewhere. She searched high and low, up and down. She retraced all her steps a hundred times from the day she drowned, but it was nowhere to be found. It was gone, lost with her old self. And now there were things going on in her body that she could not understand. Fighting against her instincts and not listening to them had only made things worse. The fish was one of the best meals she had ever had, and Anya thought about how easy it had been to catch, despite its speed. Feeling restless, she decided to put her body to the test. She went a floor down and propelled herself through walls, bent metal and destroyed everything in her path in vain attempts to make herself feel better. None of it helped, none of the hate helped. There was only so long she could stay awake, and soon she surrendered her mind to sleep.

~

The next few days were the same lonely torture. She tried to starve herself, fighting the temptation to catch another delicious fish despite their delicious scent. Anya had taken to staring out of the window where Tomas had been. From here she could see the ocean, and all the others down below. To her surprise, there were children playing together. Adults conversing, swimming and hunting. There were moments when the sense of dread dissipated, when curiosity in this underwater world and its inhabitants took over, only for thoughts of fear and failure to remind her that she hated them all, that she would have rather died than leave the Ark. The constant turmoil, obsessive thoughts, anxiety and sickness continued day after day, night after night as she starved herself.

On the third day, Anya noticed a very young monster playing, laughing and pointing at another one doing back-flips and tricks. After a while, the toddler did one too. She remembered being that old, and she remembered doing summersaults on the surface. Anya saw the first glimpse of their humanity, and realised that the children, like her, may not have chosen their way of life. Amidst thoughts of self-loathing, she began to question everything, even her own prejudice. They sat together, ate together, told jokes together, slept together. It was another way of life, a different way. Anya watched them play strange games along the ocean floor, and she could hear them talking, worrying about each other, praying with each other ... she knew then, that they may be human, after all.

Anya began to tell them apart: they all had oceanic names and rituals. There didn't seem to be any tribal structure, any hierarchy, and that scared her. They all had strength and worked together. As much as she tried to project a place of darkness and sorrow, the luminescent glow of green and blue scales, of wild and colourful coral made her see beauty, no matter how she fought the feeling. Slowly, every ounce of resentment began to disappear, and it was replaced with curiosity. Still, she spent each day and night alone, trying to sob but unable to do so. She would give anything to feel human again.

The hard-reptilian body that she cursed, the sharp claws and ultraviolet sight, all became a natural extension of herself. She could strike out through the water, accelerate and weave. Echolocation was a thing of instinct and so was her new-found way of speaking and listening. She could often hear those down below, catch their conversations and switch them off. She could whisper, and she could shout. The scent of prey had become stronger. Anya's attempt to hunger strike had been broken time and time again by the odd small fish that she'd caught within the office walls, but now she dreamt of a bigger catch, and in the morning when the monsters were all asleep, she decided to make a move. She had the most relentless urge to swim, and so she did. She burst from the window at pace, flying through the water. Forwards, backwards, up and down she went, eating as many fish as she desired. Strong and confident, she began to explore the bottom where the coral reef had glazed over humanities past. There were clownfish, octopus, seahorses and stingrays in a host of bright colours. It was beautiful, it was mysterious, it was unlike anything she had known on the surface. There, everything was dark, cold and miserable, desperate. The only animals left were seagulls and the only fish were too small or too sickly to be close to the surface. This place seemed to be a haven to its people, but as she saw them wake, she fled back to the safety of her tower for fear of being seen again.

"You are one of us," said Hali.

Anya looked around but she could not see her.

"I am not!" she spat back, but deep down she knew that denial was useless. Her hands were green and scaled. Her hide was webbed and shimmered in the moonlight.

"Talk to my people, feast with us. In time you will know we mean you no harm."

"I don't want to –"

"You do, I can sense it. We see more than you know, and so can you." As quickly as it came, her voice was gone again. From afar Anya watched the group swim together; they had no qualms or arguments. Food was plentiful and there was no need for warmth. Everyone had whatever they needed, they seemed friendly now, and she could tell them apart, the children, the elders and all in between. Each had a different hue and everything around them looked beautiful. As much as she wanted there to be, there was no hate or judgement in their eyes, only a welcoming warm yellow glow. It made Anya think of how the tribe had looked at her on the Ark. Those glaring eyes following her foolish declaration to be a Hunter, the disgust at her infected chest, the doubts and downright denial about her being what she wanted to be. How they whispered, how they bickered with each other and fought over scraps of food in the cold.

The men were the worst, making the women marry as young as sixteen, have inferior roles in the tribe, and serve their husbands' hand and foot. They said it wasn't service, but it was. Anya had looked at them all and knew she could equal any man among them. It was easy to wonder how life would be up there if men's and women's physical strength were matched, even though nature intended their strengths to be revealed in different ways.

She took her time picking out monsters from the crowd below, making up stories about them, and one stuck out to her: he was the largest and tallest of them. She imagined he would be another Tyson; he stood tall and proud, clasping some sort of trident in his hand. He was the only one to stop and stare as if he knew exactly where Anya was, but his gaze did not linger before he instructed his tribe and they moved on through the water and away.

Anya felt that this place may be a haven after all, but her newfound idea was constantly questioned by her memory of the monsters chasing after her, teeth glinting in the sun, and screaming as Uncle Isaac came to the rescue. She also knew that one of them had torn out Gregory's heart, and he was a kind man, a good man.

Anya took her time, considering what to do for hours, before going to the other side of the office block. From there she could explore, far enough from the creatures not to be seen. She swam fast, trying to drain her inexplicable energy. Anya soared at great speed, cutting through the water, chasing fish and other sea life. It was a part of her now, a part that was growing. Everything about the Ark became dark and grey in her mind, except for her family. She started to remember the cold and the injustice of the Ark. Hali was right, and as much as she didn't want to be, Anya was now a part of another world. She swam through it. Lived it. Breathed it. She flew through its endless beauty, the shining coral and the glimmering wonder of it all. She spun and flipped, almost dancing through the water until she turned around and noticed the office block was nowhere to be found. She was lost.

## 10

## COLOSSAL

All alone in the deep dark depths, Anya strayed further away from the underwater civilisation. In minutes the colourful coral and fish that had taken back the old office blocks disappeared. Swept into an undercurrent, Anya was dragged miles from the shallows. She did not know it was dangerous for the water dwellers to swim beyond their boundaries, and that if they did, none went alone. Anya drifted in ignorance of what was around her; she swam all night, desperate to get back to somewhere familiar, but there was nothing recognisable around. When the seabed dropped like a cliff edge into the abyss, the current only swept her further and further away and Anya quickly lost track of what was up and down. There was nothing. Just a blank dark blue infinity.

"It can't be any worse than there," she said with her mind – something she still wasn't used to. She meant, of course, the shallows. The place that had taken everything, friends, family and home. Still, something felt strange about leaving; there was a subliminal connection she could not explain, a connection to the other creatures. She reminded herself they were strangers, monsters, the enemy, but even the office block wasn't as bad as being all alone. Every so often she looked at her green skin. At first it had made her wretch but now she was used to it. Anya made the decision to dive down deep into the abyss, pass through the darkness in the hope of using the seabed to navigate. Maybe Hali would be able to communicate with her and guide her back.

At the bottom, however, in the darkness, everything changed. There were no bright and beautiful creatures, only great spider crabs, viper fish and frilled sharks. Everything had awful teeth or sharp claws, and very quickly Anya became their prey. She darted away from the open space and made for a fissure in the rocks. She was afraid and alone, with no way out, surrounded by fang-toothed fish, eels and little monsters. These creatures were a different breed, much bigger since the great flood. Just as humans had changed, much of the sea life had adopted a darker form, too. Either side of her, blackened coral, cursed and enchanted, moved, slow and subtle. A barbed dragonfish, black, with long green teeth, snapped its jaws. Anya dodged out of the way, close to the coral's sharp needles, where one wrong move would end her, then she swam back out of the crevasse and well away from the wicked creatures. Floating up into nothingness, she rested, relieved not to see anything coming for miles.

"Come on, you can do this, you can get out of here.

Think, think. The monsters navigate somehow, how do they do it? If only I wasn't so useless." Her words were no use and they echoed into infinity. Then a strange feeling came over, as if something was watching her, and sent a shiver down her spine. She turned around, looked left, right, up, down – there was nothing but blue. Then a great eerie shadow was cast upon her, but still when Anya looked up there was nothing but dark empty ocean. She was afraid, truly afraid that something was toying with her.

"Hali, this isn't funny, you proved your point: I'm no good on my own so just take me back to the office block. I won't be any trouble." Anya looked around but her voice was met with an eerie silence.

"Far from home and all alone in my waters," said a dark and mysterious voice, echoing through the deep as Anya felt the weight of its power. She turned, desperate to find its source, but there was nothing. She wanted to speak but found it impossible, as if she were caught in a trance. "Sadness, great sadness in you, child; and hunger," it continued.

"Hali, please. I want to go back now, take me back. Just please don't leave me out here." Anya's voice trembled as she struggled to speak; her fear turned to a deep inertia only made worse by her lack of sleep.

"Your tired eyes can rest now, I will watch you," said the voice with a sinister slither to it and then Anya realised it wasn't Hali at all, but something else, something playing tricks on her.

"No, no," Anya mumbled, trying to break free, to push her mind beyond the dangers of slowing down, for the mystery foe brought a sense of dread and terror.

"Rest child, rest …"

"I said no! Reveal yourself!" Anya shouted, as if breaking free of a curse; and then, out of nowhere, an unholy figure slowly took shape. From its camouflage came an enormous monster, a deep rocky red colour, a great devilish beast with eight tentacles waving in the water, and great green eyes. Anya froze, unable to break its gaze, or even to think or speak. It took hold of her and made time melt away with a potent hypnotism beyond Anya's understanding.

"Look upon me with disgust all you want, but I was here before man and will be here long after."

"What, what are you?"

"A jurassicess, older than your race, as old as time. A kraken … and you, you are a human, or were …" The kraken's pupils pulsated, it could see more than just that instant, and something it saw brought the beast great fascination.

"You know who I am?"

"I know who you were, what you are and what you could be. None of that matters now, though, none of it matters at all …" The kraken's tentacle came from behind and wrapped around Anya's leg, a slithering wet thing but somehow it went unnoticed, "I'm lost. How do you know what I am?"

"We are all lost, and I know all. Recently turned, recently burned, I see." The jumble of words made Anya lose focus as the tentacle brought paralysis. She floated;

helpless prey caught in the grasp of a great beast. "You must pay the price of trespass, you must."

"Please, I didn't know. I'm lost, I want to go home."

"Go home? To the place you despise? This makes no sense."

"I don't despise my home! I despise the shallows, I love my home," Anya said in confusion as the kraken toyed with her emotions, like a viper playing with a mouse.

"So, you have chosen?"

"The Ark is my home."

"So many places, such little time, for you. Scales or skin, it all bleeds the same …"

"Humans are different, and the Ark is … the Ark is …" It was getting harder and harder to make sense, to stay focused. Anya was strong but not strong enough to fight the kraken's tricks whilst in its grasp.

"She may not have human skin, but tastes the same, bittersweet and all the better for I despise humans." The kraken's gaze took hold again as it squeezed her leg tight. Anya could feel the krakens dark loathing for humanity. Despite her newfound strength, she could do nothing to escape as she stared into its eyes.

"What did humans do to anger you?" asked Anya, her voice a whisper.

"Humans burned trees, killed animals, poisoned the seas and turned on each other. Humans were a plague, and now they are almost gone. Death to all that is human."

"I didn't do any of those things."

The kraken reeled Anya in to inspect her once again, it hung her upside down, observing her every movement, her every breath, and it began to laugh as if amused in a way that Anya would never understand. "These are my waters."

"What makes them yours?"

"Tired of your questions, I've heard enough." The kraken seemed to enjoy the feeling of pulling Anya up and down in the water and passing her between each of its tentacles.

"If you are going eat me, then eat me," said Anya, not willing to plead to the kraken's surprise. Keeping a hypnotic hold on Anya, it made Anya's body still and her mind unable to lie.

"I fear a sour taste. You don't beg ... Humans beg ... Why?"

Anya remained silent. The kraken hissed, sizing her up as if ready to swallow her down as a tasty meal. Anya accepted the end, having nothing left to give as the kraken drained all her energy, giving only poison in return.

"You don't fear death?"

"No."

"Every human fears death, has things to lose."

"I have nothing to lose that I haven't already lost."

"Foolish of a soul to have no faith. Pathetic, for all life is precious, sacred until the end."

"Spare me your lesson, be done with it."

"Very well," said the kraken, before it pulled Anya close and opened its mouth to reveal thousands of weathered yellow teeth. As it pulled Anya in, there was a glimmer in the kraken's eyes as it saw her past, present and future. The kraken's vision echoed through the water and into Anya's mind.

"I see black and white. True courage, bright light. Best friends, broken hearts … Beware the trust of men and, and –" said the kraken, as if surprised by its own revelation. But then, something most foul took its attention, as something bolted through the water at lightning pace.

"Let go of her!" bellowed the mighty mind-shout of a stranger. Anya's heavily dilated pupils turned to see the trident bearing water dweller. He sped through the water strong and fast, a green blur coming to her rescue. The kraken struck out with its tentacles but reacted too slowly and met the stranger's sharp gold trident. "Let go!" he bellowed once more.

"She is mine; leave us, foul dweller," the beast hissed, unwilling to give up its prey. Anya's saviour spun around, flipped and rolled through the water at lightning pace, unstoppable and at one with the water. None of the kraken's tentacles could catch him, and whenever it came close it met his trident. The saviour came to a halt and made a gesture with his free hand, whereupon from behind him came an army of sharks in formation, ready to strike at any moment.

"Let her go or be torn to shreds!" he warned.

The kraken hissed, "she is *mine*, leave well alone."

"I said let her go!"

Too smart to do battle, the Kraken let Anya go, to float through the water, lifeless and grey from the slow strangulation she had suffered in the grasp of the beast. The saviour took her floating body and slowly retreated.

With his mind, he signalled the sharks to take their leave, and swam away with Anya, far into the upstream. The kraken, defeated, returned to the depths, hidden in darkness once more, to wait and listen until the end of time.

## 11

## POISON

Anya floated in a distant realm as the ocean's ultraviolet colours blended together. Intoxicated, and when the blur began to fade, she found a place much brighter than the quiet cold darkness of the kraken's depths. The familiar reality of sand and seaweed, the sun shining through the surface – it was a blessing compared to the dark, the unknown, and monstrous creature. Still, she was seeing double and the paralysis made her helpless. Her saviour led her lifeless body by the hand, as she stared at two hammerhead sharks that accompanied them. They blurred in and out of focus until she saw their teeth. They were fierce dark beasts with light grey fins and piercing hungry eyes. Desperate to keep her eyes off the beasts, Anya looked up at the saviour. He was a green and fearless figure, lean, but not like Tyson or Isaac.

"You're a fool, girl, poisoned and if we're too slow you will lose your leg." Blunt and to the point, the saviour said only what he needed to. Anya could not reply and thought only of the kraken: its green eyes and rock-hard red skin burned into her brain. She was lifeless and relied on the saviour to keep her going. As time went by her lips began to tremble, as did her fingers and her toes. When the feeling started to come back a piercing pain took hold in her right leg where the kraken had wrapped around her bare skin and delivered its venom. Anya had no energy; in the corner of her eye she saw that her leg was black. The kraken had burnt through her skin.

"Don't shout," said the saviour as he grabbed her arm. "These waters are not safe. The more you panic, the worse it gets. Don't look at it, look at me." He shook her by the shoulders, and she saw his wide flat face, the orange dots around his eyes and the subtle stripes of green around his features. He appeared fierce and bitter, remaining stoic at all times. Anya tried to breathe, tried to get used to the pain, but it was almost as unbearable as the surface. He took Anya by the hand, guided her down to the ocean floor and placed his gold trident upon a large rock, where it glistened. Anya was close enough to notice that the trident was missing a prong.

"Why did you save me?" she asked, her words slow for the strength of the venom. In great pain, she was desperate for an answer. The saviour said nothing and instead looked around the ocean floor for something.

"The kraken's tentacles secrete a slow paralysis-inducing toxin; it would have killed you in your past life. You will live if we get to Hali soon, but it will be painful until then."

"Then why have we stopped?" Anya murmured, trying to remain calm amidst the stinging pain and strange daze. The saviour pulled green reeds from the ground and extended his other hand as if summoning something. An eelworm shot from the sand into his hand and Anya would have flinched if she could have. He took the creature and placed it upon Anya's leg as she drunkenly tried to resist.

"That's disgusting, that's –"

"You will die before we get to Hali if the worm doesn't suck out the venom." He took Anya's ankle and attached the long fat worm, wrapping reeds tightly around it as she tried not to scream. She could feel the strange pulsating creature sucking upon her leg, and as awful as it was, she could do nothing to stop it.

"Shouldn't we keep moving?" Anya's question came as she shuddered, trying to keep her mind off the pulsating worm.

"Soon, when the worm has done its job."

"Well … thank you."

"For what?"

"For coming all this way to save me," said Anya. She was grateful to be free from the kraken's control and more herself again – exhausted and in pain, but herself again.

"I came because you entered the kraken's waters and broke our agreement. Don't thank me: what you did was foolish. Never wander from the tribe, never go out alone no matter how close by."

"I'm not part of your tribe." Anya was right, she was an outsider and he had never dealt with an outsider before, or not for a long time. If it had been up to him, Anya would not have been saved.

"You're alive. So long as you live down here in these waters, you are one of us. Be more careful next time, I won't be around to save you."

"All I wanted to do was say thanks."

"Neptune doesn't need to be thanked. I do only as I must."

Anya looked up at him, startled and confused by the way he referred to himself in the third person. She looked down to see his trident resting on a rock and then it clicked. She was unsure whether it was the toxins, the worm, or just his ridiculous name, but Anya howled with laughter. In fact, the whole situation, drowning, descending, the office block and the kraken all seemed hilarious now. Neptune just stared back at her blankly.

"Are you done?"

"I'm sorry I, I just can't … Neptune is an old sea god's name and you are not gods."

Neptune picked up his trident and lifted it high in the air. He swiped it down upon a boulder and split the rock in two. Anya watched it float away either side of him for the force, ceasing her laughter. Neptune gave a familiar stare, the same stare Uncle Isaac always used to give her, the disapproving glance an adult bestowed on a disrespectful child.

"We all suffered, we all drowned. This is the afterlife and I built my resting place after the flood. The Ark clings on, but it is its own false idol, an insult to nature."

Neptune's sour and twisted words made Anya's heart sink, and her eyes glistened with a fierce remembrance of home. Her parents built the Ark, and at the saviour's insult Anya was distraught. She hadn't had any time to grieve, to get over everything she had lost.

Neptune sensed her feelings, he lowered his trident in regret for what he had said, but he was not the type to apologise.

"You know nothing of our struggle, our fight against the elements. My father built the Ark and he was a better leader than you will ever be."

Neptune looked into the child's eyes and had nothing more to say. Underwater life had made him cold and vicious, but he had saved her life all the same.

"Days ago, I was on top of the world, I was about to change everything, then I turned into this and doomed my people. Now I get to spend the rest of my days here dreaming about what could have been."

Neptune looked down at the small surface girl with her bright yellow eyes full of self-hatred. Having lost everything, it was hard not to see himself in her, and even someone else he had lost … He swam down and sat cross-legged where she bobbed and stayed perfectly still alongside her.

"Look at me," he said, and Anya resisted as much as she could before lifting her chin. She was confused, dazed from the worm, and not feeling her usual self. "You can sit upon the ocean floor if you really try."

Anya looked at him again and with her legs outstretched, she tried to hold herself down, but as quickly as it came, it went away for her frustration. It was hard to hide the anger, to hide the pain. Here was a foolish fish man pretending he was some sea god. She felt ready to leave, to try to swim, but she didn't know which way to go.

"Where will you go with that worm on your leg?" asked Neptune as if reading her mind, "you need a healer, you need Hali."

"Hali can go to hell."

"She saved your life –"

"Saved! You call this monstrosity *saved*! Look at me! Look at yourself! We are monsters banished to the ocean to eat like animals, sleep like animals. You call yourselves a tribe. You all gave in and drowned. On the Ark we fight for survival."

"Look where that fight got you. I've heard enough of your Ark's fairy-tale, weakness, warm blooded weakness."

Anya wanted to defend her home, but a little of what he said was right. Neptune took off from the sea floor, made himself as large as possible and remained in her path. He folded his arms, closed his eyes, bowed his head and opened both his palms. The strangest noise came forth, as if something huge was rushing through the water from every direction, Anya could smell it, sense it. Then a thousand fish all of different colours flew from everywhere, forming a sphere around them. It was beautiful, magnificent, as they criss-crossed like bright shining fireworks.

"We *are* gods, Anya."

Anya watched in awe as Neptune controlled the whole shoal of fish with his mind. It was unbelievable to see a thousand different fish orbit them at incredible speed. She wanted to reach out and touch them but instead she stayed perfectly still. It was hard for her to accept that Neptune was controlling sea life with thought alone.

"We are the next stage of human evolution, free from war and slavery. An equal people who work together with no shortage of resources. I offer you the chance of survival, I offer you a place in our family."

"What good am I?" asked Anya, unable to fathom why Neptune, Hali and their tribe were interested in her in the first place.

"Hali turned you; you have been chosen."

There was one question at the front of Anya's mind: why she could not trust any of them, why she would never trust them. "I-I need to know: why did you murder Gregory? He had a wife and child; he was a good man."

Neptune's posture sank; he never thought he would have to speak of this again. As quickly as they came, he made all the fish disappear from sight, leaving the two of them alone again. "Your people came to *our* waters, they cast nets to take *our* fish. We couldn't communicate, as much as we wanted to. One nearly killed my brother, so he tore out the man's heart in self-defence."

Anya listened, unsure of what to make of it, unsure of whether to believe him.

"I banished my brother for what he did, and he is never to return."

Anya took a moment to contemplate his story; it was sad but believable. Led by Tyson, the Hunters would strike first – but it didn't mean she trusted Neptune.

"None of that matters now, you don't belong to your Ark anymore, you belong to this a world now, chosen for the next stage of evolution. I sense great potential in you, and I know this is where you are meant to be."

That was as close as Neptune could come to pleasantries. He offered Anya a hand, it stayed there waiting, and Anya looked at this monster, this scaled beast who had saved her from the kraken, she didn't know what to do next.

"My leg … my leg hurts so much."

"Then let me bear your pain," said Neptune, Anya took his hand and with a bright glow he transferred the pain from her unto himself. "Now, let me show you something else …"

With his will alone, two hammerhead sharks came out of nowhere, great beasts with razor teeth and cold eyes. They had white under-bellies, and grey backs. They whirled around Anya thundering through the ocean. Neptune brought them to a halt, as he had brought the ocean with a single thought. Half afraid and half amazed, Anya didn't know what to do until Neptune climbed on the back of one.

"This is Grey, that's Fin, they are brothers like my brother and I were. Are you going to tread all day, or ride one?"

Anya placed a hand on Fin as he took off and she clung on for dear life still unsure of whether it was really real. The sharks moved at pace, and despite her pain, Anya felt incredible, like a true predator. She let the beast do all the work, half scared to open her eyes, and when she did, she saw the many scars on Fin's back. Their journey was long, but they followed a warm current for a few hours, and after a while, to Anya's relief, the shallows came into view. They departed the sharks and took to swimming.

"Why aren't we going to ride them the whole way?" she asked.

"Some are afraid of the sharks, especially those who can't bond with a creature."

Anya could understand why, when they reached the office block, and all the adrenaline wore off Anya felt incredibly tired.

"Try to rest, I will send Hali to treat your leg."

"Goodbye," she replied, before Neptune swam away.

Anya watched him go as she slowly made her way back up the old office block to the top floor, there she lay close to the window. Every moment that went by seemed an eternity as every moment she was without Neptune the pain became stronger. It was severe, so bad she felt overwhelmingly grateful, but she also wondered how he had coped with the pain. Anya held on, she didn't shout, scream or fight. Instead of lashing out or trying to run, she sat in silence. She thought of the kraken and how lucky she was to be alive. How strange it was for the beast to take her … She felt that it was a part of her now, after feeling its touch, as if it had taken something from her, and she shuddered. She tried to remember what it had said, but all she could remember was its warning.

"Black and white. True courage, bright light. Best friends, broken hearts, beware the trust of men and … and …" None of it meant anything to her. The kraken was cut away so soon by her Neptune that she would never know its final words of warning.

Now the pain was so bad that Anya struggled to breathe. She drifted in and out of consciousness, unable to do anything but float. Her eyes were heavy, her heart, too. It was dark, almost pitch-black in the office. Anya was so tired she could not lift a limb. Paralyzed once more, she lay staring straight ahead as Hali entered through the doorway surrounded by bright glowing fish that provided the most tranquil source of blue light. Hali looked like an angel and came to her side like a caring mother, her eyes glowing.

"Help me," said Anya, soft and breathless.

"Shh," replied Hali holding her head softly, "rest, girl."

Hali unwrapped the seaweed bandage, careful not to touch the damage herself as the strange worm floated dead and free toward Anya. She averted her eyes in horror, batting the worm away before looking down. The leg was infected: blood and other such darkness drifted away from it. The infection was eating right to bone. Hali shook her head as Anya winced. Then the most peculiar creature poked its head over her shoulder, a little yellow smiling face with pointy antenna, an axolotl, a sunburst neotenic salamander, red, with a yellow face.

"Just relax, look at Guillermo, he's always happy." Anya wanted to squeal but instead she did as Hali bade her and stared at the little axolotl's friendly face. "You're safe now, and you're very brave; there's a strength within you, Anya. Guillermo is going to save you, I promise."

Anya watched Hali pick up the axolotl before lowering it onto her leg. The pain was tremendous; Anya would have done anything to relieve the burning sensation. Hali took her hand and placed it upon the smiling axolotl until both her hand and the beast started to glow brightly. Hali and Guillermo closed their eyes in unison, and when they opened them again, they were blinding white. She mouthed something over and over, as if saying some sort of special prayer.

Anya found it hard to stay conscious as the pain slowly disappeared. She closed her eyes and Hali continued to carry out her mysterious work. Guillermo climbed back on to Hali's arm and back up to her shoulder.

Hali watched over Anya all night, her head in her lap as she rested. It was a mother's love; a love Anya would never have expected from her. Hali sat for as long as it took, as hours passed and the pain faded, along with the weakness and lack of balance.

"Thank you," Anya said. "Have I lost my leg?" she asked, afraid to look down.

"See for yourself," Hali replied, so Anya took a glance.

Her leg was intact, it felt whole again and free of poison. Anya looked at Hali and gave a fang-toothed smile. She understood there was more to their mysterious ways than she had thought. She turned her head to look at Guillermo upon Hali's shoulder, then raised her hand and gave it a gentle stroke. The axolotl buzzed in return.

"He likes you."

"Thanks Guillermo. Can you teach me how to –"

"This bond can't be taught, only discovered. You must find your creature. Neptune has sharks, I have this little one," she said stroking the chin of the little axolotl.

"What about the fish?"

"Well, they are just fish. I suppose it can be taught, it's like breathing, but you never tried to breathe, so don't try to move the fish. Just do."

Anya nodded, hanging off every word Hali said, and Hali looked down as though at someone different to days prior. She saw a lot of herself in Anya, this young strong-minded girl with her whole life ahead of her – who had had everything taken from her all the same.

"I know it isn't easy being down here. I know how it feels to wake up having drowned and finding yourself trapped under the ocean. I had a family, children. They will always be a part of me, but I have a new life now."

Anya didn't know what to say, she had neglected to think anyone was in the same situation as her. Unable to find words, she froze for a moment, before embracing Hali. She in turn hesitated to return the gesture, but when she did so, they both felt a warming connection.

"I'm sorry I wasn't nicer to you – you saved my life. I just … I just miss the Ark."

"We all miss home, Anya, and not one of us wants to look like this – but think about what we can do.

Neptune says you will be strong; there is no limit to what you can accomplish down here."

Hali's sharp-toothed smile didn't scare Anya; Hali's reptilian ways were becoming more natural to her and she started to see the very human side underneath her aquatic exterior. Everything was changing and becoming so much more. The kraken, the sharks, the healing … It was a new world, one of which she still had little understanding. Anya was still disheartened, her memories of the Ark left her understandably so, but she began to show a new resilience. Instead of acting like she knew everything, she began to realise that there was much she could learn. She made a promise to herself: instead of spending so much time hating everything, she would try – she would at least try.

"What can I do?"

"Whatever do you mean?"

"To show you I'm grateful. I want to spend time with your tribe, move fish, discover the whole ocean."

Anya's sudden motivation made Hali laugh, and for a moment she didn't know what to suggest.

"At daybreak I will send someone to you, to show you the reefs, teach you our ways – but only if you are ready?"

Anya hesitated; her experiences beyond this office block had so far been terrifying. There were many things hiding in the deep dark waters that she was unprepared for, no matter how strong she felt. There was, however, no going back, so she met Hali's question with a fang-toothed smile and said – "I'm ready."

## 12

## KAI

I n the morning, Anya awoke to the brightness of daylight shimmering through the water. Her leg seemed back to normal and she felt its scaly surface with her claws just to make sure. Anya was hungry, starving, and knew she could wait no longer to eat for the scent of a succulent fish filled her nares. She took off with speed and strength through the office block to follow the scent as if reborn. Two floors down she, burst into a room filled with fish that had become trapped overnight. Diving towards them, Anya watched in dismay as they all flew away from each other. Anya took turns launching herself, spinning back and forth and flying every which way to try to catch each of the little blue-tails whole.

She stopped herself for a moment and looked into the eyes of one that faced her. Anya extended a claw in the hope of achieving what Neptune had found so easy. She opened her palm and concentrated, trying to move it with her mind – but nothing happened. Anya tried again and again before shaking her head in frustration. Then, when she was off guard, she heard the strangest noise, some sort of squeak. Making for the window, she saw a spotted dolphin, speckled grey, with a smile on its face, swimming around in circles. For a moment she could not believe her eyes, but then she the short skinny water dweller, green with streaks of blue on his back alongside the dolphin. They chased each other around, up and down, left and right. The creature laughed whilst the dolphin squeaked and whistled merrily. They were communicating in the way Neptune had with Grey and Fin, and like Hali had with Guillermo. Afraid of being seen, Anya stayed hidden behind a desk, watching them intently; she was jealous of such a bond but timid, too, despite making progress with Neptune and Hali.

Anya panicked and retreated further into the office to hide. When she found the courage to peek out again, the dolphin was staring right at her through the missing windowpane. There was something comforting about such a majestic creature, no one on the Ark had ever come this close to one. Anya waved her hand around to break its glare, and the dolphin swam in circles, smiling and squawking. She wanted to tell it to be gone, but how could she? Instead she turned to disappear further into the building but then she heard another voice.

"Don't go, you will make Polka sad," said a young male voice. Anya turned to see a boy, right behind her and upside down, mimicking a seated position. He was small, slim and his eyes more orange than yellow. Stripes of blue came down over his shoulders. He seemed only a child, closer to ten than twenty. With one look, the dolphin came back and nuzzled up against him.

"Is that its name?" asked Anya, taken by surprise, unable to get used to the boy being upside down. It hurt her eyes, but the boy seemed unfazed, as if it were no different to being upright.

"Her name is Polka Dot, Polka for short, she's a spotted dolphin and she knows when she's being made fun of. She's the smartest creature in the whole damn sea." Polka seemed to whistle in agreement. This was not the first time Anya had seen a dolphin, but now, down here, her perception of them was entirely different, as it stared at her with a very human gaze.

"That's a silly name for a dolphin, fish boy."

"Fish boy? I'm a waterman! And Polka is a fine name, take it back," the boy said, folding his arms and ushering himself into a relaxed supine pose, yet seeming unable to stay still.

"There's no way that you're a man."

"Well, no, not yet, but some day, when my beard comes in ..."

Anya shook her head, cringing, unable to fathom whether the boy knew what a beard really was. She had to remind herself that he was just a child.

"Fine, I take it back."

The boy extended his arms, back-flipping in celebration. Polka barrel-rolled alongside him before whistling, as the boy smiled with large fanged teeth. He signalled with his hand and Polka approached Anya, to swim around her in circles.

"My name is Kai, it means ocean in Japanese – I guess you think that's stupid too, huh?"

"A little," said Anya, barely able to concentrate, too distracted by Polka, who kept swimming and nuzzling up against her. Polka made her smile and even laugh for the first time in too long. There was nothing quite like the sweetness of an innocent creature to make any bad situation better. Kai could see the positive impression Polka was having on her, and his large bright orange eyes seemed to fill with promise.

"So, you've been here for quite a few days?" said Kai; he seemed concerned for Anya's wellbeing, but there was a childish quality to his tone. Anya, like any sixteen-year-old, felt too mature to be dealing with this. On the Ark you grew up fast or drowned, but Kai seemed to have it easy, like the kids of old; she half expected him to make mention of the kraken, but it appeared Neptune and Hali had not told him what had happened.

"I have."

"The others worry about why you haven't come to see them. We're a nice people – why don't you?"

"No." Anya shuddered; she did not want to let anyone down again. On the Ark she had ruined every-thing, and these people did not need that.

"Well, what is it you're waiting for?"

"I don't know," said Anya – but she did: every-thing she had done upon the Ark had led to disaster and a deep sense of shame and guilt. She was afraid that they would not like her, not accept her, and that she would mess everything up again. "Hali is sending me a guide, someone strong who can teach me the ways of the water; maybe they can help me figure things out."

"Ohh," Kai replied, scratching his chin. Still upside down, he looked left and right, searching for someone who might join them. He waited for them before realising that it was him. "Ohh," he extended his arms in celebration and shouted, "Ta-da!"

Anya looked all around, expecting her guide to be behind her now, but no one was there. She turned back, to find Kai's expression of joy still there, that big cheesy grin which knew no hardship and only easy childhood. Now it clicked and Anya realised that the guide who was meant for her was, to her disappointment, Kai.

"You?"

"Me! And you are going to be the best pupil! I will teach you everything. What do you want to learn first? Wait, no, I'm the teacher! Let's just go swimming, you, me and Polka."

"Aren't you a little young to go swimming on your own?"

Kai and Polka shared a serious look; Kai was offended at first, before he and Polka began whispering to each other, with the dolphin giving an occasional squeak before they both burst into laughter.

"What's so funny?" Anya asked, for fear of missing out.

"I'm one of the strongest and fastest members of the tribe. I speak to dolphins – trust me, I can take care of myself better than you can. You're like a new-born baby."

"I drowned. I didn't choose to. I didn't choose to leave my home."

Kai scratched his head and slowly drifted upside down again. He looked at her with sadness, knowing her pain all too well, and Polka stopped smiling almost mimicking his expression.

"Hali told us you were drowning, and that there was no other way. Yet you blamed her for saving your life."

"Did she tell you that?"

"No, I see it."

"She terrified me," said Anya.

"At least you got to experience the other world and know what breathing air feels like. I was born here. I've always lived this way."

It occurred to Anya now why Kai did not stay still, why he moved so often upside down or at odd angles, constantly shifting his body. Kai had never walked or breathed before.

"I'm sorry, I –"

"Don't be. Do you miss the surface, Anya? They told me of the raft, the daily struggle, the bitter cold and the fight to live. Me, I can't even figure out how you stand up there, no sir."

He surprised her. Kai was smart for his age – and he had the young, hopeful eyes that boys get when they see an older girl they like. If watermen could blush, Kai would be blushing; Anya could see it. And it was cute. At that moment, Anya realised she had sensed something that no human could sense: strange vibes coming from everything, telling of its character and history. Anya had already made a swift judgement about Kai and she knew he would not last a day upon the Ark. He was soft and full of imagination, not hard work. She would also say that he was honest, and so she saw no reason not to answer his question with honesty.

"I miss the people, but they were stuck in their ways – ways that only harsh weather can bring."

"Well, my people are kind and loving. They would never hurt you."

Anya would not trust them or anyone else ever again but he seemed honest, it was becoming easier for Anya to forget Kai was a monster, for she was one too, now; and maybe, just maybe, they were no worse than those upon the Ark. She saw the human within him and kept having to remind herself that this place, these beings, were not normal.

"Have you ever seen the reef?"

"No, the adults on the Ark told us about the reefs, how beautiful and bright they were before pollution killed them all."

"Then you must," said Kai, turning and taking off like a rocket through the window that Tomas had broken. Polka Dot looked into Anya's eyes as if trying to say that everything would be okay. She rubbed Anya's side with her nose, before squeaking and coming up behind her to push her in Kai's direction. Anya swam, but hesitated for a moment at the window.

Polka dot shot right past her. Anya tried to breathe and swam forward to meet them, despite the feeling that she should stay inside. She swam high above the tribe, trying hard to keep up with Kai and Polka Dot. Anya was taken aback by the beauty of it all, the bright blooming colours, the thousands of different under-water creatures.

At first, she worked hard to keep pace with Kai, but he was too fast. They were moving faster than she had ever thought possible, and the influx of cold water at such pace felt so satisfying.

"Breathe. Let the water flow through you, take in all the sights and sounds. You might even hear a species that wants to bond with you, or they might hear you. Be careful what you wish for, though, some of them are too strong to bond with. The first dweller to try to tame a shark got eaten."

Anya tried to listen; she found it hard to get the kraken out of her mind, but sure enough, with deep breathing she was able to do so. Every obsessive negative thought floated away the further Kai pushed ahead, and he kept looking back to test her. Anya flew further and further, trying to match him for pace, but he was too far ahead. He hadn't lied about how fast he was. When they reached the reef, she stopped in wonder. It was unlike anything she had ever seen, fluorescent oranges, yellows, neon-blues that no human eye could begin to compre-hend. It was beautiful, and despite its depth it wasn't dark in the slightest. Anya saw the beauty water could bring. The man-made surface humanity had left behind was a bland and crumbling thing, but down here the world was alive. There were blue jellyfish, red pufferfish and blue sharks. When they went further down, Anya could see the speckled yellow starfish, the orange coral bursting with life as octopuses moved along changing colour, and the stingrays skimming the ocean floor, hardly disturbing the sand. Despite humanity's apparent destiny to destroy the planet, Mother Nature had triumphed after the flood. The sea had flourished, free of oil, free of machines, and free of man.

Kai caught up with her and he took her by the arm. Anya turned to face him and saw the reflection of the whole reef in his eyes; it made them almost human.

"Have you ever seen anything so beautiful?" he asked, and Anya was in awe trying to take it all in. Kai seemed about to gesture. It took Anya a moment to realise what he was doing: he was encouraging four sea turtles to appear, all in a line, almost hovering. They swam around her, as did the fish and jellyfish. Kai started to do what Neptune had done, but on a smaller scale, and with more beautiful fish. Anya wasn't in pain this time like the last time, so she could appreciate the moment; it was hypnotic, it was incredible, beyond anything she could have imagined. Telekinesis provided a way of bonding with sea creatures – it wasn't make-believe, it was real. They could communicate with each other and the ocean, and perhaps in ways never thought possible.

It was at that moment Anya's feelings of awe disappeared. She brushed off Kai's hand and pushed away. As she did so, all the sea creatures scattered; only Polka remained. Kai looked at Anya, unable to fathom why, for it was not in his nature to make inferences. It was not in the nature of any of these sea creatures to understand the struggle that Anya had been through.

"This is too much for me," Anya said. She wanted to cry but was unable to. She was anxious, afraid of losing any more. Having drowned twice and lost her home and family, to be left here with monstrous strangers. She wanted to move forward, to move on and to trust, but she could not.

"What do you mean?"

"I want to go home."

"I don't understand, I —"

"You will never understand, Kai, none of you will," said Anya, heartbroken from the loss of her family. She moved away from him to explore the reef alone and find some solitude. She journeyed along, looking at all the creatures, stingrays and starfish. There she floated and took it all in, appreciating the quiet. Kai was nice enough to give her some space for as long as he could, but kept a watchful eye, until finally he approached again.

"Kai, I want to be alone."

"No, Anya, really, I —" he said, pointing behind her; but Anya was in no mood for children's tricks.

"I said I want to be alone!"

"Turn around!"

Anya turned, and to her amazement there were three bright rainbow fish following her every move. They were entranced, captivated, as Kai came to her side and gently raised her hand. Moving it left to right, the three fish stared back following her hand with their eyes, but they didn't move as she wanted them to. Anya hung her head in frustration, but Kai was determined that she keep trying. No matter how hard she tried, how determined she was, it wasn't happening. For a moment, one trembled, before going on its way again.

"You will get it. It's a bond, a harmony between us and other creatures, it takes a while to learn."

Anya quickly became frustrated; she gave up and didn't want to try any longer. Her mind just wasn't clear enough to do anything. "It's no use, I can't control anything."

"You will. You did well for a first go, imagine what you could control in a few months!"

"Months?" She sighed.

"It takes time, but soon you will be like meeeee!" said Kai, and all of the ocean life danced around them as he somersaulted. Anya shook her head, unable to bear his cringeworthy nature once more. In response to her frown, Kai ceased his games.

"So, if you can control fish with your mind, what's the point of hunting them for food?"

"There would be no fun in just getting the fish to swim into your mouth, silly," Kai replied.

Anya looked upon the reef shining in the midday sunlight. For a moment her mind drifted, and then she saw a turtle staring at her. It was green and blue, sparkling in the water, the turtle's eyes reminded her of Lord Turtle Head and she smiled. She thought for a moment about whether Lord Turtle Head did have some strange bond with sea turtles, and whether he was right all along. She tried to approach the turtle, but when she did it swam away at speed and she felt alone in the reef once more. Anya wondered about the Ark, she remembered where she had heard of the reefs. Aunt

Lyn talked about breathing equipment, large tanks, flippers, family holidays, and how most of the reefs were destroyed. It was a subtle reminder of the Ark, the warmth of Uncle Isaac's arms battling against the wind and cold. Jake and his long surfer hair came back to her, too … She missed their voices, the wind and rain.

"Anya, what's wrong?" asked Kai.

"Nothing," she replied, and Kai was too young to see through her white lie.

"Well they asked me to ask you if … if you want to eat with the tribe tonight. Will you feast and play with us?"

Anya looked at this innocent sea creature. Despite his reptilian skin, sharp teeth and claws, she saw a child. She thought long and hard about her answer as she hid her sadness. She was afraid to say yes, but she was also growing tired of the cold dark office block.

"I'm going back to the office block, Kai," she said, to his surprise. Kai looked upset. Quivering, he bit his lip, trying to hide a stutter. He was born underwater and thus didn't know about the struggle and the loss first-hand, but somehow, he could sense the fear in Anya's heart. It was easy for water dwellers to sense each other's feelings, some more than others. Kai understood Anya's pain, and the fact that she wasn't quite ready.

"Whenever you need me, I'll be waiting," Kai said, before swimming back to his home. Anya followed in silence, unsure of what to say. They parted ways high above the great crossroads. Anya expected Kai to try to persuade her to stay and meet the others, but instead he let her make up her own mind. She retraced her path back to the office block, back to where it was safe, although she didn't want to. She wanted to go with him, to be free of the office block, as all it stood for was loss and regret. Still, she swam toward it and not away, knowing Kai was watching her from behind. She didn't turn, she just kept going.

## 13

## DWELLERS

Anya floated within the office block. It had become such a dull, grey place, plagued by bad memories. To escape in her mind, she thought about her time with Kai and the reef's wondrous beauty, replaying every event from the day she drowned until today, over and over. This time there was no sense of hatred toward those she once called monsters. Her thoughts and feelings had changed so much since her first night alone; her memories of Hali's shadow in the mirror before the roof collapsed had once brought fear, but that fear was gone. In its place, she remembered the touch of a healer, a kind and caring soul that saved her from drowning and then again from the kraken's grasp. And the horror of fleeing the shallows and those crazed, screeching monsters was no more either; now, the kraken was the monster and Neptune her saviour. The more time that passed, the more Anya reflected; with thoughts of self-discovery, of peace, instead of anger and fear.

Evening was coming and the office block became dark and claustrophobic, too small a cage for such a creature. Such power and strength longed to be free of any constrictions. Anya still thought of the Ark and her family, but it was more a distant dream now. It was as if the more time she spent in this new body, the more her old thoughts and feelings drifted away. Still, she took the meditative stance that the elders adopted upon the Ark, crossing her legs and holding her knees. Closing her eyes, she listened to the ocean; it made her calm. There were strange noises very far away, almost as if something was trying to call her … and then the laughter of children and the chatter of adults. "Papa, Papa, I love you, Papa," said a little one to its father. That reminded Anya of a time now lost.

"… And there we were, five of us, surrounded by sharks. I thought they were going to eat us! Then Neptune with the might of his mind tamed those beasts and now they are but friends," said one of the females, to a crowd of what Anya knew were gasping children. She didn't understand how she knew, but she did.

"I remember, back in the days of land, you kids wouldn't have handled walking or working or doing anything!" said one of the older males in a lecturing fashion, in the tone of a kind father trying not to be too harsh. In response came the laughter of two children.

Anya remembered that the Ark's elders, too, told the young about how they would not have been able to handle whatever their generation had handled. Anya grinned at the irony, and at the memory of walking and moving upon the surface. She didn't feel guilty for eavesdropping, for the voices made her feel less alone. Humans hadn't been built for such isolation, and the more Anya listened, the more she learned. Instead of trying to block everything out, she wished to learn the ways of her new body and soul, and so, with her eyes closed, her mind began to paint a picture of distance. She took a moment to listen, trying to work out exactly what it was that let her hear from this far away. It was the waves: sound waves. Each mind had some sort of receptor, and each one sent and received. Sound painted a picture of the world and blended with vision to form an enhanced sensation of perception at which Anya was a novice. And yet she was slightly better than before at limiting it and turning down the volume. Then she noticed everyone had taken to silence, so she waited intently for what was to come next.

"It wasn't always like this, we didn't always have food in our bellies, good places to sleep and clean ways to live." Anya knew the voice: it was Neptune, commanding everyone's attention. "The world above was cruel, vicious and unforgiving, even without the great flood. We used to say the earth drowned, but now we know it's been born again – *remember*."

"*Remember*," the crowd replied in unison.

"We used to fear the elements; now we embrace them – *remember*."

"*Remember*."

"I shall see you at the feast," said Neptune, before the crowd erupted in chatter again and Anya lost Neptune's mind as quickly as it came. She wondered about the feast; it was humorous to think of a feast underwater, for there would be no cooking. She floated in the office block all alone and then tried to search for Hali but there was only silence, so Anya looked for Kai and found his voice.

"Yes! Woohoo!" he shouted, as if celebrating something. Anya immediately tried to stop searching for him, as it felt like he knew. "I can see you!" said Kai with the same enthusiasm. Anya cringed, not quite in the mood to deal with his unstoppable levels of energy; he was quickly becoming the little brother she never wanted.

Within seconds, Polka shot through the window at speed and tumbled to a halt in Anya's arms. She didn't see Kai following. He put his head around the corner and peered in.

"How did you know?"

"I just know when people are looking for me; I can see them, too. Only a few others can. So, what do you want?" he said, with those big round eyes offering such promise. Anya desperately tried to come up with something fast, for fear of disappointing him.

"I just … erm … wanted to see you?"

"Did you hear that, Polka? I think Anya's our new best friend," he said, as he flipped and spun around in the water. "In that case, is my new best friend ready?"

"Ready for?"

"Dinner!" Kai shouted in his childish, ecstatic way.

His request was a surprise, to say the least. After how cold she had been, how reclusive, Anya did not feel that she deserved it, but there were only so many times she could say no. On the inside she was relieved to speak to another person again, for the office block was lonely. Kai froze in his celebrations, with his big cheesy smile on his face, whilst Polka danced around him. Anya knew that this time he would not take no for an answer.

"Fine, fine," she said, extending a hand. Kai took hold of it and swam fast down to the crossroads. Since Anya's descent, she had not fully explored the area. It was strange for her and would be strange for anyone who had lived long enough to see the surface. There were traffic lights, tarmac, cars and billboards, all submerged and covered in algae. Old shopping carts, letterboxes and telephone kiosks, telling the tale of the time before the ocean took back what it had once lent to the world. Anya saw seahorses, starfish, little bits of bright life all around, as Kai led her to what was an old town hall. He let go of her at the steps and went on ahead.

Anya stopped for a moment, taken aback by the old grey building as it shimmered with green algae and sea life, its high stone steps and pillars eroded with time. She had never seen such a building before; most were far more modern than these tall looming arches and old stone steps. She swam inside to meet Kai and a whole new world opened up to her, a world of white marble. Everything that hung upon the walls was covered in a murky sea dust. There were still pens on desks, telephones stained with rust, and more family photographs of those lost in the flood.

Left alone in the hallway, Anya could hear the intimidating voices of many, but she pushed herself onwards. Through the archway the room opened up into a huge chamber, where two hundred water dwellers floated either side of her, deep in conversation. Benches lined the walls all around the room. There was no roof: it had collapsed in the flood, and the setting sun now spilt through the cracks, making the green scales of the water dwellers glimmer. Neptune was sitting with a number of other close companions around him, his trident set down at his side. As Anya entered, there was a brief silence.

"Ladies, gentlemen, fish and friends, this is Anya, she is our guest. Please show her the utmost hospitality." With Neptune's words every one of them looked at her for a moment as she floated awkwardly on by in silence. It was a strange sight, and it would be an understatement to say that Anya didn't feel welcome. Many of them just kept staring; they did not smile or laugh or offer any form of welcome. There were a few, however, who bowed after a moment or two, before they erupted again in chatter. Soon the dwellers were back in their happy little worlds, and it took Anya a moment to realise that this was their normal behaviour. On the Ark there were no strangers, no survivors from outside. If one ever did show up, they would be forever distrusted, so she could understand the reaction of these creatures to some extent. Everything about the way the Arkers lived seemed so full of stress and desperation to survive. Anya brushed the memory away and moved on, hoping to make friends of some of the strangers. Then Hali swam down to her side and gave her a smile.

"Anya, my dear, how are you feeling?" she asked.

"I feel better," Anya replied, eyeing Guillermo on Hali's shoulder, forever grateful for its magical intervention, but still baffled by the mystery of its powers. Then a purple and orange octopus took her attention, it floated on by before making its way back to its partner and wrapping itself around a reptilian arm. Two stingrays brushed along the floor, chasing each other, such creatures were a hard thing for Anya to get used to.

"You look better, stronger. Sorry if not everyone welcomes you as they should; no one knows what to think after the incident – but I wouldn't worry, they will warm to you," said Hali. She couldn't help but notice that most of Anya's attention was on Guillermo, so she reached up and rubbed him on the nares. "You may have one of your own soon."

"Doubtful …"

"Oh, my dear, I see it in your eyes: what you have is not in all of us." Hali could see things that others could not, just like how Kai knew when others were watching him. Anya felt so suddenly reminded of Aunt Lyn. With the thought of her aunt came an unexpected feeling of panic, and everything stopped for a moment. She shuddered as everyone's eyes turned green, giving her a sharp reminder of the kraken's power. A split second later, everything was normal again.

"Anya is everything alright?" asked Hali as she touched her shoulder, trying not to cause a scene. "The kraken doesn't have you anymore, you're safe now."

"I know, I just –"

"What did it say to you?" asked Hali with concern.

Anya nervously rubbed her arms and tried to

remember the kraken's words. It was hard to recall, it seemed so long ago.

"You look better, Anya, how's the leg?" said Neptune, interrupting them both with his deep voice. He was a dark and imposing figure who made Anya rather self-conscious with his stare. His strength reminded her of Uncle Isaac, but there was something else about him. He was always so guarded and Anya couldn't help but think that he was hiding something.

"My leg is fine," said Anya, forgetting that the poison had gone almost to the bone before Neptune saved her.

"I'm glad you came; I imagine you have wondered how we feast?"

Anya had indeed wondered how they feasted, given that there was no fire, no drums and no dancing. She also thought it was strange that Neptune knew that she had wondered about such a thing. He looked at her, at everyone as if he knew something that they didn't.

"I do."

"All will be explained in time. Now, tell me. How was the reef, and how was Kai?"

"Good, he … umm … is quite energetic but–"

"Sometimes we need someone like that to get you through where you've been."

Anya supposed she did need Kai, more than she knew. His constant positivity wore on her at first, but in truth, now he was away from her, she missed him.

"What about the reef itself?"

"The reef was beautiful. I managed to make three fish turn."

"I'm sure you will befriend sharks in no time," said Neptune. "Now I must address the group." He turned and swam to the middle of the room and hovered above everyone else. "Friends and fish. Tonight is special, tonight we have a new guest. A guest who hails from the surface, a friend for life. Let us today show her a new way! We do not have tables, we do not cook, we do not have flame, but we know how to eat. It's time to feast!"

Neptune raised his hand and his tribe followed suit. Vibrations grew, shaking the benches, the building and the earth as their energy combined, and suddenly a thousand fish flew in from above and filled the room with wild patterns. It was a magnificent sight to behold. Anya watched as those around her swam up to catch and eat as many of the fish as possible, picking them out of the water and stuffing their mouths endlessly. She joined the chase, picking out all different sizes and colours. It was a delicious banquet the likes of which Anya had never known. A hint of magic filled the hall as she watched the others move around her. Even toddlers swam on by, looking adorable, with squished little reptilian faces, making short sharp uncoordinated movements. It was a remarkable rainbow of fish, and the feast seemed truly endless. Near the end Anya was stuffed, and her belly swollen, when Hali came to her side.

"That was ... that was *incredible*."

"I know," said Hali with that motherly smile, before guiding Anya down to a seat. The thought of staying seated in the water seemed impossible, and Anya held on to the underside of the bench to keep herself in place. A thousand fish bones had settled on the floor and three tribe members, led by Neptune, moved with such force that it created a current which pushed all the bones upwards. After shaping the water with their hands, the bones flew back out of the roof.

The room was alive while everyone sat on the benches, talking and laughing with each other and telling stories. A few moments later everyone quietened down; there was eager anticipation all around, but Anya had no idea why. The adults began to sing, holding a note in harmony, a rich vibrant tone that flowed through Anya's mind unlike anything she had ever heard. A unique acoustic hum brought wonder, as more joined in and an entire choir formed. It started low, with a gentle lift from minor to major. A girl not too far from Anya's age, with stripes of orange down her back and across her side, came forth. In the light her eyes glittered white as she drifted to the middle of the room, while the music around her built, layer upon layer.

The mysterious sea angel extended her arms and legs in a ballet pose. She floated perfectly still in the water, pirouetting, one handheld high, one leg bent to meet her other knee. Her hands moved as if in air not water, flowing free. It was a dance, but not one Anya knew, like she knew the sharp, staggering dances of the Ark. It reminded her of the Hunters' spear dance, but even then, they were miles apart. This was something else. The girl moved with a holy grace, spinning round, lifting her legs, spinning again and diving. Cutting through the water with perfect form. She was not a girl, not a monster, but an angel, and if Anya could have cried she would have, as the music built, and the dancing accelerated. Time seemed to disappear with her movements and with the uplifting rhythmic hum of the choir, before the beautiful crescendo brought her back down. The angel spun slowly, before picking up speed again as the voices returned and lifted her once more. Sand swirled about, creating a whirlpool around her. Faster and faster she went, becoming a blur. It went on and on, a beautiful green and blue blur that Anya could have watched forever. There was something so gentle, so beautiful about the choir and the dance. Anya was lost in the moment as the angel slowed down along with the choir. Revolving like a slowing spinning top, she finally came to a halt, ending with a bow. When the dance was done everyone got up again to reunite with family and friends, but Anya sat alone, star-struck by what she had seen.

## 14

## THE GAME

Anya sat for a while, as families and friends busied themselves around her. They moved around as she clung to the underside of the bench, all the while her eyes fixated on the orange-striped angelic water dweller being congratulated. Every so often another scaly figure came between them, but Anya didn't even blink. The angel's performance, her display of art, was unlike anything Anya had ever seen. She had never known such grace, there had never been a moment on the Ark like it, and it seemed odd that everyone else could simply move on. She noticed the difference between the water dwellers and the Ark's tribe. Though they were strong, the water dwellers were gentle, too, and because of the beauty of the music and dance she forgot that any of them had ever been monsters. Yes, they were human after all.

After another moment of sitting, hypnotised, Anya let go of the bench and floated through the crowd, squeezing past strangers, to go to the angel, although she did not know what to say.

"Can I help you? Anya, is it?"

Anya couldn't find the words; she was speechless, staring at an artist, a figment of beauty that had captivated her imagination.

"Yes … I … I liked your dancing." Upon the Ark, Anya would have cringed, never daring to say something so stupid – but now she could say nothing else.

"Thank you."

"It was beautiful." It was the first time Anya had ever found real meaning for that word. Aunt Lyn had used it, true, but not once had Anya ever found a reason to say such a word on the Ark.

"Listen, Anya, me and some of the older young fins are going to play water-wheel, if you want to join us?"

Anya didn't know what to say. She thought about playing with others. She didn't play well with the other girls on the Ark, she was never good at sports, and the sports up there were rough.

"I-I probably have to go back to –"

"Come on, you have to try! It's easy."

Anya gave her a sharp-toothed smile, and to her own surprise she agreed. It would feel good to meet new people, as it felt good to be so full of music. So they left the hall and followed the rest of the young crowd whilst the adults stayed behind.

"Sorry, I haven't even asked your name."

"It's Pearl."

The name did suit: Pearl's eyes had glimmered white while dancing, but now they were more orange. There was an odd quiet grace to Pearl; she wasn't swift and erratic like Kai, but slow and so calm.

"Could you teach me some time?"

"To?"

"To dance," said Anya nervously.

"I can."

The thought of learning new things made Anya forget about the Ark just long enough for her to feel like her old self again. She followed Pearl back out of the doors and onto the reef; on the far side of Atlantis was what the young fins called the water-wheel stadium. It was once a football stadium, a huge metal contraption long overgrown, the grandest building Anya had ever seen, bristling with gates and surrounded by rusted metal food vans. She swam over the top of the stands and down into the arena, surrounded by thousands of seats. There was of course no pitch now, just rugged seabed covered in debris and reeds. Sand and coral had brought it to life and gathered there were twenty young fins all ready to play the game, and all staring at Anya, unsure of what to make of her.

"Hey! Anya! It's me, Kai. Over here!" He shouted from a crowd, which he stuck out of for being the smallest.

"Right, listen up. You all know the rules: one end of the street to the other!" Pearl shouted. That surprised Anya, as before she had seen nothing but her gentle nature.

A large metal disc cut through the water, spinning down towards them. Anya pushed herself backwards just in time; it missed her and crashed to a halt in the sand, causing quite a storm. Anya looked down, and as the sand settled, she saw a large heavy metal wheel, rusted and orange.

"I don't want the new kid," came a deep voice, and Anya turned to see the one who had made the throw, so close to her, with a mean unwelcoming look on his face.

"Don't be so rude, Cliff!" said Pearl. Anya disliked him already. It was no surprise that he would have the most bland, dull sea name. Cliff floated down, remaining distant yet revealing his size, a broad strong figure, dark green and covered in white speckles. He was built more like an adult than Kai or Pearl.

"We don't like outsiders," said another voice similar to Cliff's. It was his brother, Crash, who looked just as intimidating. The kids then split apart, Anya on Pearl's side while the others joined Cliff and Crash. Anya found it difficult not to take what they said to heart: she *was* an outsider, after all, and she had seen things none of them were strong enough to face. As she debated a retort, Kai and two others joined her side, and they too looked similar. "We are Bow and River," they said, pointing to each other in unison. Anya noticed that they each had one red eye and one yellow, and their skin was more blue than green.

"So which one of you is Bow and which one's River?"

"Bow's the boy, River is the girl," Kai said, attempting to whisper.

Anya couldn't tell them apart. They looked exactly the same, so she shrugged and turned back to Pearl.

"What do I do?" she asked, desperate for instruction.

"It's our turn to serve. Take the wheel, spin around and launch it in between the two teams up in the air. Then we fight for it. Cross the line to score a point," said Kai, an ecstatic ball of energy ready to play the game.

Anya took to the disc, picked it up and dragged it into the middle, desperate not to embarrass herself, desperate not to do what she had done time and time again. She took a firm grip with her claws and started to spin around like a discus thrower as the water rippled around her.

"Now, Anya!" Pearl shouted, and so with all her might Anya swung the disc up into the air. She couldn't believe her own strength as she watched the large hunk of metal fly upward. She stood in a wide stance, marvelling at her work, not paying attention to what else was going on.

"Three! Two! One!" shouted Kai, and all ten of them took off in a flash. Anya watched in awe as high above they flipped, dipped and soared through the water, flying up after the wheel. Cliff got up there fast, but not as fast as Kai, who had hold of the wheel until Cliff booted him back. They took to throwing and then tackling each other, passing the disc at pace until Bow or River intercepted and made their way to the opposition's goal. Anya looked on, unsure what to do; she floated near the start position, afraid to intervene. Cliff flew past all of them and using his brute strength took the wheel, flying toward Anya's team's goal. With a spinning turn, he threw it like a Frisbee once more to show off instead of placing it down with a wicked fanged smile on his face.

Anya watched the wheel hurtle down and without time to think she sprang into action. Catching it on the line, she spun back around and began soaring towards their goal. This time she moved along the sea floor, staying low. Cliff and Crash came for her on either side. "Up here!" Kai shouted, and Anya threw the wheel. Kai caught it and was spun round by the force. He pushed on, before throwing the wheel down for a goal. Screaming in celebration, he came down to Anya to celebrate. She felt ecstatic and huddled with her team to get ready for the next play.

"Beginner's luck, land dweller!" shouted Cliff, his brother Crash laughing alongside him. Anya turned as if ready to strike but Pearl grabbed her arm.

"They aren't as tough as they look, Anya, remember that," she said.

Cliff served next. He threw the wheel high and his team flew out in formation ahead of him. First to the wheel, they palmed off each member of Anya's team, tackling them out of the way. Then Cliff took the wheel and three others crowded in front of him like a shield as they swam in formation. Kai, Pearl and the twins took turns trying to break the barrier, but each of them bounced off ineffectually. Anya soared at speed up high and over the shield, heading right for Cliff, but he turned, and she met his shoulder. Then Cliff threw her back down and went on to score a goal.

"You're weaker than I thought, land dweller," said

Cliff, egging Anya on once more.

"Stop it, Cliff!" said Kai, darting through the water before Crash held him back.

"It's just a game, just a bit of fun. Relax, Kai," said Crash.

Each of them retook their place but tensions were high as Pearl went to serve. Anya needed the fire, the fury and the doubt to drive her. She didn't want to hold back, and so, when the wheel went up, she boosted herself into the air with all her might. To Kai's amazement she was the first one to the wheel. Anya grabbed the wheel with one hand to everyone's disbelief as the other team came at her; she batted them away with hitherto unknown strength, before soaring for the goal. Cliff floated directly between their goal and her, but Anya picked up speed, with no intention of slowing. Just before meeting him head-on, she pulled the wheel down to her feet and kicked off against him, causing Cliff to fly backwards. She kept moving through the water with power and speed all the way down to the opposition's goal and scored. Her team celebrated, and Crash and Cliff looked on in confusion. Anya was faster and stronger than any of them had thought.

They went back and forth for the next hour, and for the first time in her new form Anya started to tire. Still, it was different from human fatigue; before, she would have only lasted ten minutes and moved with a fraction of the speed and strength upon the surface. The game went on and on. Cliff had stopped antagonising her and gave her respect where it was due. The disc hurtled around and was booted off in all directions, and nasty pushes and tackles took place, all in the spirit of the game. Pearl scored one last goal to even things up and Anya was ecstatic. She had never been picked for anything, nor ever won anything on the Ark.

"Sudden death!" everyone shouted in unison around her. Kai explained that one player from each team had to make it to the middle to fight for the wheel one on one, and then bring it back to their teammates.

"Anya, you do it," said Pearl.

"No, I couldn't possibly, I –"

"You can, Anya, I saw the way you move," said Kai.

"He's twice my size."

"It isn't about size down here," he responded, and that resonated with her. She put her shoulders back, floated straight ahead and put her hand in the middle. She turned to face her adversary – and it was of course Cliff who was ready and waiting for her.

"Are you ready?" everyone shouted as if it had been rehearsed. "Three! Two! One!"

The two of them burst off their lines on the seabed, flying toward the wheel. Anya got there first by a fingertip, but Cliff snatched the disc and put himself between her and it. Anya launched herself again, but he batted her away. She tried once more, and Cliff hit her with the wheel. Anya did a flip and wrapped herself around his arm, loosening his grip, then she batted the wheel back down to the seabed. Cliff dived down and they began to wrestle, tangling with each other. He threw her off, but she kept coming back for more. Cliff put one of his feet on the wheel and kept beating her away again and again. But Anya would not give up – on the Ark, she had always got into fights with the other girls, and sometimes more than one at a time.

Anya reached down to the seabed and launched a cloud of sand upward, blinding her opponent. No one could see a thing, and when the dust cleared, when Cliff could open his eyes, he turned to see Anya flying with the wheel towards her own goal. He didn't even have time to move. He scowled, then smirked, for it was only a game.

"Anya! Anya! Anya!" her team shouted, swarming her and lifting her up as she laughed and smiled. Then Cliff's team came over, and at first, he looked intimidating, being more bulky than most.

"Hey, good game," he said with a fanged smile.

"Here, this is yours until the next time we play," said Pearl as she handed Anya a trophy left-over from the flood, some old rusted thing from a sport long gone. She held it tightly as they carried her back to the town hall.

"So, Anya, when we feast all the young fins stay together: we're all going to hang out tonight, not stay with our families. You can be with us, if you want," said Pearl, with Kai alongside her.

"I think I will," she said with a smile.

Anya felt warm, with a full belly and good people around her. She laughed at Kai's jokes, Cliff's stories, and Pearl's funny sea songs. They ate more fish and talked of plans to build a new world. Anya missed her family, but looking back at the day, she thought it was probably the best day of her life. If Anya could have cried, she would have.

## 15

## ADULTS

In the morning it took her a moment to take in the green reptilian scales and remember the joys of yesterday. How much fun it had been at the feast and playing waterwheel with the others. Anya turned to see the young fins sleeping around her: Kai, Pearl, Cliff, Crash, Bow and River. She didn't want to wake them and stayed quiet. She looked upwards, at the divide between sea and air that kept her from the Ark. Anya was starting to find peace in meditation when the purple octopus swam by; it circled her, turning orange as it did. The pesky thing kept swimming away and coming back, so Anya followed as it propelled itself along the sea floor, changing from purple to luminous orange. She went down the streets, around corners and through small buildings, until she noticed it was leading her to a large dweller she hadn't met. Anya hid around the corner and peered around it, noticing the dweller's stocky shape.

"I know you're there, land animal. Patricia never

fails as bate," said the dweller, as Patricia the octopus drifted down to rest upon the dweller's shoulder. "Come on now, I don't mean you any harm – my name's Marina."

Anya had no reason to hide herself any longer. She came out from behind the wall. "There you are – sorry I didn't say hello to you last night; many of us didn't; I'm guessing you had a lot to take in."

"I guess I did," Anya replied. "What do you want?"

"You're appearing in front of all the grown-ups today, so we can discuss your intentions. The whole lot of us. We will vote, that's how we make decisions."

"My intentions?"

"Judge your character and whatnot, if you're going to be playing with my kids."

"Which ones are yours?"

"Cliff and Crash – oh, and this little one here, Conway." Marina put an arm behind her back and pulled out a very small and cute baby dweller with huge eyes and one fang. It wriggled and crawled all around her before firing itself off for a swim, and only then did Patricia the octopus leave Marina's side to retrieve him. Anya watched as the colour-changing octopus played the part of a nanny. It was all very difficult to take in, although, as strange as it was, she had seen stranger things these past few days.

"Hali says we can trust you but I'm very protective of my boys, they are as good as gold. I don't want them corrupted by some land animal; do you understand?"

Anya thought about that for a moment and remembered how unwelcoming they had been at the start of the water-wheel game, only then did she realise that this was without doubt their mother.

"I understand," she said, not wanting any trouble.

"Now, Anya, it isn't going to be easy for you around here, you know. Most people haven't seen a land dweller for, well … for years. Most of the oldies, well, most of the men, don't speak about the surface."

Anya wasn't surprised, since the males on the Ark were the same.

"Is there anyone in particular I should look out for?"

"Well … come to think of it, all of them," Marina replied.

At that moment Hali came shooting down from above to join them. "Marina, are you trying to scare her?"

"Not at all, Hali, just telling her how it is."

"Oh, and how is it?"

"I'm just telling Anya to be kind to my boys and how she should be careful, with her being recently from above and all."

Hali shook her head and folded her arms. "I watched them play water-wheel yesterday and it was your boys who needed to be kinder."

Though Anya didn't say it, she was mighty grateful for Hali's intervention as she was feeling more off than usual today.

"That being said, some of the men are a little resistant to the old ways and don't like being reminded of them, especially after the *incident* with your people, Anya. Anyway, none of this is really important, we're having a meeting and I wanted to see if you would like to join us."

"I guess that sounds okay," Anya said, and so they went back to the crossroads and into the town hall for the meeting. None of the other children were present. It was a grown-up affair for those who had taken their sea names. Anya entered and found that all the grown-up water dwellers were there, many with their tamed beasts. Neptune with Grey and Fin, his twin hammer-head sharks. Hali was with Guillermo, Marina with Patricia the octopus, and there were many more. One dweller had a giant lobster, another a colossal crab, one of the older dwellers had a porpoise. The best of all was an old man who rode a stingray around the room as if it were a magic carpet. Anya had to duck to get out of the way. Then a huge fat dweller by the name of Russell swam in behind him. Anya could not believe her eyes: it was a walrus, and she winced thinking of Elder Frederick's cloak.

Soon though, the magic seemed to disappear with the overwhelming number of adults who took to the many rows behind her. Those sat ahead were the likes of Neptune, Russell, and many more she didn't know. All colours of blue and green with eyes from red to yellow. Anya noticed that none of them appeared too friendly, but she brushed it off as it grew quiet, and as to her right, Hali gave a caring nod of reassurance.

"Welcome, one and all," said Russell.

"Welcome," they all replied.

"Today is a special day, a day on which we welcome someone new. I'm sure Anya is keen to see how we run this place. Now, as you all know it's been twenty years since we last had someone new with us, and we all know how that went … Anyhow, Anya, every water dweller is equal and has the right to vote and speak in this here hall of ours." Russell scratched the chin of his walrus and looked around the room. It was easy for Anya to feel their awkwardness, a tension in the air, but it was hard to know the cause. It was unclear whether it was paranoia, or some newly acquired sixth sense, but the males around her were staring in the most uncomfortable of ways, all except Neptune.

"There are two hundred of us in total," said Russell. "Of the two hundred, we have thirty children and one hundred and seventy adults. Of the two hundred, eighty of those are bonders, people who can communicate with advanced sea life. No one knows how we became water-dwellers, we're just the lucky few who found the next stage of human evolution. Does it feel good to learn about the water dwellers?"

"I suppose so," Anya replied softly.

"Very well. And what about your Ark?"

*The Ark,* Anya thought, afraid to even begin.

"Maybe this is a little soon," said Hali, trying to protect her.

"No," Anya replied trying to summon her courage. "The Ark is, or was, my home. It's cold and wet, we're hard and tough. We brave the elements every day."

"What about rule-making?"

"What about it?"

"Who makes the rules?"

"My …" Anya remembered that it was her uncle

and his council, but beyond that she had never thought of such concepts. Still, she had to be brave, she had to face their questions. "A council."

"Consisting of?"

"The leaders of each of our professions, Hunters, Makers, Cooks and Carers."

A number of the male dwellers scratched their chins and whispered amongst themselves, while Neptune remained silent and rather distant. This whole thing was so strange to Anya that she didn't know what to say next.

"Are they elected?" asked an unfamiliar voice, a tall but thin male who didn't have his own creature. "Forgive me, my name is Dorian."

"Not exactly, it's strength that rules the Ark."

"How fascinating," continued Dorian, although he didn't seem fascinated in the slightest.

"Where do you sleep in the cold?" asked Russell, taking the attention away from Dorian.

"In hammocks, and if it's very cold, sleeping bags."

"Sleeping bags? What are they made from?"

"Seals, whales and fish leather," Anya said, forgetting the offence that it might cause. There were a few sighs all around. She started to feel interrogated and wanted to leave. It was clear that many of the dwellers opposed the use of animals for such things.

"Blasphemous," Dorian whispered.

"What would you expect us to do, freeze?" Anya replied.

"Enough!" shouted Neptune, ending the debate.

"The Arkers do what they must to survive, as we do what we must to survive; let that be the end of it."

"Very well," said Russell. "Now, let's not tread lightly around the real issue here," said the large overbearing walrus man. "There was an incident between the Arkers and us. Do you know anything about this?"

Everyone leant in close; even Neptune seemed to take notice.

"I don't really know, I wasn't there, I only know what I heard."

"And what did you hear?"

Anya was afraid of getting it wrong and being on her own again, doomed to the office block only made it worse. She found herself drawn to Neptune, her saviour, "four Hunters went to explore the shallows, and only three returned."

"Is that all?" asked Dorian.

"No," she tried to remember, but what the Arkers and Neptune had said seemed to blur together. "The Arkers were scared of monsters. They came for fish, there was an altercation, an accident."

They all began to whisper, making her feel uncomfortable, but Anya stayed strong, for she had known deep down this moment would come. Russell, Dorian, Marina, Hali and all the others seemed satisfied with her answer, but Neptune leaned in, eager to hear.

"Who do you consider struck the first blow?" asked Russell.

"I-I don't—"

"Leave the poor girl alone," Hali blurted as everyone turned to her, she covered her face with her claws in regret of her outburst, "Anya has assured us that what happened was an accident. We don't need to upset her anymore, what's done is done."

At that moment, Hali flew toward the exit, and it appeared that if she could cry, she would have. Everyone looked to Russell to make some sort of decision on what to do, and even he was lost for words for a moment.

"Let her go, she has been through enough. Hali and Enki were very close, Anya."

"Hali is right, it's in the past. My brother, Enki, had a choice, he did something unforgiveable and will never return. I'm sick of speaking of it and I will speak no more, understood?" asked Neptune.

"All dwellers have the right to a trial, and you didn't grant that opportunity to your brother…" Russell said, seeming rather sceptical as he stroked his chin. A silence cut the room with an undertone Anya was too unfamiliar with to understand.

"Enki is a murderer; I didn't dare bring him back."

"I think that's enough," said Marina interrupting the pair. "Thank you, Anya, what you say corroborates our understanding of events …"

Anya looked at each of them and wondered how one of them could tear out an Arker's heart. She didn't say anything, but her timid frown foretold her lack of comfort for the situation. There were so many watchful eyes on her, eyes she didn't know or like, and they all seemed to blur together into the Kraken.

"Anya of Ark, guest of the water dwellers, we thank you for your contribution," said Russell, reminding himself that the meeting was about her. "In time, you may consider relieving yourself of your surface name and taking a sea name. Only then can you become a full part of the water dwellers' world."

"Thank you," said Anya.

Everyone readied themselves to take their leave; it had been tough, but Anya saw why she had to go through it.

"You did well," said Marina, but then she appeared as if something was wrong. Marina began to swim around all over the place trying to find something, and Patricia the octopus was doing the same. "Conway! Conway! Where is Conway?" she shouted in panic past the water dwellers making their leave.

"Marina, I'm sure he will be with his brothers," Russell replied, but Marina would not stop panicking. Within minutes she had everyone searching the town hall, under all the old rustic benches and in every closet. There was no sign, and in the end the children were called. All two hundred water dwellers searched far and wide for the baby, but there were no signs of her.

Cliff and Crash soon joined the search in panic, as their tiny brother was nowhere to be seen. Everyone split-up to search the entire town, even Anya. They went from building to building, searching high and low. The child's name could be heard echoing through the sea, but no one could hear him. Everyone kept saying how strange it was that they couldn't hear the child, as children often mind speak very loudly; something wasn't right at all.

Anya searched too, but she had the strangest feeling, like a sixth sense to search one of the only places she knew, the water-wheel stadium. She took her time swimming through turnstiles, going down corridors, interrupting schools of fish, seeing the bar areas, toilets, and all sorts of corroded history.

"Conway!" she would call, "Conway!" To no avail.

Anya went past picture frames of old teams, of jerseys and footballs in cases now flat. There were rusted trophies too, and she thought of how much Jake would love to have one. Anya swam back onto the pitch to see the stadium properly in all its glory. It was a beautiful beast, a huge open space, and she could only imagine the games that had come to pass. She had a strange feeling, as if something was watching her. She saw something in the reeds on the pitch's faded halfway line, so she swam down to investigate.

"Conway! Conway!" Anya called again. She pushed through the reeds, and there, with a mouthful of sand, was the little tyke with its huge yellow eyes, giggling away. Anya tried to pick him up, but he swam away. She sped after him and took hold as he climbed all over her. "I'm glad I don't have to put up with this every day, Conway, that's for sure." Anya laughed: the kid was cute, and she turned to leave, when all of a sudden, a strange feeling took over. Something came at her in a flash, something sharp, and when she turned around, she saw a blue swordfish, razor-sharp. She only just managed to thrust herself out of the way as it came back again and again. Anya swam for her life with Conway in her arms; she made it to the stands as the swordfish charged again. Swimming over and under seats she went, but the fish wouldn't stop, it was coming at her with no holds barred.

"Help!" Anya shouted, "Help, I have Conway, help!" The fish came at her again; she was out of breath now, tired, and the fish kept coming. It made one last dash to take her down and she saw no other option than to dodge the sword and meet the fish head on with tooth and claw. Anya was ready, she waited for the next charge, and here it came, three, two, one …

From the side, Dorian flew in. Smashing into the swordfish, he sank his teeth and claws into its side, and it flailed back and forth. With one hand on the sword to stop another attack, he wrestled it back and forth until the fish came to rest. With his kill in hand, Dorian hovered triumphant.

"You are going to have to learn to defend yourself, it was just a big fish," he said, taking a bite of flesh and swallowing it down. Dorian then tore off a chunk and handed it to Anya, but she didn't take it. "What's wrong?"

"It tried to kill me, it tried to kill me. It was you, wasn't it, you hate me!"

"It wasn't me, silly girl. I can't control fish or anything else for that matter … and I don't hate you, I hate the surface."

Understandably, Anya was rather shaken; it was easy to see that he didn't like her.

"Conway! Conway!" Marina's mighty voice bellowed across the sea.

"Go on, run along now. Be the hero," said Dorian, and so, with Conway in hand, Anya went back. She didn't mention her ordeal to anyone but received the dwellers' favour for rescuing its youngest fin. Still, as she swam, she kept thinking about the swordfish, it would never attack anyone like that normally, it wasn't in its nature, and she wasn't able to stop it. Anya felt that someone, somewhere had intended to kill her, or to send a message, but she didn't know who, or why.

## 16

## NEPTUNE

Months went by and Anya spent every moment with the water dwellers. She started to find her place as she befriended the young fins and was closest to Kai and Pearl. Friendship here was not cold and short-lived as it was upon the Ark. Down here it was a warm and friendly affair; people didn't hide how they felt and instead they embraced. Sometimes Anya thought about the swordfish attack, but it seemed a distant memory as her social life started to blossom – even Crash and Cliff started to welcome her. She took to speaking with Hali every day, even if it was just for a moment, and the pair had started to feel a deep connection to one another.

The days seemed longer in the ocean than upon the Ark. Above, there was a mad rush to get everything done, a constant fight against the elements and each other. Here, there was plenty of time to spare, for food was not a problem, and nor was staying warm or caring for the old. There was no need to craft and no need to dry. Anya's curiosity knew no bounds. Pearl and Kai tried to fill her time with teaching her ways to control fish and even trying to dance, but only so much time could be spent on such things. Anya wanted nothing more than to move the ocean with her mind, but apart from that day when she had moved three fish together on the reef with Kai, she had not moved a single one.

Curiosity had taken over and her fascination with Neptune had grown. He was quiet and mysterious, solemn, as if something was always concerning him. He acted for his people but there was something strange about him, something Anya could not put her finger on, so she followed him. She knew when he ate, when he rode with his sharks, conversed, planned and rested. Every day, Neptune went east, crossing the deserted town, past large schools of rainbow fish. It was a quiet and eerie place where his sharks rested, and no one else ever seemed to follow him there. Neptune wanted to be alone there, but Anya spent a little of each day getting closer to him, with complete disregard for his unspoken wish. To Anya the journey was a playground, a stealth exercise and a maze. On certain days she would spend hours waiting for an opportunity, or some sort of pattern to the sharks' nature. Every day she went another block further on, to another street sign, a little closer to Neptune's secrets, and her wild imagination always pictured what they could be. Could it be food, treasure or some great relic of times now passed? Maybe he was deceptive, betraying his people. Anya's mind shot around endless possibilities in the hope of a great discovery.

On the seventh day, different sharks were dotted

about on her journey. Though seeming friendly to water dwellers, they were Neptune's eyes and ears. With stealth in mind Anya had to be ready. She dived through the drive-through window of the derelict fast-food restaurant ahead and swam through the ventilation onto the roof. She was silent and swift. She darted at speed into a clothes store where some garments still hung on rusted hangers. Circling the stands, she didn't react to the mannequin ahead and stayed close to the floor. Then she took to the street, darting beneath each car, careful not to disturb the hammerheads floating aimlessly above her. At the last rusted jeep, she launched a rock back behind her to distract the sharks' attention whilst she made it to the next building.

This one was much larger, and also more peculiar. Anya saw the old dark overgrown checkouts and long wide aisles, but most of the products were either gone, or open and empty. She swam down to pick one up: it was a tin of peaches, and it broke her heart. Fruit; real fruit. Anya had never tried any fruit, but Aunt Lyn had spoken of the succulent sugary taste a thousand times. The Ark was gone, though, a distant dream. She wondered how they were and hoped for the best. They would be far from here, she guessed. She hoped Tyson would be a fair leader, and she prayed for many fish for them. Anya didn't so much as hate Tyson for what he had done but pitied him. He had acted out of fear, but she couldn't help thinking of her uncle.

As much as Anya wanted to keep moving to track Neptune, she could not. Instead, she tore open the tin of peaches with her razor claws and split it in two.

Taking out one of the orange peaches, the juice swirled around her as she ate it whole. Sickly sweet, it tasted awful compared to raw fish on the bone, and that made her feel even worse, for Aunt Lyn found them delicious and Anya would have too, had she still been on the surface. Now she found them revolting. She left the tin behind and moved on. Ahead was an aisle of rusted metal tools and she promised herself that if the Ark ever came back, she would swim up and leave them on the edge, along with any tins and anything else of use, and maybe also a sign to let them know that she was okay. She kept going all the way to the end and found another exit, a smashed window, so she headed out and passed through long reeds until she reached the other end of town. Ahead was flat, open land, and right in its centre was Neptune sitting on a rusted swing. He was right next to a climbing frame once brightly painted in red, yellow and blue, now rusted and overgrown. Anya swam in silence toward Neptune with caution, not wanting to surprise or disturb him. She felt good for getting this far without him knowing; now she was only a few metres away.

"Do you know what this is?" asked Neptune, his voice low and solemn, without any sense of joy, and Anya was disappointed at having been discovered.

"How did you know I was here?"

"I knew what you were up to the moment you stared a moment too long at the first hammerhead, days ago."

That made Anya feel a little stupid: for days she had tasked herself with outsmarting Neptune and surprising him. It was all she had to concentrate on, her only goal while living down here. She had had to do it, just to stay sane.

"I said, tell me what this is."

"A park, a playground?" asked Anya, half doubting her own knowledge.

"Take a seat."

At this invitation, Anya joined him. He was deep in thought and had not even looked at her; his shoulders sank, and he appeared a different person now, lacking his strong demeanour. "No matter how much I want to, no matter how strong I am and how many sharks I have, I will never be able to swing again."

"What's so great about a swing?"

"A swing set is a child's first taste of flight and fear of falling. Every child should get to swing at least once. It isn't even the swing I miss, it's the angel I used to push."

Anya stopped. She felt like an intruder as the tragedy hit home. It was easy to forget that most of those down here shared the same feeling of loss as those on the Ark.

"Does it ever get easier?"

"Some days."

"Who was she? If you don't mind me asking."

"My daughter. Her name was Miriam and she was strong, like you." The way Neptune said her name was full of adoration but tainted with sadness. It pained him to say it and it pained him to remember, but every day for at least an hour he would come here and reminisce. "Who do you miss most?"

Anya sat and thought for a moment, her claws upon the rusted chain. Their names made her so sad, and she didn't want to be sad anymore.

"Jake, my brother. Aunt Lyn. Uncle Isaac. Even my bunkmate, Riley."

"I'm sure they miss you too."

"I know they do but they think I'm dead. How do you do it, how do you get by without her?"

"Not a day goes by when I don't think of Miriam, when I don't come here and think about how things could have been different; but then I leave the thought of her here, for there are people who need my leadership, as much as I want to stay and remember."

For the first time Anya felt she knew something about Neptune. He wasn't some almighty being free of imperfections – he was real. His answer was honest. That was how he did things. He turned to her now and looked her in the eye, and she saw a very human side to him, one suffering with grief. Anya thought about her brother, Jake, how much she missed him, and then she remembered that she knew something else about Neptune. It was his brother, the one who tore out Gregory's heart, whom Neptune had banished forever.

"What about your brother, do you miss him too?"

At Anya's question, Neptune's expression shifted; he didn't share the same thoughts for his brother that he did for Miriam, that much was clear. His grip on the chain tightened and his eyes shifted around uncertainly.

"Brothers are brothers ..."

"What was his name?"

Neptune hesitated, unsure of what to say. He hadn't

said his brother's name since that fateful day, and he wanted nothing more than to forget it. "Enki, that was his sea name," he said it with great difficulty, "but never mind him, I must commend you for making it so far. You went around my sharks and showed your strength. There is more to you than meets the eye."

"Me? No, trust me, there isn't."

Neptune laughed, shook his head and pushed out into the open spaces of the old park, elevating himself above her. He crossed his arms and with his open hand summoned a few small fish around them. They were hypnotised, mesmerized.

"Are you ready for a lesson?" he asked.

Anya remained seated, lacking any belief in herself, and Neptune summoned one fish forward. "Hold out your arm and draw a circle," he continued.

Anya got off the swing and swam up to meet him. She hesitantly brought forth her hand and began to draw, albeit half-heartedly. It was no surprise to Neptune that she could not move the fish at all, so he flung it at her, and the fish slapped full pelt against her green-scaled forehead.

"Ow! What did you do that for?"

"You aren't trying."

"Of course I'm trying!"

The sea around her seemed to become a little darker, a little colder, as Neptune lowered his brow. "You don't know where it comes from, you don't know what it means. It comes before emotion, before instinct. Do you want to know where true power really lies? It comes from control."

At that moment Anya felt a rumble, a whoosh, and the hammerheads flew out from the reeds and into the open. They circled above at speed before making their way down. One of them thundered right past Anya, forcing her backwards as she flinched. The first time, she thought it was an accident and closed her eyes to hide her terror, but the second time she saw its teeth, each time it came closer. Then it came head on, jaws wide open, a predator of the sea.

"Neptune, make it stop," Anya said, but Neptune did nothing as the shark hurtled towards her. "Neptune, *please*." Anya moved to the side, but the shark adjusted and continued its attack, its razor-sharp teeth ready to tear her in two. Anya could not move for the fear, and at the last moment she looked into its cold dead eyes as the shark narrowly missed her.

"Why? Why did you do that!" Anya shouted with fury as she made fists and tensed up.

"Don't you see?" asked Neptune, but Anya saw only a disregard for her life.

"I see alright: you're mad! A lunatic. A fanatic. I want no part of this," she said angrily. Neptune didn't speak, he raised a hand and pointed behind her until she turned around. There, a thousand sea creatures were frozen on the spot. A whole ocean bent to her will just long enough for her to realise what she was seeing; and then the ocean moved again.

"Your power is in your rage," said Neptune with conviction. "On the day you awoke in our herd and ran to the office block, when you shouted at Hali, I felt the whole office block freeze."

Anya was disappointed with him more than anything, but he had given her a lesson she must learn. Still feeling uneasy, she backed away as if to leave, unable to admit to anger being the source of control.

"Wait, Anya, we're only just getting started," Neptune said, but Anya continued to swim away. "Anya, wait," said Neptune again, once more raising his hand, and this time Anya stopped, unable to move despite her eagerness to leave. But it was nothing more than an instant, a blip, gone as soon as it had come, and Anya shook it off before swimming further away.

"I thought you were different," she said. "Your people are good and kind, your world is a heaven, yet here you are frightening little girls in order to see their powers."

"Anya, I ... That's not what I meant ... you need to be strong."

"Then let *me* find my strength," said Anya, before making a clawed fist and bolting in a flash back past the old buildings. She was angry and upset, for she feared that Neptune was the same as Tyson. *How can he be kind if he tried to instil such fear?* she wondered.

As Anya went back to find Kai and Pearl; she knew she could never mention this encounter to them. And she never wanted to see such power again.

## 17

## ORACLE

Another month went by in the blink of an eye as Anya continued to swim with the water dwellers. Strangers became friends and everyone was kind, healthy, well fed and strong. She became good friends with all the other children, especially Pearl and Kai. Pearl and Kai taught her about the water way of life: its tranquillity, its peace; and Anya never wanted to leave. Thoughts of the Ark became few and far between as she was lost in the wonder of a new world. When she did think about her aunt and uncle, her brother, the worries went away and in their place was the feeling that they were okay.

Anya awoke in the water dwellers' sleeping circle with her legs crossed, having sunk to the seabed in a meditative position. In time she slept better than on the surface, for there was no rough, uneven rotting wood, only soft sand and calm water. Across from her, Kai was still asleep, but Pearl was staring right at her. It was the night after the third feast, when Anya had helped move some of the smaller fish, Pearl had danced again, and they had played waterwheel. Anya looked across to Pearl with a silent smile before they rose and swam toward the water-wheel pitch, passing the vast sandscape and debris of times long past. There they found the perfect clearing far enough away so that nobody else could see or hear.

Pearl floated opposite Anya and hummed in a sweet angelic tone. She raised both hands and extended one of her legs behind her body up in the air and pointed her toes. Anya mimicked her pose as a novice would, slowly extending her leg, her arms and toes staying slightly less still, but nevertheless with grace. Together they spun, a swift motion in unison, like clockwork. A succession of slow lyrical movements followed, bending at the knees, guiding with the legs, an arabesque, a pirouette and an assemblé. Pearl's voice picked up pace as they ran and jumped together, leaping through the water as majestic shining creatures. Taking the lead, she began to spin, and Anya did the same. Round and round they went, picking up pace until dizziness took hold and Anya stumbled backwards. Pearl came to a halt laughing at how hard it was for Anya to take to such a dance.

"It's not funny! I just don't move like you do."

"You're an awkward mover, you need to be mellow, to relax," Pearl said as she moved her hand from hip to shoulder and back down again with a smooth flowing motion that Anya would never be able to perfect. "Did you dance on your Ark?"

"Oh, erm …" Anya began, unprepared to speak of

her old home. "Warrior dances, with spears, cries of war and heavy drums."

"Drums?"

"Yeah, drums. You know, the …" Anya thought about explaining but then realised that she could never describe such sound. Only the living made sounds in the sea, humans, dolphins or whales from far away. There were no instruments, and they didn't need any, not with a choir like that. "Drums," she added, "dried skin stretched over wood and hit with a stick."

"Ew," Pearl replied, which reminded Anya of just how precious Pearl was. "Sometimes I forget you're a savage."

"Me, a savage? You've never worn clothes! Or cooked, or cleaned or –" A fish then flew at Anya so fast she could not even blink before it slapped her across the face, cutting her words short. It knocked her off balance and Pearl burst into laughter. Anya took control of the fish and fired it right back. Pearl deflected it with a smug look, begging the question whether that was the best Anya could do. They burst into laughter, as best friends often do. Then Kai shot out from nowhere just above them; he moved fast and stumbled over his words.

"What is it, Kai?" said the girls in unison.

"I had … I had a dream!"

"We all have dreams," replied Anya.

"No, not like this. In the kelp forest is the biggest fish you will ever see!" Tired but ecstatic, unable to control himself, Kai had an unrelenting excitement in his voice. Polka swam on by and around him chuckling as she did; she approached Anya and they exchanged a hug before Polka did the same to Pearl.

"We don't go as far as the kelp forest on our own," said Pearl, bringing a sense of the rational to Kai's fantasy. Anya thought back to the last time someone had asked her to go somewhere she wasn't supposed to. That fateful day when she crashed into the edge of the world, the office block. A day of wonder, exploration and friendship, but one cut short by drowning, dread and a narrow escape. Anya shuddered, remembering the fear of being chased; but then she thought of Jake and Tomas, and smiled. Every day she mourned, every day she healed, and now she only prayed for the best. The thought of adventure and escape took over. Though the sea was vast, she had only seen the merest droplet, and part of her felt caged. Anya had seen the reefs, algae, beautiful creatures of every shape and size, but never had she seen a forest, although the Arkers told wondrous stories of them. She remembered sitting as a little girl, huddling in the cold, listening to Elder Frederick tell her of rustling leaves, whistling birds and swaying trees.

"Anya, is everything okay?" asked Pearl, interrupting her trail of thought.

Anya shook her head and turned on the smile she had perfected over the past few months.

"I'm fine."

"Well, I'm going, I have to. Either on my own or you come with me," Kai continued.

Anya and Pearl looked at each other and shared a quick, wordless conversation. Pearl rolled her eyes,

Anya, however, turned to the young dweller with a heart bigger than his head, and said, "Let's go."

"Yes!" Kai exclaimed, making wild backflips of celebration. Polka zoomed past for Kai to grab hold, and they boosted off at speed. Anya followed just behind, and so did Pearl.

Journeying east far away from the town wasn't something dwellers did alone, especially not a young adult. Past the stadium they ventured, across endless sand that washed over humanity's buildings. Nature's brush strokes over man's feeble attempt to paint something – something that was finite.

About two miles down there was a torn billboard for a movie that the three of them would never understand, no matter how many elderly water dwellers might try to explain cinema to them.

The sands ended at a rocky cliff edge. Despite being able to swim so well, Anya had a strange fear of falling, and her heart skipped a beat. She froze as if taken by the kraken, and felt its gaze, for although it was probably many miles away, it could be lurking anywhere. Pearl took Anya's claw, and with a smile reassured her that everything would be okay. They moved on, and to Anya's relief they stayed high. To her surprise, the drop's black rocks disguised a canyon half a mile wide that rose again on the other side but stretched forever left and right. Together they made the crossing and the black rocks became jade green. Anya had to do a double take, as just a little further on were trees, green and glorious, sparkling in crystal water. She had never seen so much green.

"What is this place?" she said, breathless for the beauty.

"This is the kelp forest," replied Kai.

"What's that noise?" asked Anya. There was a strange whistling sound moving through the forest, an endless tone.

"The whisper?"

"Yes."

"The forest is alive," said Kai.

"It isn't really alive," said Pearl. "It's just the sound of rippling water on kelp."

Kai smiled, for he knew there was much more to this place for the water dwellers. "Come on, we need to catch the fish of my dreams, the biggest fish alive!" he said. He was so excited that he swam ahead of them both as Anya tried to keep up. She passed between the reeds and before she could tell him to wait, Kai was gone. She turned and found that Pearl was gone too. She looked every which way but there was only forest as far as the eye could see. On the seabed were large crabs, big yellow bog-eyed fish, and all sorts of majestic creatures.

"Kai! Pearl!" Anya shouted. She heard them faintly in the distance and tried to swim toward the voices, but it was no use. A blue and yellow eel slithered by, and then a family of seahorses. She was lost again but tried to remain calm. A grey blur shot past her; she flinched and shut her eyes, and when she opened them the creature darted out of sight like a ghost. Her first thought was a swordfish, but then she thought of a hammerhead shark. Anya waded through the kelp trying to find her friends, lost in a never-ending maze. It seemed hopeless, until she realised that swimming above might be the way forward, and so she did. From here she scanned the area below until she saw a streak of blue amidst the green that could only be Kai. Anya swam down towards him, and, greatly relieved, placed an arm on his shoulder. Kai shuddered, before pulling her close.

"I saw something," he said, his voice a trembling whisper. This was the first time Anya had ever seen him afraid.

"What?"

"Something *big*." Kai placed a finger to his lips as if to silence her, and turned in all directions, desperate to keep an eye out. Taking Anya by the claw, he led her out of the forest at speed.

"What about Pearl?"

"She will be fine, let's go!"

They both made it out of the forest and went a few metres further, before turning to shout for Pearl. Pearl didn't call back, and to their dismay they heard something rustling through the kelp towards them. Anya could sense Kai's fear, and that made her more on edge as some beast made its way towards them, perhaps having already got to Pearl. Right when the creature was at the forest's edge everything stopped as it revealed a grey nose. A little sea-lion poked its head out, making them both laugh and feel very embarrassed for taking things so seriously. Pearl, having watched the whole debacle, pushed through the tree line in hysterics. She was beside herself about how afraid they had been of a baby sea-lion.

"I can't believe the look on your faces!"

Anya and Kai went from hysterics to feeling slightly embarrassed. Pearl continued to make her way to them, pointing and laughing, paying no attention to Anya and Kai's expressions. In a flash, something cast a huge shadow over the sea-lion. It burst from the left-hand side and took the sea-lion in its grasp. It was a beast. A black and white beast. A killer whale, striking with pace and precision. The sea-lion was no more, and Pearl, frozen in disbelief, looked on to see blood as the killer came close. She took off and swam towards her friends as Kai and Anya froze too, unsure of what to do. Neptune had made it clear that such beasts were a danger to the water tribe: they didn't like humans and especially not water dwellers.

"Swim! Swim for your lives! They eat dwellers!" shouted Kai. They fled as fast as possible from the mighty black beast behind them, gaining no distance as the shadow of the killer came closer. "Look!" Kai pointed left and right, to where two more closed in on either side of them, while three closed them off ahead. The wolves of the sea were pack-hunting. Surrounded, Anya felt the same fear as when she had fled the water dwellers with Jake and Tomas. The urge to fly, the yearning for it all to stop, took hold, but the beast was too fast.

Fleeing was no longer an option, and now Anya thought of Dorian and how he had gone head to head with the swordfish. She turned to see the killer whale soaring toward her with its wide-open mouth and cold black eyes. Defiant in the face of death, she was prepared to meet it head-on. Time stopped. Anya could claw, charge, kick or evade, but instead she closed her eyes. She lifted a hand in the open palm position, the one she had seen Neptune use. She tried rage, she tried anger, but when she opened her eyes the black and white beast was still charging, mouth open and ready.

There was nothing she could do to escape now, in that moment, Anya thought of Aunt Lyn, Uncle Isaac and Jake. She returned to a place of peace and tranquillity. For a moment she was blindfolded upon the log, practising for the spear dance in the morning sun with a cold refreshing breeze against her skin. It was heaven, it was grace, but in the same breath she was back in the water with her eyes closed and her palm facing the beast.

When she finally opened her eyes, the impossible had happened. The killer whale had stopped right in front of her, mesmerised by her hand. Kai and Pearl watched in disbelief; this was the first time a water dweller had come so close to such a beast without injury. The orca came closer and rested its nose on Anya's hand, and she felt the beast's agitation, its hunger. The other orcas gathered around her as Anya made the first feel calm.

"I don't believe it," said Kai, unable to contain himself.

"Shh," Pearl replied, holding him back, not wanting to interrupt the bonding process and scare the beast away.

Anya looked into the black eyes of the beautiful creature, the smartest, most intelligent predator in the sea. The beast bowed down before her, and as her hand and its snout made contact, she saw everything the orca had ever seen. It was the whale from her dreams, and their bond would be eternal, from birth until the end. A bond drew them together, never to be torn apart. Serendipity bound them, and Anya knew what must be done. She moved towards the beast and climbed upon its back. It took off with one mighty thrust of its tail, gentle and slow at first. The orca picked up pace, gliding through its infinite playground as they moved together, powerful and strong. Anya watched as on either side the other orcas gathered, powering through the ocean together in formation, ruling their kingdom.

"Anya!" Kai shouted, and Anya turned back to see her friends, having forgotten everything else for a moment. Pearl and Kai watched in wonder, knowing that no one had ever tamed a whale before. It was magic, and the creature moved with pace.

"What will you call him?" asked Kai.

"Her name is Oracle" said Anya with a smile. The other orcas swam around them, but Kai and Pearl knew that they were no threat: Anya had broken a barrier and made friends with one, so the rest simply followed. The others looked smaller, younger, and the three of them supposed Oracle must be their mother.

"No one has ever bonded with an orca before … you might be more powerful than Neptune."

Kai was right: no one had ever accomplished such a feat. Kai's dolphins were intelligent and stronger than they looked; Neptune's sharks were more simple-minded, but fierce. No one had ever thought bonding with an orca possible, and no one would believe it unless they saw it.

"Anya, ride her back to the others," said Pearl.

"No, I don't think so," she said, remembering her last talk with Neptune, how she despised the fear he inflicted. But without him she might never have found Oracle. Anya had never before understood the link with animals that others shared; she had thought it was control, as Neptune said, but he was wrong. It was a common language. A connection of love that could not be described but only understood through feeling.

Anya and Oracle thundered back the way they had come, across the ridge and back to the water-wheel pitch. Oracle soared at speed toward the tribe, and as she did, she circled around the crossroads. Many looked on in wonder. Anya would never forget the look on Hali's face – but Neptune was nowhere to be seen.

"Anya, you're … you're …"

"This is Oracle," she said calmly, as she and Oracle approached.

"This isn't possible, no one has ever …" said Hali. Anya was turning out to be more powerful than she had ever imagined. Her speed, strength and her connection to the ocean seemed unmatched. Hali tried to suppose the reason why, maybe it was the age she had turned: a sixteen-year-old surface dweller. Anya was more powerful than a young fin or a turned adult. She didn't say anything, though, and instead hid her concern beneath a proud smile.

For the first time Anya was the centre of the water dwellers' attention; everyone young and old came to pay homage to her bond with the whale. They greeted Oracle with a smile and the children played all around her. Anya couldn't help but wonder what her uncle and aunt, her brother, her mother and father would say if they could see this. For the first time down below, she felt a true sense of pride.

It was toward the end of the day, as things were quietening down that Oracle became unsettled.

"I told you that you had great strength," said Neptune from behind Anya. He approached with his hammerhead sharks by his side. Grey and Fin seemed to float almost lifelessly, and for the first time Anya realised the extent of Neptune's control. Both Polka and Oracle had their own personality, but Grey and Fin didn't. There were many things Anya wanted to say, she remembered the way the hammerhead had come at her, teeth first despite her protests. She wasn't afraid any more with Oracle by her side, but the whale was agitated.

"I found a way to tame her from a place of peace."

"She doesn't look too tame," he replied and rightly so.

Anya tried to quieten her new friend, but it was clear she found something about Neptune or the sharks unsettling. There was tension in the water, for a moment Anya almost felt that Neptune was threatened, but quickly the sense was thwarted away.

"My brother trained Fin the way you tamed Oracle, but their bond was weak, and now Fin calls to me, but killer whales are much stronger than sharks, they say. Now excuse me, I must go."

Neptune turned to swim away without saying goodbye as Anya looked on, "I'm sure they are," she muttered.

"Anya," Kai touched her arm and reminded her that everyone else around was acting normal. "It's time for Oracle to go home and rest. She will come back tomorrow, if you wish it."

Anya didn't know what to make of his words, she didn't ever want to part with Oracle. She would never be without her again if she could, but she knew Oracle was a mother, and had her own children. Oracle had grown more restless at the sight of the sharks, so Anya turned, took hold of her dorsal fin, and again they were off together to explore the ocean. She turned back to see the water dwellers looking on, but all she looked for was Neptune, and although he wasn't there, she still felt his presence.

## 18

## HUNTRESS

Anya was a novice; she was afraid when she first came eye to eye with Oracle. No one had bonded with a creature so intelligent, so majestic, and it made even Neptune worry. Anya had taken to her bond unlike any that had come before her and it brought Hali a great sense of pride. Everyone was in awe of the majestic killer whales; no one had ever been so close to an orca before, some older water dwellers said that their distance came in return for being kept in tanks. Before the flood, there were only a handful left in captivity, and none in the wild. With the flood came their release and their will to stay away.

Anya was greeted by Oracle every day and would hunt as part of the pod, the wolf pack. Together they ruled the sea, smashing through the ocean and eating prey. Anya learned their way of hunting: to surround prey from every side and close in. She saw them communicate, show love, tease, and they even dreamed when asleep. The pair were inseparable, and the time Anya spent with Oracle made even many jealous. Neptune remained distant, and though he would never say it, he knew he might not be the most powerful water dweller anymore.

Every day Anya became more powerful, be it with Oracle, in mind-hunting fish, or water-wheeling. When Hali first called her a huntress, albeit nonchalantly, she didn't know what to say. It was the stigma attached to the word on the Ark, for there it was a joke. Now the word filled her with a sense of pride, but despite her new-found place with the water dwellers, she would never forget where she came from. She thought of her brother, Jake, and his calm, easy-going attitude, Aunt Lyn's sweetness, Uncle Isaac's strength and leadership, even Tomas and his quiet courage. It wasn't always the happy times, though, for she also remembered her ceremony, the trial, and Tyson sending her into the abyss like it was yesterday. Sometimes she wondered about the hellish future everyone above was living somewhere far away, but such thoughts came and went, drifting on by. Over many months it got easier. Now it was just a few distant thoughts of a past life during fragments of her day. The trick was to think of this life as more an afterlife, no matter how tragic that sounded. Still, she dreamed of them; her feet upon the rotten wood while running after Jake; holding Aunt Lyn by the leg; and the smell of cooking fish upon the fire. Sweet childhood innocence filled her mind. Then the storm would come, and she would wake.

Every day, the dream of leaving the water dwellers and trying to map the entire ocean, to see it all with Oracle, became more appealing. There was so much to see and creatures much deeper, much more prehistoric, to behold. She loved her new people, but she did not fit in; they had not seen what she had seen, and only Oracle could really understand her.

It was in the eighth month when Anya dreamt of something strange, something beyond her imagining, that would change the course of history. She had taken to falling asleep amongst the orca on the outskirts of town. Upon the surface, storms reigned, but below it was quiet in the deep black ocean. When the night was at its darkest Anya began to dream. Her dreams always felt so very real, and recently they were more intense, frustrating her often, for every night the same thing happened. Anya felt the sensation of lying down on something uneven and dry. There was an odd wind, and a strange smell, as the sound of seagulls and waves crashed and retreated in a way she had never known before. No matter how hard she tried to open her eyes, nothing happened. She lay still, and when she could see, all was bright and blinding. A coarse fresh breeze and curious smell took over her senses as she took a warm breath. Claws became hands, and, clenching her fists, something strange was clumped inside them. She sat up in shock from the crash of water close by and the keening of seagulls. Everything around her was bright and yellow, almost blinding. Bringing her hand close to inspect the strange substance against her skin, she could not believe it: it was sand, dry sand just as the elders had explained. The sand spread and poured away, every grain escaping her grasp, returning to where it belonged. Ahead of her she watched darker grains meet the gentle crush of blue ocean waves in constant rhythm.

Below were her legs and her toes. Olive, freckled skin replaced reptilian scales, and her long brown hair, dry and vibrant, flowed in the wind. A bright red polka-dot dress clashed with everything else in its brightness and beauty. When the pain of the brightness faded, Anya saw the sunshine again and felt the rush of wind against her skin. The feel of sand between her toes was an odd sensation. When she went to stand like she did upon the Ark, she fell, having grown so used to the constant movement of the ocean. Her feet were like jelly for the lack of motion. She struggled to walk around until she fell down once more, then she took to balancing with her arm out, as if on the log, but there was only dry land below. The beauty was breath-taking as water clashed upon rocks, upon the beach, and then she turned to see that behind and there were trees, ginormous trees, the elders has explained them but she had never come to understand until now. A mixture of fear, excitement and disbelief took over. When the exhilaration took hold fully, her consciousness came back.

Anya awoke to the blinding swirls of colour being replaced by the dark morning ocean. She struggled to breathe as the warmth of dry land and sunshine all but disappeared. In came water to her lungs. Though every-thing had disappeared, Anya felt it had been real. Land took her mind, every ounce of her thoughts. She had seen it, she had smelt it, and it had felt so real.

That morning, Anya didn't wake Kai or Pearl. Instead, as much as she didn't want to, she went to Neptune for answers. She found him spending the morning alone on the edge of the town as he did every day, clearing the seabed in the hope of building a monument from gargantuan rocks. When Anya approached Grey and Fin, they stared down at her in a statuesque fashion. This time she was not afraid, for despite the fear of the last time they had met, Anya believed her powers would protect her.

"Ah, the most powerful dweller in the sea who curses my lessons. How can I be of service?"

"I had a dream."

"Oh? And what sort of things were we dreaming of, more orcas?"

"No, no not at all. It was … it was land."

"You are too young to know the land," said Neptune, before going back to throwing rocks. He didn't smile at her reference to land, but Anya knew how men hide the truth of their emotions. She saw something strange in his eyes; all the adults on the Ark and the water seemed to share that same look of desperate heartbreak at the mention of land and hide it all the same.

"I saw it, it's real, I know it's out there somewhere."

Neptune's expression lost any humour it had had; he was angry but saddened. Every good memory of land was tarnished, every good moment washed away by memories of the water rising, cold hopeless dark nights, and days spent searching for his wife and daughter. It was a manic test of faith to keep a raft afloat every day, fighting a losing battle until it sank. Anya saw the lack of joy in his heart. She could see Neptune was afraid of land; that the very mention of it made him sick. This was the first time she had been able to read him so clearly, and she saw something strange inside him, a kind of darkness.

"The whole surface is submerged, gone, Anya. There is nowhere left."

"But look how close the surface is," she said, pointing upward. She was right: the tallest building teased the air; there had to be more somewhere, had to be.

"But there's nothing left. I'm telling you; land is no more. Our people are past needing land, we've evolved without it, and even if we did find it, we could never step foot on it. We would die of our burns; you know it, I know it – hell, the whole tribe knows it. Each one of us, to our shame, has made for the surface and learned the same lesson. Even I, though I'm by no means proud of it. I can't have my people consumed by dreams of land. Besides, down here is a paradise free of humanity's wars and quarrels, for we are the next stage of evolution."

As much as Anya was growing to dislike him, he was right, but still something in the sound of his thoughts and the look in his eyes made her doubt him. Neptune came to her and placed a webbed hand on her shoulder, looking down at her as Isaac used to. It was hard not to flinch.

"I need you to be strong, I won't be here forever. I will need you to take my place someday," he counselled, and Anya's chin sank before he lifted it up again. "You are the one who will have to lead us when I am gone, you are the only one strong enough to protect our people."

"I thought the dwellers had no leader …"

"If you learn to read between the lines, you may see that they do."

"I don't know what to say."

"Say you wish to learn, say you wish for me to teach you my secrets, there is much you do not know."

"What about Kai and Cliff?"

"None of them can do what you can do."

Anyone else would have been foolish to question Neptune's offer, it should have made her happy, but it didn't, nothing could. Today, the sadness brewing beneath the surface of her mind came forth with the vivacity of her dream. The use of her powers, her bond with Oracle, friendships gained, and her new way of life weren't seeming to have the positive affect that she envisioned. Underneath everything seemed a sadness that might never be cured.

Anya looked into Neptune's eyes and tried to work out why she wasn't happy. He hadn't given her the answer she wanted about land, but there was something more, a glint in his eye that made her feel slightly uncomfortable. It echoed from when he had tried to unlock her power with his sharks. She couldn't trust him again. There was guilt in his eyes that he couldn't hide, and Anya knew that guilt. She realised that the water dweller in front of her was just a man, nothing more, and the kraken had told her not to trust men. The only man she could ever trust was Uncle Isaac, so Anya turned around and took off at great speed.

"Anya, Anya!" Neptune called out as she sped away. He started to follow her, and then Oracle flew through the water, whooshing past him, and in a flash, Anya was gone.

Whizzing through the water, she was on a journey to find the truth. She clung on to Oracle and felt the bond as the orca clicked and squeaked to comfort her. There were a thousand things racing through her mind, and Anya summoned the wolf pack to swim with them. Together they rode through the abyss as the most powerful force in the sea. There was only one place Anya wanted to go: a deadly place. Where the kraken took hold of her and forced the life from her.

Anya led the pack in to the unknown, they stayed above the ridge, and then made their way to the depths that had struck fear into her heart the last time. Now she was no longer afraid; now she was eager to face the mighty foe. Anya reached the depths and floated above Oracle as the killer whales remained in formation on either side.

"Where are you! Where are you!" she shouted impatiently. She looked around everywhere, up, down, left and right. She waited and waited, then she led the Orca to the ocean floor, and they swam in a circle to create a current. The sand unsettled, spiralling up into leaving a spectacle of dust in the ocean that spread to reveal the deadly shape of the kraken. Its glowing eyes opened and stared down at Anya in the hope of hypnotising her.

"So, the girl has awoken. How you've grown – but still so unhappy with both worlds? How sad," said the kraken looming over her, wanting nothing better than to eat her but knowing all too well the threat of killer whales.

"I know your tricks, they won't work anymore, I'm too strong."

"Strong, perhaps, but an immature strength without cunning."

Anya hadn't come here for mind games; she looked into the eyes of the Jurassic beast and found she could resist. The kraken continued to move, slow, subtle and with grace, almost dancing in hypnotic movements, but Anya resisted its tricks and charms no matter how hard it tried.

"I came here for your help."

"I see pain in you, and worry."

"Your words make me worry. You talked of black and white – that's the orcas. What about the trust of men?"

"Humans have a way of taking words and making them serve themselves. You see a weakness in another – what does he hide from you?"

"Neptune? I don't know, tell me!" Anya shouted, losing all patience and respect, knowing full well that if she had to, she could take the kraken.

"False idols. Deep down, you know. I cannot tell, you know I cannot break the chain of time." With her words the kraken intertwined its tentacles around each other to imitate a bond of chains.

"I-I don't understand."

"Time cannot reveal itself to those who cannot see. Only I can see, not you, girl. Not you, guardian of orcas."

The kraken saw into Anya's soul, into her mind, and possibly into the future. It was a dangerous game Anya was playing, but she needed to know.

"Last time I was here, you were about to say something before Neptune came, what did you mean to say?"

The kraken gave a sinister laugh, as if the mortal soul of the girl amused her, and it did. Such a small, insignificant creature, a blip on the line of existence that meant nothing.

"The false idol stopped me from saying the word. That word is gone. Away with you, girl, before you learn the ultimate price of testing my patience."

"Say it, please. Just say it. What was my fortune?"

"No."

"Was it *land*? Does Neptune know that there is land somewhere? Please, I beg you, I need to know."

"It was the thirst for knowledge that drowned you. It will be land that kills you."

"Stop playing games!" Anya screamed, unwilling to play any longer as the orcas edged closer.

"I cannot say … unless …"

"Unless?"

"Unless …" said the kraken, looming ever closer and coming eye to eye with Anya. Its broken red skin towered over everything in the sea. Its green eyes glowed bright. If it wasn't for fear of the orca pack the kraken would have already taken her, torn her limb from limb.

"If you touch my tentacle again, I will show you everything you wish to know. I promise I won't sting or bite." With the kraken's words came a slithering tentacle, its tip waving in the water next to Anya. Anya became fixated on the tip as the kraken's eyes followed its gentle movement in the water. The hypnotic motion made her lose her judgement for a moment; yes, she needed to know.

Anya extended her green reptilian claw, drawing closer to the fountain of knowledge ... then, without warning, Oracle raced by, grabbed her foot and dragged her away as she kicked and screamed, wishing for the touch of the kraken. But no matter how she resisted, Oracle didn't let go, and dragged her far away. The further Anya went, the less the kraken had a hold on her mind. She could think again and the burning desire to touch the kraken faded, along with her belief in the kraken's lies.

"You saved my life, what was I thinking?" she asked herself, and Oracle just kept swimming. Anya felt tired, so tired. Oracle released her and let her float alone for a few moments until she came back. The orca's cute mouth and eyes were right up against her to make sure she was okay. Anya reached out and hugged her as she clicked and squealed.

"I love you, girl, you were right, you were right."

Oracle hummed as if to mimic the human words "I know," before barrel-rolling; then the other orcas came to Anya's side and surrounded her, nuzzling her as she giggled. Time went on, it was quiet out in the depths, Anya found it peaceful and she thought about her conversation with Neptune. He had saved her life, and played a part in what she had become, but she didn't know how she felt about him, or anyone.

## 19

## TAKE A NAME

It was Anya's birthday, she was seventeen. It had been just short of a year since she became a dweller in all but formality. The ways of the water had become second nature, but she still counted the days. Today was no different from the last: having woken early on the outskirts of the water-wheel pitch, she stared across and noticed Pearl and Kai were still asleep. Anya didn't dare make a noise to wake them; instead she looked to Oracle by her side. Anya searched her feelings, she tried to stay positive but every day she felt no better. The only thing that kept her going was Oracle, and even then, she felt confused. Neptune had called it "control", and the last thing Anya ever wanted to do was control such a sweet thing. She felt it was something different, a bond, and yet the thought of Neptune's words still made her feel guilty. There was something holding her back, still holding her back as it always had.

Anya hadn't spoken to Neptune for many weeks, only the odd word here or there; she felt that might be the reason for her feelings, so she swam off to find him on the outer reaches of Atlantis. He was throwing large rocks over the cliffs as his sharks brushed rubble off the edge. Fin who was once his brothers shark looked tired, whereas Neptune's first bond Grey appeared in much better health.

"I'm surprised you've come, Anya, after our last conversation," said Neptune without turning around. Anya shrank inside, remembering the things she had said. With time to reflect, she saw that it was the kraken that worried her, not Neptune, and she felt ever so guilty for that.

"I came to say I'm sorry, I came to say you were right about land."

Neptune dropped the large boulder he was holding; it sank and shook the sea floor as sand rose around their webbed feet.

"It isn't about being right, Anya, it's about protecting our people."

"They aren't –"

Neptune swayed in the water, turning to face her. "They *are* your people. They will *always* be your people. You play our games, sing our hymns, move fish. The first to bond with a killer whale, more powerful than me – don't you dare say that they aren't your people."

Neptune came closer, and though he was taller, they saw eye to eye, as everyone did within the water. There was no strength in size. Anya didn't know what to say; she was stuck obsessing over his words, unable to make sense of them, unable to find a place of acceptance for herself. Her low chin and sunken shoulders gave her a defeated posture.

"Everything I did, I did to help you. I helped unlock your power. Do you know what I see when I look at you?" asked Neptune.

"No."

"I see strength that doesn't know its strength. I see courage that doesn't know its own courage. I see a leader, a fighter who knows what it's like to be at the bottom, to face death over and over. Today is the day, Anya, your birthday. You are a water dweller, take your sea name," said Neptune extending his claw to reach her.

Anya hesitated for a moment. She knew this day would come, the day she would be asked to join them. She thought about it all the time, and considered what to say, but it only made her afraid, haunted by her sixteenth birthday upon the Ark. It was a daunting request; part of her wanted to say no, to take Oracle and go off to explore the ocean, but another part of her loved this life.

"I will," she said, "I will."

That was the first time Anya had ever seen Neptune smile. Looking beyond his green scales and his scars, it felt good to see him smile. He moved forward and held her, and Anya hugged him back, but all she could think was how much she missed Uncle Isaac. After a brief embrace she made her way back to Pearl and Kai to prepare; it was only a few hours until the feast and she had to practise. She found the duo playing with Polka, and Pearl was dancing as Polka spun around her squeaking as she did.

"Where have you been?" Pearl asked when she saw Anya.

"I've been, busy," Anya replied.

"Too busy for your birthday?"

"Surprise!" Kai shouted, they both embraced her and there was laughter all around. Anya's didn't know what to say.

"Today's the day I take my sea name," said Anya, more in shock than excitement.

"Yay, Anya!" said Kai, ecstatic to hear such news; he celebrated by swimming round and round with Polka.

"I'm proud of you, so proud," said Pearl. "We got you a present," she continued before diving down to the sand and taking something. Anya's heart raced for her mother's emerite necklace, but it sank when she discovered that whatever it was, wasn't glowing green.

"It's a pearl necklace, pearls from Pearl, do you get it?"

Anya tried to fake a smile, but it was easy for Pearl and Kai to see she wasn't happy.

"What's wrong? Do you not like them?" asked Kai seeming rather bothered.

"No, it's just, they reminded me of something from above, that's all."

"Well, they took a long time for us to find, especially with us having to sneak around you."

"They're beautiful," Anya said. She put them on around her neck and tightened them to keep them from floating free. Anya felt strange: she wasn't happy, as much as she wanted to be, and that only made her feel guilty. Today should be a day of celebration, her birthday, the day they asked her to join the family, the day she led the feast – but she felt guilty. Guilty for having no appreciation, for the novelty of water was wearing off. Pearl took her by the hand and Anya managed to shake off the dark feelings she had kept hidden since her descent.

"Right, I have to go" said Kai, "I have to teach some young-fins how to move fish."

"See you soon Kai," Anya replied, and she watched him go.

"Come now, we don't have much time," said Pearl.

"Time for what?"

"To dance."

That made Anya smile as Pearl led the way back out into the fields; here she took Anya by the claw and spun her round. All her thoughts seemed to melt away in Pearl's arms. Everything that was so wrong upon the surface went away as their hands, their eyes and their fang-toothed smiles met. Anya felt at peace for a moment, as if all her worries disappeared.

"It's time," said Pearl.

"Time for what?"

"Spin like I spin." Anya looked back at her uncertainly, but Pearl nodded and gave a smile of encouragement. Anya closed her eyes and took up her pirouette stance. With a few deep breaths she turned her claws ever so slightly in the water, thrusting her hips and her feet, and so the motion began. Slowly but surely, she went around and around, faster and faster. The sand began to move around her, but quickly Anya felt dizzy; she couldn't let go and she stopped to catch her breath.

"You're holding back," said Pearl.

"I'm not."

"You are, what's stopping you?"

Anya looked at her best friend, someone she had admired for the past six months, who had taught her new things every day, listened to her, made her laugh, cry and strive to be something better, made her see the beauty in this vast ocean.

"I'm scared! Everything has happened so fast, the Ark, this place, Oracle. I don't know if I'm ready for it."

Pearl swam close, so close that her eyes were glowing, and blue glimmered off her scales in the morning light. She took a hand and placed it upon Anya's cheek to feel the warmth and strength of their connection.

"You were always ready, Anya. I don't think you need to practise anymore; you surprise everyone every day, even me."

Anya faked a smile to hide the fear. It wasn't that she wasn't grateful, she appreciated everything Pearl had ever done. But something was missing although Anya could not say what it was. Pearl reached down and scoured the sand; she dug out a silver headband. She lifted it up and gestured for Anya to take it.

"Is that for me?" Anya asked, and Pearl nodded with a smile.

"I can't take this."

"You will," said Pearl as she came close, placing the band on Anya's head before moving away once more.

"Where are you going?"

"I can see you need some time to think, to relax. I'll see you tonight," said Pearl, and then she swam away. There went one of the most remarkable people Anya had ever met. She watched her go and smiled before reaching up to summon Oracle, who came flying by in seconds. Anya extended a hand and grabbed her fin as she passed, thus flying away with her. It was good to ride, liberating, and it always seemed to clear Anya's mind. They swam together, hunted, foraged, played and laughed all day. Time flew, and when Oracle returned Anya home something strange happened. When Anya turned to say goodbye, Oracle didn't move. She stared back, hovering in silence, just staring with her pitch-black eyes, and bowing her nose slightly.

"Go on, shoo," said Anya, but still the beast didn't move. Anya came forward once more and stroked her great friend, rubbing her down, but Oracle didn't smile, squeak or click in the same way as usual. Something was wrong and Anya knew that orcas sensed things far beyond the realm of humans or water dwellers alike. She turned to swim away but Oracle was right behind her now, following her every move.

"You have to go! Go back to your family," said Anya, and finally Oracle began to move away. Anya swam along the seafloor; the feast would be soon, and she had to be at the old town hall early. She moved through the water alone, swimming silently except for her own thoughts. Something glowing in the sand made her stop, made everything stop. In the corner of her eye she caught a green sparkle from the seabed.

Anya darted down to investigate and scooped up a

handful of sand. To her disbelief, it was her mother's emerite necklace, warm and bright. Anya stopped and remembered the day she had lost it, the day she had drowned. She remembered the day Jake had given it to her, the days she had watched it hang in Aunt Lyn's shack on stormy nights as a child. For the first time in a long time Anya felt truly homesick as she clasped the necklace tight and then wrapped it around her right arm. Thoughts began to race in her mind, of her lost family, of Jake, Isaac and Lyn. How cruel it must be for Tyson to rule over them, and yet, despite the Ark's hardships, she missed it now more than ever.

Time melted after she wrapped the necklace around her arm and the feast came in the blink of an eye. Anya entered the town hall late, having dawdled in the entrance. A nervous sickness took her belly which she hadn't experienced since the trial. In the hall it was silent; everyone was already waiting for her, sitting in anticipation of the opening dance. Anya swallowed her pride, put on a brave face and entered to take centre stage; she could feel their eyes watching and judging. She looked through the crowd and found Pearl's bright blue eyes, Kai's childish smile, Neptune's courage and Hali's love. She touched the necklace before taking a deep breath and felt a little better.

One voice from the choir to the left began to sing the most beautiful tune. Another voice followed, and another, until an angelic harmony of *a cappella* chords formed. They sang with such emotion and vivacity. Layer upon layer of sweet harmonic tones rose and fell as Anya stood still with the yellow eyes of all the water dwellers upon her. For a moment she froze while the music took off without her, and then she began. She twisted and turned, cutting through the water, racing back and forth along the seabed. She pranced and leapt as everyone looked on in surprise. She was afraid, she was unsure, but she had danced with Pearl every single day and if she had an ounce of her dance partner's grace, she would do just fine.

Every movement was perfect as she cut through the water with speed and precision in perfect flow. Nearing the end, she only had a few movements left and went into a spin as the crowd began to roar. Then she heard something strange underneath all the song that took her mind off her work, but she corrected herself as the crowd's roar took over. Anya focused … *It was probably nothing*, and so she started to spin again, faster and faster, as Pearl did. Around and around at speed, with such grace that a circle of sand started to twist around her; so fast that she became a blur as everyone looked on in awe, singing and cheering. When she slowed to a halt to bow, the crowd erupted and then gathered round, embraced her and praised her, for today was a joyous day.

The sea people continued to sing as each of them accepted Anya into the tribe with a palm to the chest and Neptune placed a seashell crown upon her head. But under all the shouting and the praise, Anya swore she heard something strange. It was something quiet, an animal in pain, perhaps, or crying. It forced her to zone out from all the cheers and greetings. There was a sinking feeling inside her, and despite all the happiness around she sank further away. The noise struck a strange fear into her heart, but it went away again with the booming voice of Neptune.

"Anya, you have become a member of our water tribe in all but formality; we are one family and we now invite you to join us. Your powers have become stronger every day, you have risen to every challenge and even mastered the orcas. It would be an honour for you to join our tribe officially and take a sea name."

The crowd roared again but Anya appeared distant as if she were waiting, listening for something to go wrong, but nothing did. She could barely think for the chatter of the crowd and she gazed at Neptune again as if trying to understand what he was asking.

"Anahita … Anahita will be my sea name," she said, as if it was meant to be. She had heard the name as a child, in an old Persian tale about a goddess of the sea. Neptune took his trident and placed it down on either shoulder, then he lifted her hand in the air in triumph.

"I pronounce you Anahita of the water dwellers!"

The crowd erupted; they cheered, danced and sang. Kai and Pearl came forward to hug her, but it seemed as if Anya wasn't there at all. The crowd parted again to take their seats, for it was Anya's turn to bring the feast. Everyone waited and watched as she closed her eyes, concentrated and began to control the movement of the water, the pattern of the fish. Everyone waited with anticipation, eager and hungry; they could not contain their excitement. And then Anya heard it again.

This time it was clear, for the crowd was silent. Somewhere in the ocean, cries carried through the waves, and she knew who it was. She opened her eyes in distress to stare at Pearl and Kai. There were a thousand things she wanted to say, a thousand and one, but she didn't have time. She pushed herself up into the air towards the hole in the roof and threw down the crown of shells. Everyone gasped. Hali looked on in shock and Neptune felt a terrible sense of shame. He couldn't bear to look. Then Pearl tried to swim after her.

"Anya!" Pearl shouted, but Kai grabbed her by the arm to hold her back.

"Let her go," he said, but despite his strength Pearl broke free and swam for the roof, but then a thousand fish flooded in, knocking her backwards and blocking her path. The dwellers tried to clear the storm of fish, but it was too strong. Pearl fought to get out, but she was lost in the maze of fish; no one could slow them down, and no one could find an exit.

Outside, Anya swam alone for she knew what she had heard. It was the cry of a girl she used to know: Riley. She never thought she would miss her, but she missed her now. The Ark was here, close by, and so she swam to the old office block at lightning pace. It was right there, the old window that Tomas had knocked out. All she wanted to do now was go home, all she wanted was to be with her family. She couldn't bear to live down here without them, she couldn't live to know the suffering they faced, so she set out to go back from where she came. It was so close now, but Oracle came from her blind side and put herself between Anya and the window.

"Girl, please don't do this now, you're breaking my

heart," said Anya, but Oracle wouldn't back down. "I love you so much, but I have to do this. I have to find my family and see if they're okay."

Anya trembled; she was afraid. She came forward to embrace Oracle once more and the whale's black eyes seemed to understand. Anya kissed her goodbye and swam through to the office block. She turned to face her friend one last time and saw that Oracle hadn't taken her eyes off her, for she knew what Anya was about to do.

"Swim, swim, girl" Anya said, and Oracle, with great reservations, started to swim away.

"Anya, wait!" said Pearl, her voice echoing across the sea. "Please don't do this! Don't leave us!" At every attempt Pearl made to get closer, Oracle blocked her way.

As much as Anya wanted to turn back, she wanted to embrace Pearl and thank her for everything, to tell her how afraid she was and how she wished she didn't have to go, but she just kept swimming. She made it past the old bookcase to the hole in the roof. There she stopped and felt her necklace upon her wrist for courage.

With one mighty stroke she flew from the water to the bright and burning daylight where, after a moment, the water upon her skin dried. Screeching, she burnt beyond pain as her lungs spluttered, unable to take in the air. Steam rose like flames as she tried to cry. The sun scalded her as the smell of roasting flesh filled her nostrils. Her webbed hands went red in the sunlight as Anya felt a pain so ferocious that the idea of jumping back through the hole, or lying down under the water, became all she could think about. As much as she wanted to, though, she stopped herself from retreating from the Ark. Having heard her family, her friends, and despite the dwellers, despite everything, all she wanted was to return to them and to see them again, in this life or the next.

Her head pounded in the heat, and blind panic took over. She couldn't breathe and suffocated as she crawled along trying to stay above the water. With every ounce of energy, she made her way to the edge, where she lay burning and broken, looking up at the sunset one last time. Her throat, lips and eyes were dry; inhaling brought nothing but dust that turned to cement inside her. Anya reached out her hand one last time in the direction of the cries that carried from the Ark, one last defiant act, and then she closed her eyes, at peace, forever.

In her last moment Anya was finally able to feel again, she saw her brother, her uncle and aunty, and they were standing together on land, outside a house, well dressed, dry and smiling at her. Then she saw her mother. She looked beautiful and elegant, wearing her necklace. The emerald twinkled brightly, and her hair flowed long and blonde like Jake's. Her father was in a suit as he picked her up and hugged her.

"Mother, Father, I –" she began, before her mother put a finger over her lips.

Her mother held her close and said, "The storm is over now, you can rest."

## 20

## LIFE

E ver since the great flood, nothing had stayed above water. Nothing more than the odd sea creature coming up for air – flying fish or turtles. Everything above, no matter how hard it fought to stay, ended up below. The flood took with it nine billion people, every home, every profession, every history book and every life. It was merciless, sparing only those most desperate souls. Its origin was unknown, and no matter how much both sides begged for the old ways, they were gone, while the water would always be.

Lying peacefully where both worlds met, upon the shallow edge of the roof, Anya's body faced the sky. Burnt dark green scales dried in the sun, and the only features that told of her humanity were her cold blue eyes, which returned with her passing. She was naked but for her mother's emerite necklace in her hand, her headband and pearl necklace. In her last moments, she had clutched it tight to her chest and its shadow was the only thing that guarded her from the sun. There was to be no grave, no ceremony, no hymns, no prayer and no churches. No one would mourn and no one would cry, as no one would ever know. Lying burnt and broken in the midday sun, Anya's body waited for a wave big enough to knock her off and the sea to swallow her whole. Every now and then a small one would come by and wash over her, but her body quickly dried again.

There was not a sound except for the waves, no one to give her a final goodbye or write down the tremendous and unlikely tale of Anya Fairheart. The girl who crossed the boundary between land and sea, who could mind-speak, hunt with telepathy, echolocate and bond with killer whales. Here she lay, alone, with so much promise stolen, on her seventeenth birthday. No one would bury her, and no one would dare to retrieve her body.

As the wind whistled and the waves passed, the hot sun beat down upon the water and Anya's emerite necklace sparkled. Its light twinkled in her cold blue eyes as she lay there pale and lifeless. A large wave washed over Anya, who suddenly sat up and spluttered saltwater. Her thick brown hair hung over her face, knotted, tough and heavy. Anya ran her hands through it in disbelief whilst looking down at her body. When she looked up again, her eyes were blue and reflecting the ocean. With the knowledge that she was on the surface, she began to laugh in hysterics, and then she began to cry huddling up to her knees. Shaking and in disbelief, she felt her freckled olive skin and her hands, soft to the touch. Her face, lips, ears, warm once more. The overwhelming sensation of the surface took hold, she wanted to rejoice, but she was too hungry, thirsty and fatigued.

Anya struggled to her feet on human legs as if for the first time. She stood tall and proud with a smile and then she looked to the ocean.

"I'm alive!" Her voice echoed across the sea, "I'm alive!" She looked down to see, to her horror, that her feet were still green, with long claw-like nails under the water's surface.

"No no no," she pleaded expecting to turn back and have to go back under, but then she lifted a foot in shock, and when she did, it turned human again, as if the scales had melted away. She did the same with the other foot and it happened once more. Kneeling down in disbelief, she placed her hands underwater, and they changed too, from human hands to dark green claws and then back again: skin to scales, and scales to skin. Lifting her hand out of the water, she memorised the feeling of being submerged, and concentrated; her eyes flickered yellow as her hand went back to being reptilian, although now it didn't steam or burn. She had turned it back again by the power of thought alone.

Then came the scream that had forced her out of the water. Riley was out there, muttering and murmuring, and the sound travelled across the ocean. Anya didn't know whether she was really hearing or whether it was in her mind. It didn't matter now, though, all that mattered was being alive and breathing fresh air again.

Anya shook her head, closed her eyes and winced before opening them again; she felt better than ever before, either upon the surface or below. Turning, she ran to the office at incredible speed and launched herself into the air, before diving down into the sea. Anya soared at incredible speed with webbed hands and feet. When she broke the surface, she became human again, before slicing back under. Liberated, she could do anything she desired, free to live, free to breathe and free to swim.

Hovering at the water's edge, she closed her eyes and thought of Oracle. Anya rose out of the water and stood – below her feet was the whale. She surfed on her back, reacting to the orca's every move. Anya screamed in celebration as Oracle leapt into the air and dived back down again. They flew together, as one unstoppable force bound forever.

It was freedom, bliss, and then Anya saw something that took her breath away. The Ark, her former home, floated in the distance, a majestic wreck of civilisation. It was everything she feared and everything she loved. Right then, right there on Oracle's back, she knew what had been missing and she had never thought she would get it back, but now, with every stroke, it came closer. Hopes of seeing Aunt Lyn, Uncle Isaac and Jake filled her mind. There was no turning back, no other way, and as her thoughts raced through her mind, so did the wind. The closer she was, the stormier the weather became. The waves crashed, rolling and folding, trying to consume Anya, but she was too strong, stronger now than ever before. The sky grew dark and thick with cloud as it took away the daylight. Then the rain came down amid cracks of thunder and jags of lightning as the weather tried to tell her how things were going to be. Though what had scared her once, didn't give a second thought to now; she was fierce, ready, unfazed. She kept swimming, moving with Oracle until the Ark was within her grasp. She looked up and saw the south tower bending in the wind and rain. She knew Wilson was watching her from above, but he didn't sound a bell or alarm – no, he simply watched, for the night was young.

"I won't be long, girl," Anya whispered, before Oracle whistled goodbye. Anya made her way under the Ark, swimming at first and then climbing underneath the framework as Jake had taught her. Moving in silence with much more grace than before, she pulled herself up onto the edge. There was a hut here, used for drying clothes, so she took some leathers and quickly dressed. She went back into the water and edged along to the feet of a Hunter on watch. His name was Dren. The Hunters had kept watch ever since Gregory's passing. Dren was a large dark brown-haired young man with a stooped brow; he looked tired, pale and skinnier than he used to be. He looked straight ahead instead of down below, and Anya was about to strike when his companion Leon approached.

"Are you going to stand there all night, brother?" asked Leon.

"As long as Tyson says so."

"And how many nights after?"

"Does it matter?"

"It does," said Leon lowering his voice to a whisper, "we're wasting away out here, we need to be fishing, not keeping watch."

"There are no fish," said Dren.

Anya didn't know exactly what they meant, but when she looked past them and saw a Hunter positioned every ten feet around the Ark, she knew something wasn't right. She went under without holding her breath and took her green form. Climbing onto the Ark was useless: they would take her and gut her like a fish. Instead, she closed her eyes and listened for familiar sounds, but sadly she could hear no voices of family or friends. Then she heard the familiar chop and tear of rotten wood, over and over. She had an idea, and instead of hopping over the side she swam underneath to find the source of the disturbance.

On the underside of the rotting raft, she got as close to the sound as possible before breaking through the floating base layer just below the surface. Smashing a fist through the rotten wood, she grabbed the leg of her target so fast they hadn't time to scream. A stocky body fell from above into the framework; Anya caught him as if he were light as a feather and threw him into a more supportive part of the wooden scaffolding, then dived on top of him to cover his mouth. Tomas mumbled something, before realising he was looking at a ghost, and upon this realisation his expression went from one of horror to bewilderment and finally disbelief.

"Shh, if I take away my hand you have to be quiet!" hissed Anya.

Tomas's flickering eyes quietened; he nodded, and so Anya took her hand away.

"Anya, Anya! It's you, its –" She covered his mouth

again, afraid his voice would attract someone's attention. "I thought you were dead, I thought –"

"No, Tomas, I'm alive," she said, and it brought a smile to her face as well as his. "I'm alive and I'm home."

"Where have you been?"

"Swimming, mostly … I wish I had more time to explain."

Tomas raised an eyebrow; in the shallow moonlight he caught a glimpse of yellow in Anya's eyes and gulped.

"Miles said they dropped you into the sea without a chance of survival; he won't talk to Tyson anymore; the Ark is mad. I prayed you would find driftwood, Anya, and you did."

"I found so much more," she said, remembering Pearl, Kai and the others. "I can't keep this from you, Tomas, someone must know. I can turn into one of them, those underwater beasts."

"Those monsters?"

"Water dwellers, Tomas, water dwellers. They are human, good souls, like you and me."

Tomas moved away from her, well aware that they had touched, and unhappy at the thought. He was scared of infection, illness, or worse.

"Don't worry, I can't give the condition to you, only Hali can …" Anya realised that the name meant nothing to him, and then she realised that something about Tomas wasn't right, just like Leon and Dren, he was skinny and malnourished.

"What's wrong with you, Tomas? You look hungry."

"Ever since the shallows, we can't catch fish like we used to."

"What do you mean? Has Tyson's leadership sorrowed the Hunters?"

"No, the fish swim away from our nets and spears."

His words ignited a thought in Anya's mind that brought disbelief. There could be only one reason for this: fish were simple-minded creatures that begged to be caught. The only people who could change that – who could make the fish change course – were the water dwellers. Her heart sank.

"Can you get me to my uncle? He will know what to do," she said, desperate to seek his wisdom again.

"Your uncle and aunt are being kept near the Hunters' barracks and are being watched. They would be on us in a heartbeat."

"What about Jake?"

"Now Jake I can do," said Tomas, before turning and beginning to swing from pillar to post using all his remaining strength.

Anya's face lit up and she followed close behind. "Where is he?" she whispered, conscious of shadows between the cracks in some of planks up above.

"He has been banished to the tower with Wilson and will take his place when the old man passes."

Anya snarled at the thought of her family imprisoned. Tyson had made a powerful enemy of her, one that would stop at nothing to free them, to undo every wrong and bring order back to the Ark. She thought it all over in her mind as they climbed through cold wet shadows within the Ark's skeleton. Tomas was beginning to tire; he turned to see Anya right behind him, unable to fathom why she was able to keep up with her petite frame. Then he came to a halt and gave her a nod. He pried a nail from the floorboards. Rain splattered off the deck as clouds thundered above; most had taken to their shacks to shield themselves from the storm. Tomas continued to struggle, so Anya lent a hand, knocking plank from nail with ease. Then she passed right by him and used him as a stepladder.

They approached the bottom of the tower and Anya watched it bend in the wind and rain. This was worse than her first climb. A storm was coming, and she was afraid of storms. Making this journey in such weather was suicide – but the supply cage was all the way at the top, in the dark grey clouds. She asked Tomas if he wanted to come with her, and to their dismay Leon suddenly appeared from around the other side of the crow's nest.

"Hey! You, you're supposed to be –" said Leon, staggering in the rain. Anya flew up into the air and back down, knocking his head against the tower. Tomas couldn't believe it and tried to back away as Anya picked up Leon and went to place his body in a barrel.

"Anya, what have you done?"

It was at that moment, that a turtle shell raised out of the barrel. Lord Turtle Head looked at the pair of them and then at the unconscious Hunter. He did the same again. "Anya," he whispered, "you came back. I knew you were alive, one of my turtles …"

"I know, Lord Turtle Head, I know. Can we talk about that later? For now, I need you to be quiet."

"Whatever you say, put him in the barrel over there, I've always wanted a barrel buddy."

"Thank you, Lord Turtle Head."

"No, thank you, queen of the sea."

Anya smiled and thought back to her sea name Anahita, and the thought occurred to Anya that maybe the man in the barrel was just trying to hide away from the voices he could here down below, but she didn't have time for that right now. "You have to climb with me, Tomas." He shook his head in disbelief, unable to fathom the idea of the climb. Tomas liked nothing more than to be at floor level on the Ark. He had not swum since the shallows, and he had never dared to climb.

"I can't, Anya, I'm too afraid; and besides, they will kill me for what you have done, I'm just a Maker."

Anya came close to him and gave him the soft smile he adored. "You are brave and gentle, Tomas, not what they tell you to be. Now, get on my back and close your eyes."

Tomas nodded before reluctantly climbing on her back. To his surprise, she was strong enough, despite him being twice her size. He closed his eyes and felt her leap, then leap again.

"How did you get so strong, Anya?"

"Swimming" she said.

"I don't believe it, front crawl or breaststroke?" he asked before opening his eyes to see that upon the third leap Anya had scaled much of the south mast. They towered above everything and Tomas tried to scream, before realising he had no voice.

"I want to get down, I want to get down," he said

over and over, as if in prayer, when he found his voice. Still they kept going, as Anya leaped almost weightless off indentations in the wooden mast. She felt no fear, no anxiety, no self-doubt. This her climb and her Ark. At the top, she flung Tomas over the side before climbing over herself. Wilson was staring out to sea on the other side. Anya looked around for Jake and assumed he must be in Wilson's small hut on the right; she didn't know what to say, how to greet her brother, or the old man.

"I saw them try to kill you, but they failed," said Wilson. He turned around to face her, still wearing his sailor's hat and coat. His pale skin and white beard were icy in the wind and rain. "You were turned, but you turned back again? Tell me, Anya, how?"

The storm beat down on Anya's face as she stared at Wilson, lost for words, her hair heavy and wet, her eyes shining blue as strikes of lightning flashed. Wilson saw her story in her eyes: the heartbreak, pain, and determination, her lips trembled as she knew that one day, she would have to tell a story no one would believe.

"Tyson dropped me into the sea to die. I drowned; I awoke under the waves as a water dweller." None of the others knew what that meant. "A creature with reptilian skin. They … they are human" Anya confessed as tears that she had waited months for came rushing from her eyes.

"Anya?" In disbelief Jake stood outside of the hut, lost for words. He ran forward to embrace her with a brotherly love.

"Jake," she replied as her tears poured down. She

buried her head in Jake's chest and the past six months became a distant thought. "I'm sorry I wasn't strong enough ... they took me."

"Sister, you're alive. I thought you were dead."

"I was, I-I died twice, once to go under and once to come back, but now it's different, I can choose. Jake, I swam with orcas, lived underwater and moved fish with my mind!"

Jake wiped away her tears, and it took Anya a moment to realise that they didn't believe her, not even Wilson. She did the only thing she could: as the rain smashed down, she closed her eyes and opened them once more. Now her eyes were yellow, her skin reptilian and claws took the place of her hands. They all gasped, before she changed back with a sharp breath.

"By the gods," said Wilson.

"There is no cold, no fighting, but there is warmth, endless food and places to sleep. It's a magical haven – but it's nothing without you. I'm going to save this place, end hunger and free our family." Anya was moving too quick for any of them to keep up.

"There are too many. They will take one look at your reptile skin and gut you. What makes you think you are strong enough?" asked Jake.

"Trust me, I'm stronger now."

"Strength is one thing, but convincing them that your form won't harm them, that they can live in peace, is another." Wilson's wise words made Anya think for a moment about what she could do to win the people's favour.

"I have an idea of how I can convince them."

"The Hunters sleep with spears; Tyson rules by fear, not like your uncle," said Tomas, straight and to the point.

"Where is Uncle?" asked Anya, desperate to see him.

Tomas looked over the edge, then he gasped when he saw the Grand Stage. The whole tribe was gathering, every Hunter armed with a spear. Behind them stood every Cook and Maker. They looked so tired and skinny. Anya saw Isaac and Lyn standing upon the stage bound by rope, and Tyson next to the elders with his crew. Alongside him was the young Hunter Anya had knocked out cold and placed in a barrel down below. Other Hunters were making their way to the crow's nest with a giant saw as rumours of the infectious sea girl spread.

"They plan to chop down the tower," said Wilson.

"What do we do?" asked Tomas, more panicked than Anya had ever seen him.

The metal cage used for shipping goods began to free fall and ran and jumped faster than anyone else could turn around. She caught the rope which had been cut from the bottom and used her claws to halt its descent. "Get in, quick!"

Jake and Wilson stared in confusion, finding it hard to believe what they were seeing.

"Don't worry, Anya swims now," said Tomas, but that didn't provide a good enough answer.

"I'm strong, now get in, we don't have time."

Wilson approached the cage first, "are you sure about this?" he asked.

"You don't have a choice!"

They all felt the saw begin its work against the tower as it swayed in the rain. The Hunters cut through the structure supporting the crow's nest. Anya was still holding onto the rope and had it with both hands. Wilson, Jake and Tomas would not. She had to think fast as she turned to each of them: her brother, her friend and the old man.

"Do you trust me?" she asked. Jake and Tomas nodded but Wilson stayed still, staring at her with those cold eyes. "Get in the cage," she said as the crow's nest juddered. The three of them ran into the cage and looked at her rather hopelessly, Jake held the bars and watched her.

"I'm going to lower you down," she said.

"Anya, what about you? –"

"There is no time for this!" The tower shook as the wood below weakened and she let the cage freefall; the three of them screamed, but with an iron grip Anya halted its fall, skidding to the edge of the crow's nest as she did. As she lowered them down, everyone below watched in horror, except Tyson, who took a sick sense of satisfaction from their peril. The elders stood upon the Grand Stage in silent disagreement, most were afraid to show their discontent at killing three innocents.

"Tyson, this is madness," said elder Frederick.

"Shut up, or I"ll have you walk the Iron Lady's plank," he replied.

No one else voiced their opinion, but it didn't mean they agreed. Everyone knew what had come with Tyson's rule. Mass starvation had followed, and so had the imprisonment of those he felt would rise against him. Joy took his eyes whilst his men cut down the south crow's nest as Anya fought against gravity pulling the cage down.

"Coward! Somebody stop this!" Isaac shouted, shoving his captors, but five Hunters managed to retrain him.

"She's too young," pleaded Aunt Lyn, but she too was held back. No one on the Grand Stage or below dared say anything to intervene. The women and children were afraid, as were the Cooks and Makers. Only the Hunters had spears, and a tight group of them led by Tyson at that.

"They will all be infected now! They must all fall!" Tyson shouted as everyone below waited for Anya to slip and for it to be over.

"Tyson if you do this, there is no going back," said Elder Frederick, plucking up the courage to speak again.

"Silence!" Tyson bellowed, as one of the twins forced Elder Frederick to the floor.

Above them, Anya hung onto the rope and lowered the others down despite the tower leaning more and more. She stood upon the edge using her clawed reptilian feet to hold steady as she fed Jake, Wilson and Tomas down to the floor. It took every ounce of her energy, and no matter how hard she tried to suppress it, glimmers of green skin and yellow in her eyes came through. The crowd gasped in terror, while Tyson relished the moment. The crow's nest bent and splintered, and the cage was twenty feet from the deck before the nest cracked in half.

The trio hit the ground as the cage shattered into pieces around them. They were safe but surrounded by Tyson's men. Then came the tower and Isaac let out a bellowing scream, fearing for Anya's life. Like a tree in a forest, the tower had been cut to fall in a certain direction. It took out only a few empty shacks and the edge of the Ark, crushing them into nothingness and pitching them into the sea. Dust rose as the sea crashed and the innocent looked on in horror.

## 21

## JUST A GIRL

The crowd screamed and dispersed as the south crow's nest thundered down. The Ark split with the force, the old wood splintering in two and causing a flood and a rush of waves in-between. A chaos of screams erupted as the Ark rose and fell with the storm and the fallen nest. The last log rested on the edge before dropping into the ocean, and then there was silence amidst the thunder and the rain.

Tyson stared with menace, and then, to his surprise, a shadowy form leapt through the clouds and landed like a cat at the foot of the Grand Stage. In unison many moved away as the shimmer of Hunters' spears pointed in Anya's direction. The storm continued to rage; water thundered down, but Tyson stood as strong as ever, with his arms folded, surrounded by elders and Master Hunters. Anya looked up at him as she rose to her feet, encircled by Hunters with sharp spears ready to take her down from every angle; yet she showed no sign of weakness. She didn't want to fight, she didn't want to hurt anyone, but God, did Tyson deserve it.

The crowd looked on in silence as Aunt Lyn wept. She was unable to believe that Anya was alive. Uncle Isaac remained silent, but he was just as relieved. He was proud and happy to see her again, though he knew all too well the dangers of her return. The people were starving, the Hunters had taken control, and he feared what might become of his niece, given the seemingly mindless mob ahead.

Anya, however, stood tall and proud, with a thousand eyes staring down at her. She felt surprisingly calm as she made a fist, ready to strike out against everything Tyson had done to her.

"You dare bring your poison here to try to kill us again, monster!" Tyson shouted, as those around gasped but remained eager to hear what Anya had to say.

"It isn't poison, and they aren't monsters. It's a paradise, and they can help us, all of us."

"Lies, lies from a monster who wishes to curse us!"

"You tried to drown me, a child! You aren't fit to lead the Ark."

The storm raged as rain thundered down, but no one dared move or say a thing. They were hungry and terrified, but Anya didn't falter, she remained tall and proud as she told them all what they needed to hear.

"Those bloody screeching monsters tore Gregory's heart out!" Pierce shouted, eager to aid his leader as Gregory's widow, Fiona, let out a cry before being held back.

"Didn't you strike first?" Anya asked, but neither Tyson nor Pierce gave an answer.

"Show your true self!" Tyson bellowed, beckoning Anya's true form before the crowd.

Anya had no time to contemplate her next move, but she refused to turn, for she was still afraid to show them the creature she had become. Surrounded by spears as the Ark rocked, one pressed her skin, and in response a scale flickered on her cheek. The crowd gasped.

"Monster!" the Hunters shouted, their spears glistening in the moonlight, separating Anya from her peers, and then they all began to shout.

"Monster! Monster!"

"Wait! Listen to me!" Anya exclaimed, desperate to win over the will of the people.

"Monster! Monster!"

"Wait!" shouted Elder Frederick, "At least hear what she is going to say!" And out of respect, everyone did.

"Look around you, can't you see? Our world is one of hardship. Down below is a world free of hunger, free of cold, where children don't risk illness or death on being born, where they live in peace. They are human, more human than some of you."

"Do you hear what the monster thinks of you?" bellowed Tyson's loud voice again.

"I can end hunger, I –"

"Enough! I will give you one last chance: leave this place forever and never return."

Anya tried to push her way forward as the tips of

spears pressed against her from all angles, following her every move.

"I will not leave, not until I feed every person here."

"Then I have no choice," said Tyson. He stepped up onto the fence and eyed the crowd, drunk on power, before turning to Anya with that cold and hateful glare. "Kill her," he said … but not one Hunter moved.

Anya looked around at them all and could sense their doubt. Even if she was a monster, right now she looked like the girl she always had been.

"I said kill her or find yourself thrown from the Ark along with her."

"Don't do it!" Isaac shouted, but he was held back by more Hunters while Lyn's cries echoed across the crowd.

Anya looked around to consider her options, though she didn't have many.

"I challenge you for leadership of the tribe," she declared.

Tyson looked down upon her from the Grand Stage and began to laugh. It was preposterous to him, and he shook his head in refusal.

"I said, I challenge you, coward, for leadership of the Ark," Anya said once more.

She was a child half his size, but Tyson wanted nothing more than to end her.

"Very well, clear the way!" he said as the spearmen moved on either side. Tyson tied back his long grey dreadlocks and wiped the cold rain from his brow before hopping off the rail and jumping down in front of her, ready for battle.

There they stood, surrounded by an eager crowd, like David and Goliath. Anya put up her tiny fists and assumed a fighting stance, as Tyson did the same. Without warning, he threw a mighty foot forward, bigger than Anya's head, but she side-stepped him just in time.

Tyson swung with heavy fists, and missed again and again, only serving to make himself more enraged. Every time he struck, Anya moved around him, for he moved at half her speed. There was only so long Tyson could keep this up; he had to find another way. Snatching a spear from a fellow Hunter, he edged forward, swiping manically, with far more speed and control now, as the razor-sharp weapon flashed through the air. Anya all around the spear, above and below narrowly avoiding each blow. On the sixth strike, Tyson realised it was useless: Anya jumped into the air, light as a feather, and Tyson snapped the spear in half over his knee in anger.

"Give in," said Anya, "all you have to do is give in and we can all live together in peace."

"Foolish child! You didn't see what I saw, it tore out his heart!"

Anya froze at the image of poor Gregory looking down as blood poured from his chest, and whilst she was off guard, Tyson stomped down hard on a plank, which sent her up into the air. She tumbled down and Tyson grabbed hold of her with delight. He slammed her down onto the ground repeatedly and the crowd gasped with each blow. The people cried and looked away, desperate not to see a child of the Ark beaten to a pulp. He hit her again and again as the crowd winced, before grabbing her by the wrist and flinging her up and over the elders and onto the Grand Stage.

"Tyson, no!" shouted Uncle Isaac; but it was no use, for Tyson was beyond reasoning with. He walked slowly toward Anya's broken body, as though he had all the time in the world. She spat blood, shook her head and struggled to her feet, raising her fists once more. Defiant, she crawled to the edge of the Grand Stage, and the world lit up as lightning struck behind them. Tyson approached her as she staggered on her feet, and then he threw a mighty fist.

Anya caught it in her hand and stopped it dead. Tyson stared in disbelief, struggling to break free from her iron grip as Anya's hand turned green and scaly in the moonlight. It became clear to him that she had been holding back from the start: at any moment she could have used this strength to stop him, and now, taking one last chance, he grabbed her throat with his one free hand and lifted her into the air. With no choice left to her, Anya turned green, reptilian, and her eyes bulged bright yellow, but she didn't resist. The crowd screamed, for most of them had never seen a water dweller and looked away in horror. No one knew what to make of it, they had only heard terrifying tales of the creatures in the shallows.

"I can break free," she whispered, "I could easily defeat you, but in death I will set them free."

"Enough!"

"They will turn on you and take you down for killing a fellow Arker."

"Enough you vile creature!"

As Anya took her final breath, Cooks, Carers and Makers, mothers and fathers let their tears fall freely, and so did the girls and the boys who grew up with Anya. The younger Hunters loosened their grip on their spears, before throwing them down out of fondness for her brother. Little girls approached their Master Hunter fathers, and mothers approached their sons. Everyone looked past her scales to see the truth, that a giant had wrapped his hands around one of their children.

"She has shown her true self, look at this monster!" bellowed Tyson, red-eyed, as Anya grew weaker by the second, intent on hiding his fear of the unknown.

"No, Father." Miles, son of Tyson trembled, he had come forth holding back tears, pushing through the crowd and onto the Grand Stage. Tyson turned to his son, and then to everyone else, and he saw the horror in their eyes for the first time. "*You* are the monster," Miles said.

Tyson looked up to see that Anya had turned into a girl once more, a little girl, a child, dead in his arms, and he lost his grip. The Hunters dropped their spears as Tyson let Anya fall to the floor. Cooks, Carers and Makers stormed the stage armed with knives and pots and pans, as Tyson backed away towards the edge of the Grand Stage, in disbelief at what he had become.

"What have I done? They … they tore out his heart … they …" He fell silent as Anya began to move again where she lay on the floor, coughing and spluttering. He looked at Miles as if to say something, but the brute could not bring forth his feelings. The storm thundered behind them, crashing in rage, and a tear rolled down his cheek. Tyson opened his mouth as if to speak, but another wave came and something smashed into the underside of the Ark, knocking him off his feet and into the storm.

"No!" Miles screamed as Jake held him back. Anya got to her feet and ran, jumping into the black wall of water after him. She used echolocation, telepathy, Oracle, everything in her power to find him, but the seas were rough, and Tyson was gone. Anya pulled herself back up onto the Grand Stage. She looked for Miles, who had fled through the crowd. No one knew what to do or what to say to her, but Isaac ran forward and scooped her up into his arms.

"Anya, I love you. I'm so proud of you," he said, uttering the words he had wanted to say for so long. Aunt Lyn came forward aided by Tomas and embraced them both, she was so happy that the ordeal was over, and Anya didn't want to let go. She hugged them both tightly and felt their warmth as Jake came to join them. All around the Hunters bowed their heads as Elder Frederick arrived at their side. The moment of embrace went on, but Anya noticed everyone was starting to leave, to return to their shacks for the weather, and they all looked so gaunt.

"There is something I have to do," Anya said, and so they let her go. She climbed onto the balcony to address the whole tribe. "I promise you; I'm not a monster! I'm one of you. I grew up with you, I laughed with you, I loved you, I bled with you. I was cold with you and I starved with you. Now let us feast!"

Anya raised her arm in the air and made a fist. A thousand fish flew at the Ark from all directions, as everyone looked on in disbelief. After months of hunger it was raining fish. What was a moment of horror, turned to amazement, as the starving Arkers grabbed as many as they could. In time, the storm began to clear, and Anya watched as everyone took their fair share. The chefs readied the fire pits with forever flame and began cooking in the rain, as the drummers drummed away. Anya backed off, smiling. She could finally rest.

"Isaac, shall we begin rebuilding the crow's nest tomorrow?" asked Elder Frederick.

"I don't know why you're asking me; the storm has brought us a new leader."

Anya looked on in shock. "Me, a leader? No."

"I never chose to be the Ark's leader, and neither have you."

Anya thought for a moment, she had done a lot of thinking about the way things had become, and she didn't want the Ark to be stuck in its old ways. Then she thought of the water dwellers, just for a moment. "We will have a council."

"A council?" asked Uncle Isaac.

"A council made up of all factions and you and I will sit in judgement together."

Anya looked on from the balcony of the Grand Stage as everyone began to feast. Aunt Lyn came and placed an arm around her. "I knew you were alive; I knew it. I prayed to the sea gods and they looked most kindly on you, Anya."

"I love you, Auntie."

"I love you too," said Aunt Lyn as Anya held onto them both, so happy to return and so happy to be alive. She looked on at all the families, so happy to be fed for the first time in forever. Anya saw the Cooks' forever flames burning higher and brighter than ever before. The drums brought dancing and song, and as the Ark's people swung from rope to rope a Maker brought forth the rainbow fish cloak and draped it over Anya's shoulders in gratitude. Anya ate with her family, and she watched the Ark celebrate for hours. In the early hours of the morning, in the moonlight and the rain, Anya jumped down from the balcony, she raised her hand, bowed her head, widened her stance, and began to dance.

## EPILOGUE

For months the Ark was happier than it had ever been. Anya didn't imprison or punish anyone who had stood by Tyson, the shame was enough and so with time, they were forgiven. The new council represented the tribe proportionally from each rank, role and age group, but they didn't make a final decision without Anya's say so, and that was something she may never grow used to.

The Ark was still anchored a few miles from the shallows, every night Anya would stand in the moonlight and look out toward the office block roof. She had developed the habit of touching the pearls around her neck, just to remind her that it was real. Every day she would think about going back, about seeing those who she had left behind, but she didn't go. Her betrayal kept her away, but she would often think of Kai, and though she knew that he could sense her, he never came.

The water dwellers were a quiet and private people,

Anya explained to Gregory's wife Fiona, that they had exiled the one responsible for his crime. It would take time – years, maybe generations – but Anya hoped that the Ark and the water dwellers could one day live in peace.

Still, she faced problems, unanswered questions, as she feared the Ark's famine didn't happen on its own. Anya feared it was the work of Neptune's brother, Enki, who was still out there somewhere.

"So, are you going to teach me to swim like you green queen?" said Jake whilst taking a bow as Tomas chuckled.

"The transformation is incredibly painful."

"Is it really that bad? I really want to."

"It is."

"Well, if we could do it without the pain, or the scales that would be great."

"I think there's an easier way; if there is, we'll find it together, all of us."

"I don't like swimming," said Tomas.

At that moment, a barrel came rolling down the stairs before coming to a halt in front of them. Anya expected to see Lord Turtle Head, but there was no one inside. When she turned to the top of the stairs, there was a man in fish leathers, his hands on his hips, shaggy brown hair and a freshly shaven face.

"Lord Turtle Head is that you?" asked Anya, it looked like him, but this man wasn't wearing a turtle shell.

"The very same," he said with a nod.

"Why aren't you wearing your helmet?"

Lord Turtle Head's cheeks turned pink, "well, there's no easy way to say this, but the sky may not be falling after all. I may have miscalculated; it appears people may have just been throwing things at me."

"Oh, I had no idea …"

"I thought that you might be able to help me with another problem, everyone is telling your stories, and I want to swim with the turtles, but I'm afraid of water. Can you help me?."

"I'd love to," said Anya. She was still getting used to being home again and everyone looking to her for guidance. It was so nice to see everyone, and even Lord Turtle Head looked incredibly well. Anya looked at Jake and Tomas, Jake had taken to training Tomas to be a Hunter, he looked a lot leaner than he used to. The two of them had become friends and it made Anya smile, but when she looked past them, sometimes she saw Miles and a tremendous guilt took hold. Anya would try to find him, to apologise, but he was gone. Miles hadn't said a word to her since that day …. Anya didn't know whether it was time, or whether it would ever be time, but she set out to find him, to clear the air and then the bell rang from Wilson's tower.

"Anya! Anya! Quick, the south side, you have to see this, you have to!" shouted Riley.

Jake, Anya and Tomas started sprinting across the old wooden raft, past shack after shack, and this time Anya took the lead. A crowd had gathered at the dock, fixated upon the horizon. The old trembled, some fainted, and the young couldn't look away. Anya jumped to the highest roof, she stood tall and looked out to see the horizon, and upon the horizon was a ghost, a tall dark shadow of the past. To Anya's disbelief, it was a ship.

# AFTERWORD

*Thank you for reading Anya of Ark. I do hope you enjoyed it, and if you did, a review would mean the world. I promise that Anya will return soon in another adventure.*

*This story was inspired by my niece. I wanted to write something for her; with a character that inspires and a world she would want to explore. I wanted to challenge myself and write about a girl as tough as nails who goes to hell and back.*

*It started with a daydream of four teenagers on kayaks, having lived on a floating raft for their entire lives without comprehension of land, without knowledge of buildings, electricity, solid food, or any other home comforts such as walls, roofs, heating and hot water. I played with the idea, and Anya of Ark was born.*

*I suppose that might leave you with the question, why a world of water? Well, a teacher once told me that I'd never set the world on fire, so I decided, why not flood it instead.*

*Kristian Joseph*

## MORE BY THE AUTHOR

### Titans, Cranes & Monsters Games: Sunlight

*"The Kingdom will fall, Sovereign will burn, and the Titan will reign the sky."*

In the year 2095, the earth has spiralled into chaos and the last democracy is on the brink of collapse. Join unlikely heroes such as smugglers, immortals, and a dreamer in this action-packed dystopian tale of tragedy, betrayal and revenge.

### Titans, Cranes & Monsters Games: The Journey

*Sunlight was only the beginning, and thus begins the journey…*

The Journey will continue the fast-paced action adventure right where it left off. We rejoin our heroes as they deal with the consequences of their actions; some will learn, and all will lose.

Printed in Poland
by Amazon Fulfillment
Poland Sp. z o.o., Wrocław

63842758R00174